SARAH SCOTT

(1723-1795) was the younger daughter of the Robinson family, members of the Yorkshire gentry. She grew up at Mount Morris in Kent, an estate inherited by her mother, Elizabeth Drake, and was educated at home with her sister, Elizabeth. After her sister's marriage to Edward Montagu in 1742, Sarah travelled widely in England, both with her sister and alone.

In 1748 Sarah met Barbara Montagu in Bath and the two became close friends. They lived together until the latter's death in 1765, including the period of Sarah's unsuccessful marriage to George Lewis Scott, Sub-Preceptor to the Prince of Wales. The marriage, which took place in 1751, was legally dissolved a year later. Sarah Scott and Barbara Montagu devoted themselves to charitable works and *Millenium Hall* is based, in part, on their life together. Barbara Montagu is sometimes ascribed co-author of this novel.

Following the collapse of Sarah Scott's marriage, she wrote to support herself financially as the allowance provided by her husband was insufficient. A novelist and historian, all her works were published anonymously or pseudonymously and were well-received on publication. She was the author of five novels: *The History of Cornelia* (1750), *Agreeable Ugliness* (1754), *A Journey through Every Stage of Life* (1754), *A Description of Millenium Hall* (1762), *The History of Sir George Ellison* (1766) and *A Test of Filial Duty* (1772), and three histories: *The History of Gustavus Erickson, King of Sweden* (1761), *The History of Mecklenburgh* (1762) and *The Life of Theodore Agripa D'Aubigné* (1772).

After the death of Barbara Montagu, Sarah Scott travelled, spending some time in London. She requested that after her own death her papers should be destroyed, and therefore details of her life are few.

A DESCRIPTION OF

MILLENIUM HALL

AND THE

COUNTRY ADJACENT

Together with the

CHARACTERS OF THE INHABITANTS

And such Historical

ANECDOTES AND REFLECTIONS

AS

May excite in the READER proper Sentiments of Humanity,
and lead the Mind to the Love of
VIRTUE

BY

'A GENTLEMAN
ON HIS TRAVELS'

SARAH SCOTT

WITH A NEW INTRODUCTION BY
JANE SPENCER

PENGUIN BOOKS – VIRAGO PRESS

PENGUIN BOOKS
Viking Penguin Inc., 40 West 23rd Street,
New York, New York 10010, U.S.A.
Penguin Books Ltd, Harmondsworth, Middlesex, England
Penguin Books Australia Ltd, Ringwood, Victoria, Australia
Penguin Books Canada Limited, 2801 John Street,
Markham, Ontario, Canada L3R 1B4
Penguin Books (N.Z.) Ltd, 182–190 Wairau Road,
Auckland 10, New Zealand

First published in Great Britain by J. Newbery 1762

This edition first published in Great Britain by
Virago Press Limited 1986

Published in Penguin Books 1986

Introduction copyright © Jane Spencer, 1986

Typeset by Strewlight Photosetting, London W1 and
printed in Great Britain by Anchor Brendon Limited
of Tiptree, Essex

Set in Garamond

INTRODUCTION

S ARAH Robinson met Lady Barbara Montagu in Bath in 1748, and a close friendship soon grew up between the two women. Both were of high social standing. Lady Bab (as she was usually known) was the daughter of the first earl of Halifax and his wife Lady Mary Lumley: her brother, the second earl, added immense riches to high rank by marrying an heiress with £110,000. The Robinsons, if not quite so illustrious, were an old-established gentry family in Yorkshire, and Sarah, born in 1723, grew up at Mount Morris in Kent, an estate inherited by her mother Elizabeth Drake. Sarah's elder sister Elizabeth, who married Edward Montagu (no direct relative of Lady Barbara) in 1742, became a celebrated literary figure, the leading 'bluestocking' in the days when the term was a compliment; while Sarah herself, by far the more prolific writer, published her works anonymously. Sarah always remained deeply attached to her more famous sister, but her friendship with Lady Barbara seems to have been the emotional centre of her life.

There was a temporary estrangement from her sister in 1751 when, in the face of Elizabeth Montagu's disapproval, Sarah married George Lewis Scott, a mathematician and tutor to the Prince of Wales. Why the marriage failed we do not know, but the pair separated in 1752. The gossip of their acquaintances throws a little light on the picture. Mrs Delany wrote to her sister Mrs Dewes in April, 1752:

> What a foolish match Mrs Scott has made for herself. Mrs Montagu wrote Mrs Donnellan word that she and the rest of her friends had rescued her out of the hands of a very bad man: but for reasons of interest, they should conceal his misbehaviour as much as possible, but entreated Mrs Donnellan would vindicate her sister's character whenever she heard it attacked, for she was very innocent.

vi

Mrs Donnellan sent out delicate probes for more information, writing to Mrs Montagu in May:

> I had heard . . . that she and Mr Scott were parted, but could hardly believe it, a match so much of mutual inclination seemed to promise mutual happiness, and the shortness of the time of their union hardly allowed them to find out they were not happy, so that you are unwilling to hurt the gentleman in his character. I must conclude he is very bad, since in so short a time he could force Mrs Scott and all her family to come to such an *éclat* . . . you entirely justify Mrs Scott, and I am sure you must know the truth. I hear, too, he has given her back half her fortune, and has settled a 150 pounds a year on her; this, I think, is a justification to her.[1]

Elizabeth Montagu's worries about her sister's reputation seem to have been unnecessary. Most contemporary comments on the separation blame George Scott, and there was even a rumour that he had tried to poison his wife.

Nobody at the time seems to have seen Lady Barbara as a factor in the estrangement, but it is significant that in the partly-autobiographical *Millenium Hall*, the worst thing about Mrs Morgan's unhappy marriage is that it parts her from her friend Miss Mancel.

> The day after their marriage, Mrs Morgan asked his permission to invite Miss Mancel to his house, to which he answered, 'Madam, my wife must have no other companion or friend but her husband; I shall never be averse to your seeing company, but intimates I forbid; I shall not choose to have my faults discussed between you and your *friend*.'
>
> Mrs Morgan was not much less stunned by this reply, than if she had been struck with lightening.

Luckier, or less submissive, than her heroine, Sarah Scott did not let marriage separate her from her woman friend. Lady Barbara went with the Scotts on their honeymoon (a common enough occurrence in an age when the bride was considered to need the support of a female companion) and lived with the couple during most of their short married life. After the separation Sarah Scott stayed with her sister for a time, and then went to live with Lady Barbara. By 1755, Elizabeth Montagu was giving thanks for her sister's renewed happiness as she settled down with her friend near Bath.

Sarah Scott had been interested in writing for some time. She and her sister had been educated at home, and their early correspondence shows that they read widely. They spent some of their time in Cambridge with their maternal grandmother, whose second husband, Conyers Middleton, was Professor of Classical Languages. He is said to have been delighted with Elizabeth's intelligence, and probably both sisters' education benefited from their connection with him. Altogether Scott was better equipped for a writing career than most women of her time, despite her lack of formal schooling. Her first novel, *The History of Cornelia*, appeared in 1750. After her marriage and separation, writing took on a new importance for her as a source of income.

She had lost half the fortune she had taken with her into marriage, and the yearly allowance paid by her husband, though enough to live on, fell far short of providing the kind of life she was used to. She and her friend pooled their income: we do not know how much Lady Barbara had, but Elizabeth Montagu – herself the wife of a very rich man – considered the two women poorly provided for. Sarah Scott's letters to her sister make it clear that money was one motive for continuing her literary career. Another novel, *A Journey Through Every Stage of Life*, and *Agreeable Ugliness, or the Trial of the Graces*, translated from a French novel *La Laideur Aimable*, appeared in 1754. The latter shows Scott's interest in the problems of unattractive women, perhaps aroused when her own appearance was affected by smallpox at the age of eighteen. In the next decade Scott turned to history. Her *History of Gustavus Erickson, King of Sweden* appeared in 1761 under the pseudonym Henry Augustus Raymond, Esq. *The History of Mecklenburgh*, exploiting public interest at the time of George III's marriage to Charlotte of Mecklenburgh, followed in 1762. A third historical work was *The Life of Theodore Agripa D'Aubigné* (1772). She also continued to write novels:

A Description of Millenium Hall (1762) was followed by *The History of Sir George Ellison* (1766) and *A Test of Filial Duty* (1772). *Millenium Hall* was a fairly popular work, going through four editions by 1778, but a letter from Scott to her sister shows that she made very little money from it. She admitted, though, that as she had spent less than a month writing it her payment worked out at about a guinea a day, so it seems likely that she sold the novel to the publisher, Newbery, for twenty-five or thirty guineas.[2]

Money was important to Sarah Scott and Barbara Montagu because of the good works they could do with it. A letter to the *Gentleman's Magazine* after Scott's death testified to her generosity: 'Among many excellent qualities, her benevolence and charity were such as have rarely been equalled, scarcely ever exceeded.'[3] The two women's dedication to charity was described by Elizabeth Montagu in a letter to her friend Gilbert West, dated 1755:

> My sister rises early, and as soon as she has read prayers to their small family, she sits down to cut and prepare work for twelve poor girls, whose schooling they pay for; to those whom she finds more than ordinarily capable, she teaches writing and arithmetic herself. The work these children are usually employed in is making child-bed linen and clothes for poor people in the neighbourhood, which Lady Bab Montagu and she, bestow as they see occasion. Very early on Sunday morning these girls, with twelve little boys whom they also send to school, come to my sister and repeat their catechism, read some chapters, have the principal articles of their religion explained to them, and then are sent to the parish church. These good works are often performed by the Methodist ladies in the heat of enthusiasm, but thank God, my sister's is a calm and rational piety. Her conversation is lively and easy, and she enters into all the reasonable pleasures of Society; goes frequently to the plays, and sometimes to balls, etc. They have a very pretty house at Bath for the winter, and one at Bath Easton for the summer; their houses are adorned by the ingenuity of the owners, but as their income is small, they deny themselves unnecessary expenses. My sister seems very happy; it has pleased God to lead her to truth, by the road of affliction; but what draws the sting of death and triumphs over the grave,

> cannot fail to heal the wounds of disappointment. Lady Bab
> Montagu concurs with her in all these things, and their convent,
> for by its regularity it resembles one, is really a cheerful
> place.[4]

This life of piety, charity and friendship – expanded in
imagination by the fictional addition of large amounts of
money – was celebrated in *Millenium Hall*. No doubt because
the novel is based on the women's shared life, there is a
tradition of shared authorship, begun by Sir Horace Walpole
who pencilled into his copy of the second (1764) edition, now
in the British Library, 'This book was written by Lady Bab
Montagu (the sister of George Montagu Dunk, Earl of Halifax)
and Mrs Scott, daughter of Matthew Robinson, Esq., and wife of
George Scott, Esq.'[5] There is not enough evidence, though, to
be sure of Lady Bab's collaboration. In her letters to her sister
Scott refers to the work as her own, and only she is known as
the author of other books. However, if Lady Bab was not the co-
author, she perhaps helped plan and is most certainly the
inspiration behind *Millenium Hall*.

Sadly, the friendship it depicts was cut short soon afterwards
when Lady Bab died in 1765. Sarah Scott stayed in Bath for
about two years after this and then moved around to various
places, spending some of her time in the London society
implicitly rejected in *Millenium Hall*. She seems to have
remained close friends with a Mrs Cutts, thought by some to be
portrayed in one of the Millenium Hall ladies, and she still had a
close friend and correspondent in her sister. Around 1787 she
settled in Catton, near Norwich, where she died in 1795. She
had envisaged new ways of organising society herself, and she
lived long enough to see the French Revolution and the
stirrings of radical political movements in England . She did not
like what she saw. In particular she objected to women's public
participation in revolutionary politics – though her disapproval
was perhaps tinged with reluctant admiration. Commenting on
a political debate in Norwich in 1794, she wrote: 'a young
woman of uncommon talents of about twenty-five years of age
made a long speech in the Town Hall to about 1,500 of the

Jacobins assembled against Mr Wyndham [a Whig M.P.], and two daughters of a late Doctor of Divinity stood one on each side of her to encourage her in her proceeding'.[6] The female solidarity shown by these revolutionists was Sarah Scott's own ideal: but her hope had been for much gentler changes in society, and her vision had been of women helping to bring these changes by more conventionally 'feminine' means. *Millenium Hall* is her expression of that vision.

At the time of its publication the novel, always a popular genre, was well on its way to becoming a respectable one. The so-called 'immoral' works of early novelists like Delariviere Manley and Eliza Haywood were out of fashion, replaced by the 'moral' novel, first extensively developed by Penelope Aubin in the 1720s and made famous by the success of Samuel Richardson's *Pamela: or, Virtue Rewarded* in 1740. Sarah Scott, hoping to 'excite in the READER proper Sentiments of Humanity, and lead the Mind to the Love of VIRTUE', was joining an established didactic tradition which, according to general opinion at the time, was particularly appropriate for the woman writer. Young women, believed to form the bulk of novel-readers and always in need of good advice, were thought to be 'more agreeably instructed' by members of their own sex.[7]

What the instructions generally were can be seen in *Millenium Hall*. Like many eighteenth-century novels it contains separate 'histories' of various characters, in this case all women and all – whether initially or as a result of life's lessons – virtuous. Miss Mancel and Mrs Morgan, Lady Mary Jones, Mrs Selvyn, and Mrs Trentham have their stories related by Mrs Maynard, the sixth of the principal ladies of Millenium Hall. Self-abnegation, duty to one's elders, and an overwhelming dedication to chastity are the female virtues they repeatedly show. Thus one inhabitant of Millenium Hall has refused to marry the man she loves for the sake of his grandmother, her benefactress, who would disapprove of the match, while another has married someone she detests in order to preserve her chaste reputation from totally unwarranted aspersions. Miss Melvyn's words before becoming Mrs Morgan: 'All inclination must now be laid aside, and duty must become my sole guide and director', encapsulate the ideal of conduct usually held up to the female reader. No wonder that Clara Reeve, who put moral considerations above aesthetic ones in her historical and critical study, *The Progress of Romance* (1785), considered *Millenium Hall* 'very proper to be put into the hands of young persons'.[8]

Despite this Scott is very far from writing the usual didactic tract for young ladies. *Millenium Hall* really aims to educate *men*. The first indication of this is on the title page: Millenium Hall is a female community but its story is supposedly told us 'By a Gentleman on his Travels'. Anonymity, sometimes coupled with the pretence of masculinity, was always Scott's authorial practice. People often assume this would be the usual tactic of women writers in earlier periods, but in fact it seems more typical of the nineteenth century, with George Eliot and Charlotte Brontë's 'Currer Bell', than of the eighteenth. When Sarah Scott was writing, women novelists were beginning to gain critical esteem, and many wrote under their own names or designated their work 'By a Lady'. The woman writer was no longer a disreputable figure, and one of Scott's neighbours in Bath was typical of the new, moral, respected female author: Sarah Fielding, Henry Fielding's sister, novelist and translator from Greek, whose work was praised not only by her brother but by Richardson and by the reviewers. Perhaps Scott's attempt to avoid being known as a writer had as much to do with considerations of rank as of sex: having to write for money probably felt like a threat to her social status. No doubt another consideration, as far as *Millenium Hall* was concerned, was to hide its semi-autobiographical nature. However, probably the most important reason for the fiction of the gentleman on his travels in this novel was a functional one. His masculinity is essential to the overall effect of *Millenium Hall*.

Through the gentleman, the female utopia that is the Millenium Hall community can be viewed as from the outside, and it can be made to influence the surrounding, male-dominated world. *Millenium Hall* is a novel of ideas: its narrative is not sustained through the kind of plot interest usual at the time: the heroine's fortunes and misfortunes in love. The expected motifs are all there in the ladies' histories: attempted seduction, planned elopement, parental misunderstanding, forced marriage. Because of the framework, though, they do not create suspense or drama for the reader. We know from the start that all the women have ended up happily unmarried at Millenium Hall. Eschewing romantic interest, the narrative creates instead a utopian vision of a female community, into which the male narrator, his companion, and the reader, are drawn. The main interest of the novel is in its depiction of this community.

Learning about Millenium Hall with the narrator, we first experience it as enchantment. Its pastoral surroundings seem a 'fairy land', which makes the two men 'fancy [them] selves on enchanted ground'. The Hall itself takes us from rural delights to learned elegance. The men enter a room full of women studying or practising the arts, and the narrator thinks it is like an 'Attic school': that is, it fits his notion of the civilisation of ancient Athens. A classically-educated gentleman, he responds immediately to this recreation of a classical ideal; but he is soon to learn that the community's deeper virtue lies in its constant attempt to live up to the Christian ideal. Learning and culture here take second place to piety and charity.

The narrator enters Millenium Hall, after his chaise has broken down, to shelter himself from a sudden storm. There he is to find a more important refuge, from the harsh, acquisitive society outside. He has just returned from making his fortune – like many eighteenth-century merchants – in the new colonies. 'The hot and unwholesome climate of Jamaica' has left him rich but unhealthy. The ladies' example is to show him a way of using riches for the health of body and soul, with concern for the welfare of the whole community replacing the use of slave labour he has known in the West Indies. The ladies' main spokeswoman is Mrs Maynard, and the narrator also meets an old woman who explains how a cottage community has been set up for her and her neighbours. From these people the gentleman learns about the new society that is growing up around the Hall, making it deserve the fictional title he gives it. It is a place where one can almost believe the millennium has come.

In some ways Scott's vision may not seem radical enough to be called utopian. Her ladies do not break down class barriers: there is a big difference between the help they give to peasants' children and that offered to indigent gentlewomen. At times their patronising attitudes grate on the reader. In real life women would hardly respond with the rapture depicted here to their benefactresses' close supervision of their lives, which includes lectures on neighbourly behaviour and a daily inspection of their cottages for cleanliness. It is easy to be reminded of a later novelist's exposé of interfering 'benevolence': Jane Austen's portrait of Lady Catherine de Bourgh, who 'whenever any of the cottagers were disposed to be quarrelsome, discontented or too poor . . . sallied forth into the village to settle their differences, silence their complaints, and scold them into harmony and plenty'.[9] More often, though, today's reader is struck by how enlightened is Scott's view of a caring community. The ladies make a point of providing employment for the disabled and deformed (even if they do encourage them to seclude themselves from the outside world, this is a big improvement on showing them as freaks in fairgrounds), they particularly interest themselves in the education of poor girls, and when providing for the aged they do not just concentrate on keeping them alive (too often all our own society tries to do) but help them to have active interests: the old women help look after their neighbours' children, who 'make us mothers again, as it were, in our old age', as the gentleman's informant tells him.

The community for unmarried gentlewomen must have struck a special chord in eighteenth-century hearts. At a time when more women than before were remaining unmarried, and their opportunities of earning a living were contracting, the spinster was seen as a problem. Protestant England did not provide the alternative community of the convent, and several writers had suggested ways of remedying this. As early as 1694 the feminist Mary Astell's pamphlet, *A Serious Proposal to the Ladies*, had advocated setting up a college community for women outside marriage. Unfortunately her idea was not taken up, partly because it sounded too conventual to Protestant ears. Sarah Scott's ideas are similar to Astell's in some respects, and it is interesting that Elizabeth Montagu thought that her home with Lady Barbara was like a convent. The community of Millenium Hall is certainly not seen as a consolation for women who have failed to marry. The periodical interruptions to Mrs Maynard's inset narratives allow for the skilful juxtaposition of Mrs Morgan's plight in the outside world – hounded into marriage to a domestic tyrant – with the delights of the female community she creates with the tyrant's wealth once he is dead. The ladies declare themselves all in favour of marriage – for other people – but unmarried life at Millenium Hall is evidently Scott's ideal.

There is symbolic significance in the choice of the gentlewomen's residence. A house near Millenium Hall, bought by the ladies, is being renovated for them after successive male owners have ruined it either by hoarding or squandering their money. This is what the novel is all about: wealth, originally in men's hands, making its way into the possession of good women. What they do with it demonstrates how important women's ideas, ignored in the world at large, are to the development of a truly Christian community. The narrator and his friend are important because they show the male reaction to this. The narrator, initially sympathetic (it is significant that he turns out to be related to Mrs Maynard) moves towards a deeper identification with the ladies' aims. His coxcomb companion, Lamont, is slowly educated out of his initial scepticism. The narrator of *Millenium Hall* reappears as Sir George Ellison, the hero of Sarah Scott's next novel. In that book we learn more about Lamont's first objections to Millenium Hall:

> the persons who so much excelled him in reason as well as virtue, were women, were of that weak sex, which he had hitherto

considered only as play-things for men; a race somewhat superior to monkeys; formed to amuse the other sex during the continuance of youth and beauty, and after the bloom was past, to be useful drudges for their convenience. To be disabused of so favourite an error, galled him intolerably.[10]

Millenium Hall is primarily concerned with disabusing men of their errors about women.

Comparing *Millenium Hall* with *The History of Sir George Ellison* shows how important to Scott's vision for women is the escape from marriage. Sir George Ellison, like the ladies of the Hall, is a paragon of benevolence, and his wife joins in his work in a small way. 'Her sphere, indeed, was different and more minute; but if her charities were less considerable in expence and in their various consequences, they were however very impotant, as they adminstered to the happiness, or at least comfort of many.'[11] In complete contrast, *Millenium Hall* shows its heroines, with their all-embracing ideas for a new kind of community, teaching the narrator, who vows 'to imitate them on a smaller scale'. Being spared matrimony and its consequence, wifely subordination (not in itself challenged by Sarah Scott), the ladies of Millenium Hall can be influential guides and teachers to the men who move and hold power in the outside world. On one level then, the novel upholds the restrictive ideal of woman as a naturally virtuous creature who gets by without direct power, because she can influence men towards good by her example: but it is also, more unconventionally, an engaging account of an alternative way of female life.

Jane Spencer, Edinburgh, 1985

Notes

1. Letters quoted in *Elizabeth Montagu, The Queen of the Bluestockings: Her Correspondence from 1720 to 1761, by her great-great-niece Emily J. Climenson*, London, John Murray, 1906, II, p.5 and II, p.7.

2. This letter, along with most of Scott's extant letters, is in the Montagu collection of MSS in the Huntington Library, California. It is printed in Walter M. Crittenden's edition of *Millenium Hall*, New York, Bookman Associates, 1955, p.15.

3. *Gentleman's Magazine* 1798 (ii), p.827.

4. Climenson, II, pp.78-9.

5. See note by Edward M. Borrajo, *Notes and Queries* 7th ser., 8(1889), p.116.

6. Letter quoted in *Mrs Montagu, 'Queen of the Blues': Her Letters and Friendships from 1762 to 1800, Edited by Reginald Blunt from Material left to him by her great-great-niece Emily J. Climenson*, London, Constable and Co. Ltd., 1923, II, p.304.

7. Charlotte Lennox's novel *Sophia*, which appeared in the same year as *Millenium Hall*, was taken as evidence that women were 'more agreeably instructed' by women writers: see *Critical Review* 13(1762), p.435.

8. *The Progress of Romance*, Colchester, W. Keymer, 1785, II, p.35.

9. *Pride and Prejudice*, ed. R.W. Chapman, London, Oxford University Press, 1967, p.169.

10. *The History of Sir George Ellison*, London, A. Millar, 1766, I, pp.106-7.

11. *The History of Sir George Ellison*, II, p.215.

A DESCRIPTION OF

MILLENIUM HALL

Dear Sir,

THOUGH, when I left London, I promised to write to you as soon as I had reached my northern retreat, yet, I believe, you little expected instead of a letter to receive a volume; but I should not stand excused to myself, were I to fail communicating to you the pleasure I received in my road hither, from the sight of a society whose acquaintance I owe to one of those fortunate, though in appearance trifling, accidents, from which sometimes arise the most pleasing circumstances of our lives; for as such I must ever esteem the acquaintance of that amiable family, who have fixed their abode at a place which I shall nominate Millenium Hall, as the best adapted to the lives of the inhabitants, and to avoid giving the real name, fearing to offend that modesty which has induced them to conceal their virtues in retirement.

In giving you a very circumstantial account of this society, I confess I have a view beyond the pleasure which a mind like yours must receive from the contemplation of so much virtue. Your constant endeavours have been to inculcate the best principles into youthful minds, the only probable means of mending mankind; for the foundation of most of our virtues, or our vices, are laid in that season of life when we are most susceptible of impression, and when on our minds, as on a sheet of white paper, any characters may be engraven; these laudable endeavours, by which we may reasonably expect the rising generation will be greatly improved, render particularly due to you, any examples which may teach those virtues that are not easily learnt by precept and shew the facility of what, in mere speculation, might appear surrounded with a discouraging impracticability: you are the best judge, whether, by being made public, they may be conducive to your great end of benefiting the world. I therefore submit the future fate of the following sheets entirely to you, and shall not think any prefatory apology for the publication at all requisite; for though a man who supposes his own life and actions deserve universal notice, or can be of general use, may be liable to the imputation of vanity, yet, as I have no other share than that of a spectator, and auditor, in what I purpose to relate, I presume no apology can be required; for my vanity must rather be mortified than flattered in the description of such virtues as will continually accuse me of my own deficiencies, and lead me to make a humiliating comparison between these excellent ladies and myself.

You may remember, Sir, that when I took leave of you with a design of retiring to my native county, there to enjoy the plenty and leisure for which a few years labour had furnished me with the necessary requisites, I was advised by an eminent physician to make a very extensive tour through the western part of this kingdom, in order, by frequent change of air, and continued exercise, to cure the ill effects of my long abode in the hot and unwholesome climate of Jamaica, where, while I increased my fortune, I gradually impaired my constitution; and though one who, like me, has dedicated all his application to mercantile gain, will not allow that he has given up the substance for the shadow, yet perhaps it would be difficult to deny that I thus sacrificed the greater good in pursuit of the less.

The eagerness with which I longed to fix in my wished-for retirement, made me imagine that when I had once reached it, even the pursuit of health would be an insufficient inducement to determine me to leave my retreat. I therefore chose to make the advised tour before I went into the north. As the pleasure arising from a variety of beautiful objects is but half enjoyed when we have no one to share it with us, I accepted the offer Mr Lamont (the son of my old friend) made of accompanying me in my journey. As this young gentleman has not the good fortune to be known to you, it may not be amiss, as will appear in the sequel, to let you into his character.

Mr Lamont is a young man of about twenty-five years of age, of an agreeable person, and lively understanding; both perhaps have concurred to render him a coxcomb. The vivacity of his parts soon gained him such a degree of encouragement as excited his vanity, and raised in him a high opinion of himself. A very generous father enabled him to partake of every fashionable amusement, and the natural bent of his mind soon led him into all the dissipation which the gay world affords. Useful and improving studies were laid aside for such desultory reading as he found most proper to furnish him with topics for conversation in the idle societies he frequented. Thus that vivacity, which, properly qualified, might have become true wit, degenerated into pertness and impertinence. A consciousness of an understanding, which he never exerted, rendered him conceited; those talents which nature kindly bestowed upon him, by being perverted, gave rise to his greatest faults. His reasoning faculty, by a partial and superficial use, led him to infidelity, and the desire of being thought superiorly distinguishing established him an infidel. Fashion, not reason, has been the guide of all his thoughts and actions. But with these faults he is good-natured, and not unentertaining, especially in a tête-à-tête, where he does not desire to shine, and therefore his vanity lies dormant and suffers the best qualifications of his mind to break forth. This induced me to accept him as a fellow traveller.

We proceeded on our journey as far as Cornwall, without meeting with any other than the usual incidents of the road, till one afternoon, when our chaise broke down. The worst circumstance attending this accident was our being several miles from a town, and so ignorant of the country, that we knew not whether there was any village within a moderate distance. We sent the postilion on my man's horse to the next town to fetch a smith, and leaving my servant to guard the chaise, Mr Lamont and I walked towards an avenue of oaks, which we observed at a small distance. The thick shade they afforded us, the fragrance wafted from the woodbines with which they were encircled, was so delightful, and the beauty of the grounds so very attracting, that we strolled on, desirous of approaching the house to which this avenue led. It is a mile and a half in length, but the eye is so charmed with the remarkable verdure and neatness of the fields, with the beauty of the flowers which are planted all around them and seem to mix with the quickset hedges, that time steals away insensibly.

When we had walked about half a mile in a scene truly pastoral, we began to think ourselves in the days of Theocritus, so sweetly did the sound of a flute come wafted through the air. Never did pastoral swain make sweeter melody on his oaten reed. Our ears now afforded us fresh attraction, and with quicker steps we proceeded, till we came within sight of the musician that had charmed us. Our pleasure was not a little heightened, to see, as the scene promised, in reality a shepherd, watching a large flock of sheep. We continued motionless, listening to his music, till a lamb straying from its fold demanded his care, and he laid aside his instrument, to guide home the little wanderer.

Curiosity now prompted us to walk on; the nearer we came to the house, the greater we found the profusion of flowers which ornamented every field. Some had no other defence than hedges of rose trees and sweetbriars, so artfully planted, that they made a very thick hedge, while at the lower part, pinks, jonquils, hyacinths, and various other flowers, seemed to grow under their protection. Primroses, violets, lilies of the valley, and polyanthuses enriched such shady spots, as, for want of sun, were not well calculated for the production of other flowers. The mixture of perfumes which exhaled from this profusion composed the highest fragrance, and sometimes the different scents regaled the senses alternately, and filled us with reflections on the infinite variety of nature.

When we were within about a quarter of a mile of the house, the scene became still more animated. On one side was the greatest variety of cattle, the most beautiful of their kinds, grazing in fields whose verdure equalled that of the finest turf, nor were they destitute of their ornaments, only the woodbines and jessamine, and such flowers as might have tempted the inhabitants of these pastures to crop them, were defended with roses and sweetbriars, whose thorns preserved them from all attacks.

Though Lamont had hitherto been little accustomed to admire nature, yet was he much captivated with this scene, and with his usual levity cried out, 'If Nebuchadnezzar had such pastures as these to range in, his seven years expulsion from human society might not be the least agreeable part of his life.' My attention was too much engaged to criticize the light turn of Lamont's mind, nor did his thoughts continue long on the same subject, for our observation was soon called off by a company of hay-makers in the fields on the other side of the avenue. The cleanliness and neatness of the young women thus employed, rendered them a more pleasing subject for Lamont's contemplation than any thing we had yet seen; in them we beheld rural simplicity, without any of those marks of poverty and boorish rusticity, which would have spoilt the pastoral air of the scene around us; but not even the happy amiable innocence, which their figures and countenances expressed, gave me so much satisfaction as the sight of the number of children, who were all exerting the utmost of their strength, with an air of delighted emulation between themselves, to contribute their share to the general undertaking. Their eyes sparkled with that spirit which health and activity can only give, and their rosy cheeks shewed the benefits of youthful labour.

Curiosity is one of those insatiable passions that grow by gratification; it still prompted us to proceed, not unsatisfied with what we had seen, but desirous to see still more of this earthly paradise. We approached the house, wherein, as it was the only human habitation in view, we imagined must reside the Primum Mobile of all we had yet beheld. We were admiring the magnificence of the ancient structure, and inclined to believe it the abode of the genius which presided over this fairy land, when we were surprised by a storm, which had been some time gathering over our heads, though our thoughts had been too agreeably engaged to pay much attention to it. We took shelter under the thick shade of a large oak, but the violence of the thunder and lightning made our situation rather uncomfortable. All those whom we had a little before seen so busy left their work on hearing the first clap of thunder and ran with the utmost speed to Millenium Hall, so I shall call the noble mansion of which I am speaking, as to an assured asylum against every evil.

Some of these persons, I imagine, perceived us; for immediately after they entered, came out a woman who, by her air and manner of address, we guessed to be the housekeeper, and desired us to walk into the house till the storm was over. We made some difficulties about taking that liberty, but she still persisting in her invitation, had my curiosity to see the inhabitants of this hospitable mansion been less, I could not have refused to comply, as by prolonging these ceremonious altercations I was detaining her in the storm; we therefore agreed to follow her.

If we had been inclined before to fancy ourselves on enchanted ground, when after being led through a large hall, we were introduced to the ladies, who knew nothing of what had passed, I could scarcely forbear believing myself in the Attic school. The room where they sat was about forty-five feet long, of a proportionable breadth, with three windows on one side, which looked into a garden, and a large bow at the upper end. Over against the windows were three large bookcases, upon the top of the middle one stood an orrery, and a globe on each of the others. In the bow sat two ladies reading, with pen, ink and paper on a table before them at which was a young girl translating out of French. At the lower end of the room was a lady painting, with exquisite art indeed, a beautiful Madonna; near her another, drawing a landscape out of her own imagination; a third, carving a picture-frame in wood, in the finest manner; a fourth, engraving; and a young girl reading aloud to them; the distance from the ladies in the bow window being such, that they could receive no disturbance from her. At the next window were placed a group of girls, from the age of ten years old to fourteen. Of these, one was drawing figures, another a landscape, a third a perspective view, a fourth engraving, a fifth carving, a sixth turning in wood, a seventh writing, an eighth cutting out linen, another making a gown, and by them an empty chair and a tent, with embroidery, finely fancied, before it, which we afterwards found had been left by a young girl who was gone to practise on the harpsichord.

As soon as we entered they all rose up, and the housekeeper introduced us by saying she saw us standing under a tree to avoid the storm and so had desired us to walk in. The ladies received us with the greatest politeness, and expressed concern that when their house was so near, we should have recourse to so insufficient a shelter. Our surprise at the sight of so uncommon a society occasioned our making but an awkward return to their obliging reception; nor when we observed how many arts we had interrupted, could we avoid being ashamed that we had then intruded upon them.

But before I proceed farther, I shall endeavour to give you some idea of the persons of the ladies, whose minds I shall afterwards best describe by their actions. The two who sat in the bow window were called Mrs Maynard and Miss Selvyn. Mrs Maynard is between forty and fifty years of age, a little woman, well made, with a lively and genteel air, her hair black, and her eyes of the same colour, bright and piercing, her features good, and complexion agreeable, though brown. Her countenance expresses all the vivacity of youth, tempered with a serenity which becomes her age.

Miss Selvyn can scarcely be called tall, though she approaches that standard. Her features are too irregular to be handsome, but there is a sensibility and delicacy in her countenance which render her extremely engaging; and her person is elegant.

Miss Mancel, whom we had disturbed from her painting, is tall and finely formed, has great elegance of figure, and is graceful in every motion. Her hair is of a fine brown, her eyes blue, with all that sensible sweetness which is peculiar to that colour. In short, she excels in every beauty but the bloom, which is so soon faded, and so impossible to be imitated by the utmost efforts of art, nor has she suffered any farther by years than the loss of that radiance which renders beauty rather more resplendent than more pleasing.

Miss Trentham, who was carving by her, was the tallest of the company, and in dignity of air particularly excels, but her features and complexion have been so injured by the smallpox, that one can but just guess they were once uncommonly fine; a sweetness of countenance, and a very sensible look, indeed, still remain, and have baffled all the most cruel ravages of that distemper.

Lady Mary Jones, whom we found engraving, seems to have been rather pleasing than beautiful. She is thin and pale, but a pair of the finest black eyes I ever saw, animate, to a great degree, a countenance which sickness has done its utmost to render languid, but has, perhaps, only made more delicate and amiable. Her person is exquisitely genteel, and her voice, in common speech, enchantingly melodious.

Mrs Morgan, the lady who was drawing, appears to be upwards of fifty, tall, rather plump, and extremely majestic, an air of dignity distinguishes her person, and every virtue is engraven in indelible characters on her countenance. There is a benignity in every look, which renders the decline of life, if possible, more amiable than the bloom of youth. One would almost think nature had formed her for a common parent, such universal and tender benevolence beams from every glance she casts around her.

The dress of the ladies was thus far uniform, the same neatness, the same simplicity and cleanliness appeared in each, and they were all in lutestring night-gowns, though of different colours, nor was there any thing unfashionable in their appearance, except that they were free from any trumpery ornaments. The girls were all clothed in camblet coats, but not uniform in colour, their linen extremely white and clean though coarse. Some of them were pretty, and none had any defect in person, to take off from that general pleasingness which attends youth and innocence.

They had been taught such a habit of attention that they seemed not at all disturbed by our conversation, which was of that general kind, as might naturally be expected on such an occasion, though supported by the ladies with more sensible vivacity and politeness than is usual where part of the company are such total strangers to the rest; till by chance one of the ladies called Mrs Maynard by her name.

From the moment I saw her, I thought her face not unknown to me, but could not recollect where or when I had been acquainted with her, but her name brought to my recollection, that she was not only an old acquaintance, but a near relation. I observed that she had looked on me with particular attention, and I begged her to give me leave to ask her of what family of Maynards she was. Her answer confirmed my supposition, and as she told me that she believed she had some remembrance of my face, I soon made her recollect our affinity and former intimacy, though my twenty years abode in Jamaica, the altera-tion the climate had wrought in me, and time had made in us both, had almost effaced us from each other's memory.

There is great pleasure in renewing the acquaintance of our youth; a thousand pleasing ideas accompany it; many mirthful scenes and juvenile amusements return to the remembrance, and make us, as it were, live over again what is generally the most pleasing part of life. Mrs Maynard seemed no less sensible of the satisfaction arising from this train of thoughts than myself, and the rest of the company were so indulgently good-natured, as in appearance, to share them with us. The tea table by no means interrupted our conversation, and I believe I should have forgot that our journey was not at an end, if a servant had not brought in word, that my man, who had observed our motions, was come to inform us that our chaise could not be repaired that night.

The ladies immediately declared that though their equipage was in order, they would not suffer it to put an end to a pleasure they owed to the accident which had happened to ours, and insisted we should give them our company till the smith had made all necessary reparations, adding, that I could not be obstinately bent on depriving Mrs Maynard so soon of the satisfaction she received from having recovered so long lost a relation. I was little inclined to reject this invitation: pleasure was the chief design of my journey, and I saw not how I could receive more than by remaining in a family so extraordinary, and so perfectly agreeable. When both parties are well agreed, the necessary ceremonies previous to a compliance are soon over, and it was settled that we should not think of departing before the next day at soonest.

The continuance of the rain rendered it impossible to stir out of the house; my cousin, who seemed to think variety necessary to amuse, asked if we loved music, which being answered in the affirmative, she begged the other ladies to entertain us with one of their family concerts, and we joining in the petition, proper orders were given, and we adjourned into another room, which was well furnished with musical instruments. Over the door was a beautiful Saint Cecilia, painted in crayons by Miss Mancel, and a fine piece of carved work over the chimney, done by Miss Trentham, which was a very artificial representation of every sort of musical instrument.

While we were admiring these performances, the company took their respective places. Miss Mancel seated herself at the harpsichord, Lady Mary Jones played on the arch lute, Mrs Morgan on the organ, Miss Selvyn and Miss Trentham each on the six-stringed bass; the shepherd who had charmed us in the field was there with his German flute; a venerable looking man, who is their steward, played on the violincello, a lame youth on the French horn, another, who seemed very near blind, on the bassoon, and two on the fiddle. My cousin had no share in the performance except singing agreeably, wherein she was joined by some of the ladies, and where the music could bear it, by ten of the young girls, with two or three others whom we had not seen, and whose voices and manner were equally pleasing. They performed several of the finest pieces of the Messiah and Judas Maccabeus, with exquisite taste, and the most exact time. There was a sufficient number of performers to give the choruses all their pomp and fullness, and the songs were sung in a manner so touching and pathetic, as could be equalled by none whose hearts were not as much affected by the words as their senses were by the music. The sight of so many little innocents joining in the most sublime harmony made me almost think myself already amongst the heavenly choir, and it was a great mortification to me to be brought back to this sensual world by so gross an attraction as a call to supper, which put an end to our concert, and carried us to another room, where we found a repast more elegant than expensive.

The evening certainly is the most social part of the day, without any of those excesses which so often turn it into senseless revelry. The conversation after supper was particularly animated, and left us still more charmed with the society into which chance had introduced us; the sprightliness of their wit, the justness of their reflections, the dignity which accompanied their vivacity, plainly evinced with how much greater strength the mind can exert itself in a regular and rational way of life, than in a course of dissipation. At this house every change came too soon, time seemed to wear a double portion of wings, eleven o'clock struck, and the ladies ordered a servant to shew us our rooms, themselves retiring to theirs.

It was impossible for Lamont and I to part till we had spent an hour in talking over this amiable family, with whom he could not help being much delighted, though he observed they were very deficient in the bon ton, there was too much solidity in all they said, they would trifle with trifles indeed, but had not the art of treating more weighty subjects with the same lightness, which gave them an air of rusticity; and he did not doubt, but on a more intimate acquaintance we should find their manners much rusticated, and their heads filled with antiquated notions, by having lived so long out of the great world.

I rose the next morning very early, desirous to make the day, which I purposed for the last of my abode in this mansion, as long as I could. I went directly into the garden, which, by what I saw from the house, was extremely pretty. As I passed by the windows of the saloon, I perceived the ladies and their little pupils were earlier risers than myself, for they were all at their various employments. I first went into the gayest flower garden I ever beheld. The rainbow exhibits not half the variety of tints, and they are so artfully mingled, and ranged to make such a harmony of colours, as taught me how much the most beautiful objects may be improved by a judicious disposition of them. Beyond these beds of flowers rises a shrubbery, where every thing sweet and pleasing is collected. As these ladies have no taste but what is directed by good sense, nothing found a place here from being only uncommon, for they think few things are very rare but because they are little desirable; and indeed it is plain they are free from that littleness of mind, which makes people value a thing the more for its being possessed by no one but themselves. Behind the shrubbery is a little wood, which affords a gloom, rendered more agreeable by its contrast with the dazzling beauty of that part of the garden that leads to it. In the high pale which encloses this wood I observed a little door; curiosity induced me to pass through it; I found it opened on a row of the neatest cottages I ever saw, which the wood had concealed from my view. They were new and uniform, and therefore I imagined all dedicated to the same purpose. Seeing a very old woman spinning at one of the doors, I accosted her, by admiring the neatness of her habitation.

'Ay, indeed,' said she, 'it is a most comfortable place, God bless the good ladies! I and my neighbours are as happy as princesses, we have every thing we want and wish, and who can say more?' 'Very few so much,' answered I, 'but pray what share have the ladies in procuring the happiness you seem so sensible of?' 'Why Sir,' continued the old woman, 'it is all owing to them. I was almost starved when they put me into this house, and no shame of mine, for so were my neighbours too; perhaps we were not so painstaking as we might have been; but that was not our fault, you know, as we had not things to work with, nor any body to set us to work, poor folks cannot know every thing as these good ladies do; we were half dead for want of victuals, and then people have not courage to set about any thing. Nay, all the parish were so when they came into it, young and old, there was not much to choose, few of us had rags to cover us, or a morsel of bread to eat except the two Squires; they indeed grew rich, because they had our work, and paid us not enough to keep life and soul together; they live about a mile off, so perhaps they did not know how poor we were, I must say that for them; the ladies tell me I ought not to speak against them, for every one has faults, only we see other people's, and are blind to our own; and certainly it is true enough, for they are very wise ladies as well as good, and must know such things.'

As my new acquaintance seemed as loquacious as her age promised, I hoped for full satisfaction, and asked her how she and her neighbours employed themselves.

'Not all alike,' replied the good woman, 'I will tell you all about it. There are twelve of us that live here. We have every one a house of two rooms, as you may see, beside other conveniences, and each a little garden, but though we are separate, we agree as well, perhaps better, than if we lived together, and all help one another. Now, there is neighbour Susan, and neighbour Rachel; Susan is lame, so she spins clothes for Rachel; and Rachel cleans Susan's house, and does such things for her as she cannot do for herself. The ladies settled all these matters at first, and told us, that as they, to please God, assisted us, we must in order to please him serve others; and that to make us happy they would put us in a way, poor as we are, to do good to many. Thus neighbour Jane who, poor woman, is almost stone deaf, they thought would have a melancholy life if she was to be always spinning and knitting, seeing other people around her talking, and not be able to hear a word they said, so the ladies busy her in making broths and caudles and such things, for all the sick poor in this and the next parish, and two of us are fixed upon to carry what they have made to those that want them; to visit them often, and spend more or less time

with them every day according as they have, or have not relations to take care of them; for though the ladies always hire
nurses for those who are very ill, yet they will not trust quite to
them, but make us overlook them, so that in a sickly time we
shall be all day going from one to another.'

'But,' said I, 'there are I perceive many children amongst you,
how happens that? Your ages shew they are not your own.'

'Oh! as for that,' replied my intelligencer, 'I will tell you how
that is. You must know these good ladies, heaven preserve
them! take every child after the fifth of every poor person, as
soon as it can walk, till when they pay the mother for nursing it;
these children they send to us to keep out of harm, and as soon
as they can hold a knitting-needle to teach them to knit, and to
spin, as much as they can be taught before they are four or five
years old, when they are removed into one of the schools. They
are pretty company for us, and make us mothers again, as it
were, in our old age; then the children's relations are all so fond
of us for our care of them, that it makes us a power of friends,
which you know is very pleasant, though we want nothing from
them but their good wills.'

Here I interrupted her by observing, that it must take up a
great deal of time, and stop their work, consequently lessen
their profits.

'There is nothing in that,' continued the good woman, 'the
ladies' steward sends us in all we want in the way of meat, drink
and firing; and our spinning we carry to the ladies; they employ
a poor old weaver, who before they came broke for want of
work, to weave it for us, and when there is not enough they put
more to it, so we are sure to have our clothing; if we are not idle
that is all they desire, except that we should be cleanly too.
There never passes a day that one or other of the ladies does not
come and look all over our houses, which they tell us, and certainly with truth, for it is a great deal of trouble to them, is all for
our good, for that we cannot be healthy if we are not clean and
neat. Then every Saint's day, and every Sunday after church, we
all go down to the hall, and the ladies read prayers, and a
sermon to us, and their own family; nor do they ever come here

without giving us some good advice. We used to quarrel, to be sure, sometimes when we first came to these houses, but the ladies condescended to make it up amongst us, and shewed us so kindly how much it was our duty to agree together, and to forgive everybody their faults, or else we could not hope to be forgiven by God, against whom we so often sinned, that now we love one another like sisters, or indeed better, for I often see such quarrel. Beside, they have taught us that we are generally in fault ourselves; and we find now that we take care not to be perverse, our neighbours are seldom in the wrong, and when they are, we bear with it in hopes they will bear with us when we are as much to blame, which we may be sure enough will happen, let us try ever so much to the contrary. Then the ladies seem so pleased when we do any kindness to one another, as to be sure is a great encouragement; and if any of us are sick they are so careful and so good, that it would be a shame if we did not do all we can for one another, who have been always neighbours and acquaintance, when such great ladies, who never knew us, as I may say, but to make us happy, and have no reason to take care of us but that we are poor, are so kind and condescending to us.'

I was so pleased with the good effect which the charity of her benefactors had on the mind, as well as the situation, of this old woman, whose neighbours by her own account were equally benefited by the blessings they received, that I should have stayed longer with her, if a bell had not rung at Millenium Hall, which she informed me was a summons to breakfast. I obeyed its call, and after thanking her for her conversation, returned with a heart warmed and enlarged, to the amiable society. My mind was so filled with exalted reflections on their virtues that I was less attentive to the charms of inanimate nature than when I first passed through the gardens.

After breakfast the ladies proposed a walk, and as they had seen the course I took when I first went out, they led us a contrary way, lest, they said, I should be tired with the repetition of the same scene. I told them with great truth, that what I had beheld could never weary, for virtue is a subject we must ever contemplate with fresh delight, and as such examples could not fail of improving every witness of them, the pleasure of reflection would increase, as one daily grew more capable of enjoying it, by cultivating kindred sensations. By some more explicit hints they found out to what I alluded, and thereby knew where I had been, but turning the conversation to present objects, they conducted us to a very fine wood which is laid out with so much taste that Lamont observed the artist's hand was never more distinguishable, and perceived in various spots the direction of the person at present most famous for that sort of improvement.

The ladies smiled, and one of them answered that he did their wood great honour, in thinking art had lent her assistance to nature, but that there was little in that place for which they were not solely obliged to the latter. Miss Trentham interrupted her who was speaking and told us that as she had no share in the improvements which had been made, she might with the better grace assure Mr Lamont that Lady Mary Jones, Miss Mancel, and Mrs Morgan were the only persons who had laid out that wood, and the commonest labourers in the country had executed their orders. Lamont was much surprised at this piece of information, and though he would have thought it still more exquisitely beautiful had it been the design of the person he imagined, yet truth is so powerful, that he could not suppress his admiration and surprise. Every cut in it is terminated by some noble object. In several places are seats formed with such rustic simplicity, as have more real grandeur in them, than can be found in the most expensive buildings. On an eminence, 'bosomed high in tufted trees', is a temple dedicated to solitude. The structure is an exquisite piece of architecture, the prospect from it noble and extensive, and the windows so placed, that one sees no house but at so considerable a distance, as not to take off from the solitary air, which is perfectly agreeable to a temple declaredly dedicated to solitude. The most beautiful object in the view is a very large river, in reality an arm of the sea, little more than a quarter of a mile distant from the building; about three miles beyond it lies the sea, on which the sun then shone, and made it dazzlingly bright. In the temple is a picture of Contemplation, another of Silence, two of various birds and animals, and a couple of moonlight pieces, the workmanship of the ladies.

Close by the temple runs a gentle murmuring rivulet, which flows in meanders through the rest of the wood, sometimes concealed from view, and then appearing at the next turning of the walk. The wood is well peopled with pheasants, wild turkeys, squirrels and hares, who live so unmolested, that they seem to have forgot all fear, and rather to welcome than flee from those who come amongst them. Man never appears there as a merciless destroyer; but the preserver, instead of the tyrant, of the inferior part of the creation. While they continue in that wood, none but natural evil can approach them, and from that they are defended as much as possible. We there 'walked joint tenant of the shade' with the animal race; and a perfect equality in nature's bounty seems enjoyed by the whole creation. One could scarcely forbear thinking those happy times were come, when 'The wolf shall dwell with the lamb, and the leopard shall lie down with the kid; and the calf, and the young lion, and the fatling together, and a young child shall lead them. The wilderness and the solitary place shall be glad for them, and the desert shall rejoice, and blossom as the rose.'

At the verge of this wood, which extends to the river I have mentioned, without perceiving we were entering a building, so well is the outside of it concealed by trees, we found ourselves in a most beautiful grotto, made of fossils, spars, coral, and such shells as are at once both fine and rustic; all of the glaring, tawdry kind are excluded, and by the gloom and simplicity preserved, one would imagine it the habitation of some devout anchoret. Ivy and moss in some places cover, while they seem to unite, the several materials of the variegated walls. The rivulet which runs through the wood falls down one side of the grotto with great rapidity, broken into various streams by the spar and coral, and passing through, forms a fine cascade just at the foot of the grotto, whence it flows into the river. Great care is taken to prevent the place from growing damp, so that we sat some time in it with safety, admiring the smooth surface of the river, to which it lies very open.

As the ladies had some daily business on their hands which they never neglect, we were obliged to leave this lovely scene, where I think I could have passed my life with pleasure, and to return towards the house, though by a different way from that we came, traversing the other side of the wood. In one spot where we went near the verge, I observed a pale, which, upon examination, I found was continued for some acres, though it was remarkable only in one place. It is painted green, and on the inside a hedge of yews, laurel, and other thick evergreens rises to about seven or eight feet high. I could not forbear asking what was thus so carefully enclosed. The ladies smiled on each other, but evaded answering my question, which only increased my curiosity. Lamont, not less curious, and more importunate, observed that the inclosure bore some resemblance to one of Lord Lamore's, where he kept lions, tigers, leopards, and such foreign animals, and he would be hanged, if the ladies had not made some such collection, intreating that he might be admitted to see them; for nothing gave him greater entertainment than to behold those beautiful wild beasts, brought out of their native woods, where they had reigned as kings, and here tamed and subjected by the superior art of man. It was a triumph of human reason, which could not fail to afford great pleasure.

'Not to us, I assure you, Sir,' replied Miss Mancel, 'when reason appears only in the exertion of cruelty and tyrannical oppression, it is surely not a gift to be boasted of. When a man forces the furious steed to endure the bit, or breaks oxen to the yoke, the great benefits he receive from, and communicates to the animals, excuse the forcible methods by which it is accomplished. But to see a man, from a vain desire to have in his possession the native of another climate and another country, reduce a fine and noble creature to misery, and confine him within narrow inclosures whose happiness consisted in unbounded liberty, shocks my nature. There is I confess something so amiable in gentleness, that I could be pleased with seeing a tiger caress its keeper, if the cruel means by which the fiercest of beasts is taught all the servility of a fawning spaniel, did not recur every instant to my mind; and it is not much less abhorrent to my nature, to see a venerable lion jumping over a stick, than it would be to behold a hoary philosopher forced by some cruel tyrant to spend his days in whipping a top, or playing with a rattle. Every thing to me loses its charm when it is put out of the station wherein nature, or to speak more properly, the all-wise Creator has placed it. I imagine man has a right to use the animal race for his own preservation, perhaps for his convenience, but certainly not to treat them with wanton cruelty, and as it is not in his power to give them any thing so valuable as their liberty, it is, in my opinion, criminal to enslave them, in order to procure ourselves a vain amusement, if we have so little feeling as to find any while others suffer.'

'I believe madam,' replied Lamont, 'it is most advisable for me not to attempt to defend what I have said; should I have reason on my side, while you have humanity on yours, I should make but a bad figure in the argument. What advantage could I expect from applying to the understanding, while your amiable disposition would captivate even reason itself? But still I am puzzled; what we behold is certainly an inclosure, how can that be without a confinement to those that are within it?'

'After having spoken so much against tyranny,' said Miss Mancel, smiling, 'I do not know whether I should be excusable if I left you to be tyrannized by curiosity, which I believe can inflict very severe pains, at least, if I may be allowed to judge by the means people often take to satisfy it. I will therefore gratify you with the knowledge of what is within this inclosure, which makes so extraordinary an impression upon you. It is, then, an asylum for those poor creatures who are rendered miserable from some natural deficiency or redundancy. Here they find refuge from the tyranny of those wretches, who seem to think that being two or three feet taller gives them a right to make them a property, and expose their unhappy forms to the contemptuous curiosity of the unthinking multitude. Procrustes has been branded through all ages with the name of tyrant; and principally, as it appears, from fitting the body of every stranger to a bed which he kept as the necessary standard, cutting off the legs of those whose height exceeded the length of it and stretching on the rack such as fell short of that measure, till they attained the requisite proportion. But is not almost every man a Procrustes? We have not the power of shewing our cruelty exactly in the same method, but actuated by the like spirit, we abridge of their liberty, and torment by scorn, all who either fall short, or exceed the usual standard, if they happen to have the additional misfortune of poverty. Perhaps we are in no part more susceptible than in our vanity, how much then must those poor wretches suffer, whose deformity would lead them to wish to be secluded from human view, in being exposed to the public, whose observations are no better than expressions of scorn, and who are surprised to find that any thing less than themselves can speak, or appear like intelligent beings. But this is only part of what they have to endure. As if their deficiency in height deprived them of the natural right to air and sunshine, they are kept confined in small rooms, and because they fill less space than common, are stuffed into chairs so little, that they are squeezed as close as a pair of gloves in a walnut-shell.

'This miserable treatment of persons, to whom compassion should secure more than common indulgence, determined us to purchase these worst sort of slaves, and in this place we have five who owed their wretchedness to being only three foot high, one grey-headed toothless old man of sixteen years of age, a woman of about seven foot in height, and a man who would be still taller, if the extreme weakness of his body, and the wretched life he for some time led, in the hands of one of these monster-mongers, did not make him bend almost double, and oblige him to walk on crutches; with which infirmities he is well pleased, as they reduce him nearer the common standard.'

We were very desirous of seeing this enfranchised company; but Mrs Morgan told us it was what they seldom granted, for fear of inflicting some of the pains from which they had endeavoured to rescue those poor creatures, but she would step in, and ask if they had no objection to our admission, and if that appeared really the case she would gratify us.

This tenderness to persons who were under such high obligations, charmed me. She soon returned with the permission we wished, but intreated us to pay all our attention to the house and garden, and to take no more than a civil notice of its inhabitants. We promised obedience, and followed her. Her advice was almost unnecessary, for the place could not have failed of attracting our particular observation. It was a quadrangle of about six acres, and the inward part was divided by nets into eight parts, four of which alternatively were filled with poultry of all sorts, which were fed here for the use of the hall, and kept with the most exact cleanliness. The other four parts were filled with shrubs and flowers, which were cultivated with great delight by these once unfortunate, but now happy beings. A little stream ran across the quadrangle, which served for drink to the poultry, and facilitated the watering of the flowers. I have already said, that at the inward edge of the pale was a row of evergreens; at their feet were beds of flowers, and a little gravel walk went round the whole. At each corner was an arbour made with woodbines and jessamine, in one or two of which there was always an agreeable shade.

At one side of the quadrangle was a very neat habitation, into which a dwarf invited us to enter, to rest ourselves after our walk; they were all passing backwards and forwards, and thus gave us a full view of them, which would have been a shocking sight, but for the reflections we could not avoid making on their happy condition, and the very extraordinary humanity of the ladies to whom they owed it; so that instead of feeling the pain one might naturally receive from seeing the human form so disgraced, we were filled with admiration of the human mind, when so nobly exalted by virtue, as it is in the patronesses of these poor creatures, who wore an air of cheerfulness, which shewed they thought the churlishness wherewith they had been treated by nature sufficiently compensated. The tender inquiries the ladies made after their healths, and the kind notice they took of each of them, could not be exceeded by any thing but the affection, I might almost say adoration, with which these people beheld their benefactresses.

This scene had made too deep an impression on our minds not to be the subject of our discourse all the way home, and in the course of conversation, I learnt that when these people were first rescued out of their misery, their healths were much impaired, and their tempers more so; to restore the first, all medicinal care was taken, and air and exercise assisted greatly in their recovery; but to cure the malady of the mind, and conquer that internal source of unhappiness, was a work of longer time. Even these poor wretches had their vanity, and would contend for superior merit, of which the argument was the money their keepers had gained in exhibiting them. To put an end to this contention, the ladies made them understand that what they thought a subject for boasting, was only a proof of their being so much farther from the usual standard of the human form, and therefore a more extraordinary spectacle. But it was long before one of them could be persuaded to lay aside her pretensions to superiority, which she claimed on account of an extraordinary honour she had received from a great princess, who had made her a present of a sedan chair.

At length, however, much reasoning and persuasion, a conviction of principles, of which they had before no knowledge, the happiness of their situation, and the improvement of their healths, concurred to sweeten their tempers and they now live in great harmony. They are entirely mistresses of their house, have two maids to wait on them, over whom they have sole command, and a person to do such little things in their garden as they cannot themselves perform; but the cultivation of it is one of their great pleasures; and by their extraordinary care, they have the satisfaction of presenting the finest flowers of the spring to their benefactresses, before they are blown in any other place.

When they first came, the ladies told us that the horror they had conceived of being exhibited as public spectacles had fixed in them such a fear of being seen by any stranger, that the sound of a voice with which they were not acquainted at the outside of the paling, or the trampling of feet, would set them all a running behind the bushes to hide themselves, like so many timorous partridges in a mew, hurrying behind sheaves of corn for shelter; they even found a convenience in their size, which, though it rendered them unwilling to be seen, enabled them so easily to find places for concealment.

By degrees the ladies brought them to consent to see their head servants, and some of the best people in the parish; desiring that to render it more agreeable to their visitors, they would entertain them with fruit and wine; advising them to assist their neighbours in plain work; thus to endear themselves to them, and procure more frequent visits, which as they chose to confine themselves within so narrow a compass, and enjoyed but precarious health, their benefactresses thought a necessary amusement. These recommendations, and the incidents wherewith their former lives had furnished them to amuse their company, and which they now could relate with pleasure, from the happy sense that all mortifications were past, rendered their conversation much courted among that rank of people.

It occurred to me that their dislike to being seen by numbers must prevent their attendance on public worship, but my cousin informed me that was thus avoided. There was in the church an old gallery, which from disuse was grown out of repair; this the ladies caused to be mended, and the front of it so heightened, that these little folks when in it could not be seen; the tall ones contrived by stooping when they were there not to appear of any extraordinary height. To this they were conveyed in the ladies' coach and set down close to covered stairs, which led up to the gallery.

This subject employed our conversation till we approached the hall; the ladies then, after insisting that we should not think of going from thence that day, all left us expect Mrs Maynard. It may seem strange that I was not sorry for their departure; but, in truth, I was so filled with astonishment at characters so new, and so curious to know by what steps women thus qualified both by nature and fortune to have the world almost at command, were brought thus to seclude themselves from it, and make as it were a new one for themselves constituted on such very different principles from that I had hitherto lived in, that I longed to be alone with my cousin, in hopes I might from her receive some account of this wonder. I soon made my curiosity known, and beseeched her to gratify it.

'I see no good reason,' said she, 'why I should not comply with your request, as my friends are above wishing to conceal any part of their lives, though themselves are never the subject of their own conversation. If they have had any follies they do not desire to hide them; they have not pride enough to be hurt with candid criticisms, and have too much innocence to fear any very severe censure. But as we did not all reach this paradise at the same time, I shall begin with the first inhabitants of, and indeed the founders of this society, Miss Mancel and Mrs Morgan, who from their childhood have been so connected that I could not, if I would, disunite them in my relation; and it would be almost a sin to endeavour to separate them even in idea.'

We sat down in an arbour, whose shade invited us to seek there a defence against the sun, which was then in its meridian, and shone with uncommon heat. The woodbines, the roses, the jessamines, the pinks and above all, the minionette with which it was surrounded, made the air one general perfume; every breeze came loaded with fragrance, stealing and giving odour. A rivulet ran bubbling by the side of the arbour, whose gentle murmurs soothed the mind into composure, and seemed to hush us to attention, when Mrs Maynard thus began to shew her readiness to comply with my request.

THE

HISTORY

OF

Miss MANCEL

AND

Mrs MORGAN

YOU may perhaps think I am presuming on your patience when I lead you into a nursery, or a boarding school; but the life of Louisa Mancel was so early chequered with that various fate which gives this world the motley appearance of joy and sorrow, pain and pleasure, that it is not in my power to pass over the events of her infancy. I shall, however, spare you all that is possible, and recommend her to your notice only when she attracted the observation of Mr Hintman. This gentleman hearing that a person who rented some land of him was come to London, and lodged at one of those public houses which by the landlord is called an inn, at the outskirts of London, on the Surrey side; and having some occasion to speak to him, he went thither. The people of the house called the man Mr Hintman enquired for, who immediately came downstairs, wiping tears from his eyes; the continuance of which he could hardly restrain. Mr Hintman asking the reason of those appearances of sorrow, the good-natured old man told him, his visit had called him from a scene which had shocked him excessively. 'The first day I came here' said he, 'I was induced by the frequent groans which issued from the next chamber, to enquire who lodged there; I learnt, it was a gentlewoman, who arrived the day before, and was immediately taken so ill that they apprehended her life in danger; and, about two hours ago, the maid of the house ran into my room, begging me to come to her assistance, for the gentlewoman was in such strong fits, she was not able to hold her. I obeyed the summons, and found the poor woman in fits indeed; but what appeared to me the last agonies of a life which, near exhausted, lavishes away its small remains in strong convulsions.

'By her bedside stood the most beautiful child I ever beheld, in appearance about ten years of age, crying as if its little heart would break; not with the rage of an infant, but with the settled grief of a person mature both in years and affliction. I asked her if the poor dying woman was her mother; she told me, no – she was only her aunt; but to her the same as a mother; and she did not know any one else that would take care of her.

'After a time the poor woman's convulsions left her; she just recovered sense enough to embrace the lovely girl, and cried out, Oh! my dear child, what will become of you! a friendless, helpless infant; and seeing me at her bedside, she lifted up her hands in a suppliant posture; and with eyes that petitioned in stronger terms than words could express, Oh! Sir, said she, though you are a stranger to me, yet I see you are not so to humanity; take pity on this forlorn child; her amiable disposition will repay you in this world, and the great Father of us all will reward you in the next, for your compassion on a wretched friendless girl! But why do I call her friendless? Her innocence has the best of friends in heaven; the Almighty is a parent she is not left to seek for; he is never absent; – Oh! blessed Lord! cried she, with a degree of ecstasy and confidence which most sensibly affected us all, to thy care I resign her; thy tender mercies are over all thy works, and thou, who carest for the smallest part of thy creation, will not deny her thy protection. Oh! Lord defend her innocence! Let her obtain a place in thy kingdom after death; and for all the rest I submit to thy providence; nor presumptuously pretend to dictate to supreme wisdom. Thou art a gracious father and the afflictions thou sendest are . . . Here her voice failed her; but by her gestures we could perceive the continued praying, and, having before taken the child in her arms the little angel continued there for fear of disturbing her. By looks sometimes turned towards the poor infant, and sometimes with her hand on her own heart, and then her eyes lifted up as it were to heaven, we saw she mixed prayers for the little mourner, with intercessions for herself, till sense and motion seemed to fail her; she then fell into a convulsion, and expired.

'The little girl perceived she was dead; and became almost as senseless as the lump of clay which had so lately been her only friend. We had but just taken her from the body, sir, when you came; and this was the occasion of the emotions you observed in me.'

'The cause was indeed sufficient,' replied Mr Hintman, 'but I am glad your sorrow proceeded from nothing more immediately concerning youself. Misery will strike its arrows into a humane heart; but the wounds it makes are not so lasting, as those which are impressed by passions that are more relative to ourselves.' 'Oh! sir,' said the old man, 'you cannot form an adequate idea of the effect this scene must have on every spectator, except you had seen the child! surely nature never formed so lovely a little creature!' He continued his praises of Louisa, till at length he excited Mr Hintman's curiosity; who expressing a desire of seeing this miracle, he was carried up into the good man's room, to which they had removed her. She, who had cried most bitterly before the fatal stroke arrived, was now so oppressed, as not to be able to shed a tear. They had put her on the bed, where she lay sighing with a heart ready to break; her eyes fixed on one point, she neither saw nor heard.

Though her countenance expressed unutterable woe, yet she looked so extremely beautiful, that Mr Hintman, highly as his expectation had been raised, was struck with surprise. He allowed he never saw any thing so lovely; and the charms of which her melancholy might deprive her, were more than compensated in his imagination by so strong a proof of extreme sensibility, at an age when few children perceive half the dreadful consequences of such a misfortune.

He advised that she should be blooded, to prevent any ill effects from so severe a shock; for as she felt it as strongly as one of a more mature age, the same precautions should be used. In this he was obeyed; and it gave her such relief that she burst into a flood of tears; a change which appeared so salutary, that Mr Hintman would not immediately interrupt her. But his curiosity did not suffer him long to forbear asking her name, and many other particulars; several of which she could not answer; all the account she was able to give of herself was, that her name was Mancel, that the person for whom she grieved was her aunt; but had had the sole care of her from her earliest remembrance. This aunt, she said, had often told her she had a father and mother living; but when she enquired why she never saw or heard from them she could get no satisfactory answer, but was put off with being told they were not in England; and that she should know when she grew older.

This person had bred her up with the utmost tenderness, and employed the most assiduous care in her education; which was the principal object of her attention. They had lived in a neat cottage in the most retired part of Surrey from Miss Mancel's earliest remembrance, till her aunt, after having been some time in a bad state of health, fell into a galloping consumption. As soon as she apprehended the danger with which her life was threatened, she prepared every thing for her removal to London; but as she did not expect ever to return, this took more time than the quickness of her decay could well allow. The hasty approach of her dissolution affected her extremely on the account of her little niece, and she often expressed her concern in terms intelligible to her who was the occasion of it, who gathered from the expressions which fell from her aunt, that the motive for the journey was to find out some of Miss Mancel's relations, to whom she might deliver her before death had put a period to her own life; and where she might safely remain till the return of her parents into England.

In this resolution she discharged the only servant she kept, delivered up her house to her landlord, and after having settled all her pecuniary affairs, she set out on her journey with her little charge; but grew so ill on the road that she desired to be set down at the first inn; and her illness increased so fast she had no thought of removing; nor was she able to make any very exact enquiries after the persons of whom she came in search.

This account was interrupted with many tears, which served to render it more affecting, and Mr Hintman, as much touched as the good old man who was the occasion of his having heard it, agreed with him that it would be proper to examine into the effects of which the deceased was then possessed; and to see if they could find any paper which would in a degree clear up the mysterious part of this affair.

This was accordingly performed; but as to the latter intention without any success; for after all the examination they could make, they remained as much in the dark as ever.

They found in her trunk rather more money than was requisite to bury her in a manner becoming her rank; to defray the expenses of her sickness; and to reward those that had attended her.

The old man expressed a willingness to take the child. He said it was a legacy left him by one who had conceived some confidence in his humanity, and he could not in conscience disappoint an opinion which did him honour; though, having children of his own, he did not pretend to breed her up in the genteel manner to which she seemed by birth entitled.

Mr Hintman replied, that he should have great reason to reproach himself if with the ample fortune he enjoyed, and having no children or family to partake of it, he should suffer another to take that charge, to whom it could not be so convenient; he therefore would immediately receive her as his child; and see her educated in all accomplishments proper for a young person of fashion and fortune; as he should be able to supply all deficiency, if necessary, in the latter particular.

The old man was very glad to have the child better established than with him; though he had for some hours looked with so much pleasure on her as his adopted daughter, that no consideration, but the prospect of her greater advantage, could have reconciled him to parting with her.

In pursuance of the resolution Mr Hintman had taken, he carried Miss Mancel to a French boarding school which he had heard commended; very prudently judging that his house was not a proper place for education, having there no one fit to take care of a young person.

Louisa was so oppressed by the forlornness of her situation that she felt none of that reluctance to going amongst strangers, so usual with children of her age. All the world was equally unknown to her, therefore she was indifferent where she was carried, only she rather wished not to have been taken from the good old man whose venerable aspect, and compassionate behaviour, had in some degree attached her to him; but she felt the generosity of Mr Hintman's declared intentions; and, young as she was, had too much delicacy to appear ungrateful by shewing an unwillingness to accompany him. Mademoiselle d'Avaux, the mistress of the school, was pleased with the appearance of her young scholar, whose tears had ceased for some time; and her face bore no disfiguring signs of sorrow; the dejection which overspread it giving charms equal to those of which it robbed it.

Mr Hintman desired Mademoiselle d'Avaux to take the trouble of providing Miss Mancel with all things requisite, and to put her in proper mourning; those minute feminine details being things of which he was too ignorant to acquit himself well; and gave strict charge that her mind should be cultivated with the greatest care, and no accomplishment omitted which she was capable of acquiring.

What contributed much towards gratifying this wish of Mr Hintman's was Mademoiselle d'Avaux's house being so full, that there was no room for Louisa, but a share of the apartment which Miss Melvyn had hitherto enjoyed alone, and of which she could not willingly have admitted any one to partake but the lovely child who was presented to her for this purpose. Her beautiful form prejudiced everyone in her favour; but the distress and sorrow which were impressed on her countenance, at an age generally too volatile and thoughtless to be deeply affected, could not fail of exciting a tender sensibility in the heart of a person of Miss Melvyn's disposition.

This young lady was of a very peculiar turn of mind. She had been the darling daughter of Sir Charles and Lady Melvyn, whose attachment to her had appeared equal; but, in the former, it was rather the result of habit and compliance with Lady Melvyn's behaviour than a deep-rooted affection, of which his heart was not very susceptible; while Lady Melvyn's arose from that entire fondness which maternal love and the most distinguishing reason could excite in the warmest and tenderest of hearts.

Sir Charles was an easy-tempered, weak man who gave no proof of good sense but the secret deference he had to his wife's judgement, whose very superior understanding was on nothing so assiduously employed as in giving consequence to the man with whom she was united, by the desire of her parents, contrary to her inclination. Their authority had been necessary to reduce her to compliance, not from any particular dislike to Sir Charles, who had deservedly the reputation of sobriety and great good nature and whose person was remarkably fine; but Lady Melvyn perceived the weakness of his understanding and, ignorant of the strength of her own, was unwilling to enter into life without a guide whose judgement was equal to the desire he might naturally be supposed to have to direct her right, through all the various paths in which she might be obliged to walk; an assistance she had always expected from a husband; and thought even a necessary part of that character. She was besides sensible of the difficulty of performing a promise so solemnly made, as that of honour and obedience to one who, though she knew not half her own excellence, she must be sensible was her inferior.

These reasons had deterred Lady Melvyn from marrying Sir Charles, but when she could no longer avoid it without violating her duty to her parents, she resolved to supply the apparent deficiencies in her husband's understanding by a most respectful deference to his opinions, thus conferring distinction on him whom she wished everyone to esteem and honour; for as there was no affectation in this part of her conduct, any more than in the rest of her behaviour, all were convinced that the man who was respected by a woman of an understanding so superior to most of her own sex, and the greatest part of the other, must have great merit, though they could not perceive wherein it consisted.

In company Lady Melvyn always endeavoured to turn the conversation on such subjects as she know were best suited to Sir Charles's capacity, more desirous that he should appear to advantage than to display her own talents. She contrived to make all her actions appear the result of his choice, and whatever he did by her instigation seemed even to himself to have been his own thought. As their way of life was in every circumstance consonant to reason, religion, and every virtue which could render them useful and respectable to others, Sir Charles acquired a character in the neighbourhood which Lady Melvyn thought a sufficient reward for the endeavours she used to secure it to him; and, for that purpose, fixed her abode entirely in the country, where his conduct might give him the respect which would not be so easily obtained in a gayer scene, where talents are in higher estimation than virtue.

Sir Charles and Lady Melvyn had no other child than the daughter I have mentioned, whose education was her mother's great care; and she had the pleasure of seeing in her an uncommon capacity, with every virtue the fondest parent could wish; and which indeed she had by inheritance; but her mother's humility made them appear to her as a peculiar gift of providence to her daughter.

Lady Melvyn soon began to instil all the principles of true religion into her daughter's infant mind; and, by her judicious instructions, gave her knowledge far superior to her years; which was indeed the most delightful task of this fond parent; for her daughter's uncommon docility and quick parts, continually stimulated by her tenderness for the best of mothers, made her improve even beyond Lady Melvyn's expectation.

In this happy situation Miss Melvyn continued till near the end of her fourteenth year, when she had the misfortune to lose this excellent parent, nor was she the only sufferer by Lady Melvyn's death; every poor person within her knowledge lost a benefactress; all who knew her, an excellent example; and, some, the best of friends; but her extraordinary merit was but imperfectly known till after her decease; for she had made Sir Charles appear so much the principal person, and director of all their affairs; that till the change in his conduct proved how great her influence had been, she had only shared the approbation, which, afterwards, became all her own.

Human nature cannot feel a deeper affliction than now overwhelmed Miss Melvyn; wherein Sir Charles bore as great a share, as the easiness of his nature was capable of; but his heart was not susceptible, either of strong or lasting impressions. He walked in the path Lady Melvyn had traced out for him; and suffered his daughter to imitate her mother in benevolent duties; and she had profited too much by the excellent pattern, whereby she had endeavoured to regulate her actions, not to acquit herself far beyond what could have been expected at her years.

Miss Melvyn was not long indulged in the only consolation her grief could receive – that of being permitted to aim at an imitation of her mother – for Sir Charles had not been a widower quite a year when he married a young lady in the neighbourhood who had designed him this honour from the hour of Lady Melvyn's death; and to procure better opportunity for affecting her purpose had pretended a most affectionate compassion for Miss Melvyn's deep affliction; she visited her continually; and appeared so tenderly attached to her that Miss Melvyn, who had neither experience nor any guile in her own heart to inspire her with suspicions of an attempt to deceive her, made that return of affection which she thought gratitude required; nor was she at all disturbed when she found she was soon to look on this lady in another light than that in which she had hitherto seen her; it was easy for her to respect one whom she before loved; and she had been taught so true a veneration for her father, that she felt no averseness to obey whomsoever he thought proper to give a title to her duty.

Miss Melvyn had but very little time to congratulate herself on having acquired for a mother a friend in whose conversation she hoped to enjoy great satisfaction and to feel the tenderness of an intimate changed into the fondness of a parent. She behaved to her with the same perfect respect, and all the humility of obedience, as if nature had placed her in that parental relation; fearing, if she gave way to the familiarity which had subsisted between them when they were on an equality, it might appear like a failure in the reverence due to her new situation.

But this behaviour, amiable as it was, could not make the new Lady Melvyn change the plan she had formed for her future conduct. She had not been married above a month before she began to intimate to Sir Charles that Miss Melvyn's education had been very imperfect; that a young lady of her rank ought to be highly accomplished; but that after she had been so long indulged by her parents, if a step-mother were to pretend to direct her it might not only exasperate Miss Melvyn but prejudice the world against herself; as people are too apt to determine against persons in that relation, without examining the merits of the cause; and though, she said, she was little concerned about the opinion of the world in comparison with her tender regard for any one that belonged to him; yet she was much influenced by the other reasons she had alleged for not appearing to dictate to Miss Melvyn, being very desirous of keeping on affectionate terms with her; and she was already much mortified at perceiving that young lady had imbibed too many of the vulgar prejudices against a step-mother; though, for her part, she had endeavoured to behave with submission to her daughter, instead of pretending to assume any authority. The consequence and conclusion of all these insinuations was, that 'it would be advisable to send Miss Melvyn to a boarding school.'

Sir Charles was soon prevailed with to comply with his lady's request; and his daughter was acquainted with the determination which Lady Melvyn assured her, 'was very contrary to her inclination, who should find a great loss of so agreeable a friend, but that Sir Charles had declared his intention in so peremptory a manner that she dared not contend.'

Miss Melvyn had before observed that marriage had made a great alteration in Lady Melvyn's behaviour; but this was a stroke she did not expect and a very mortifying one to her who had long laid aside all childish amusements; had been taught to employ herself as rationally as if she had arrived at a maturer age, and been indulged in the exercise of a most benevolent disposition, having given such good proofs of the propriety with which she employed both her time and money, that she had been dispensed from all restraints; and now to commence a new infancy, and be confined to the society of children, was a very afflicting change; but it came from a hand she too much respected to make any resistance, though she easily perceived that it was entirely at her mother's instigation; and knew her father too well to believe he could be peremptory on any occasion.

A very short time intervened between the declaration and execution of this design, and Miss Melvyn was introduced to Mademoiselle d'Avaux by her kind step-mother, who with some tears and many assurances of regret left her there. Miss Melvyn had been at this school three months when Louisa Mancel was brought thither, and though a separation from a father she sincerely loved, and the fear of the arts Lady Melvyn might use to alienate his affections from her, after having thus removed her from his presence, greatly affected her spirits and she found no companions fit to amuse her rational mind, yet she endeavoured to support her mortifications with all the cheerfulness she could assume; and received some satisfaction from the conversation of Mademoiselle d'Avaux, a woman of tolerable understanding, and who was much pleased with Miss Melvyn's behaviour.

Miss Mancel's dejected air prejudiced Miss Melvyn much in her favour, the usual consequence of a similitude of mind or manners; and when by a further knowledge of her, she perceived her uncommon share of understanding; her desire to learn; the strength of her application; the quickness of her apprehension; and her great sweetness of temper, she grew extremely fond of her; and as Miss Mancel's melancholy rendered her little inclined to play with those of her own age, she was almost always with Miss Melvyn, who found great pleasure in endeavouring to instruct her; and grew to feel for her the tenderness of a mother, while Miss Mancel began to receive consolation from experiencing an affection quite maternal.

At the beginning of the winter, Lady Melvyn, who had less ambition to imitate the real merit of her predecessor than to exhibit her own imaginary perfections, brought Sir Charles to London, there to fix their residence for the ensuing half year. This made little alteration in Miss Melvyn's way of life. Sir Charles and his lady would sometimes call upon her, the latter not choosing to trust Sir Charles alone with his daughter, lest she should represent to him how unworthily she was treated; but as he was not devoid of affection for her, he would sometimes visit her privately, concealing it from his lady, who endeavoured to prevent this, by telling him, that schoolmistresses were apt to take amiss a parent's visiting his children too often, construing it as a distrust of their care; and therefore if he offended in that way, Mademoiselle d'Avaux's disgust might affect her behaviour to Miss Melvyn, and render her residence there very disagreeable, which Lady Melvyn's great tenderness made her ardently wish to avoid, as she was desirous every thing should be agreeable to her dear daughter. Sir Charles could not be entirely restrained by these kind admonitions from indulging himself with the sight of Miss Melvyn.

His lady had little reason to be afraid of these interviews, for her step-daughter had too strong a sense of filial obedience, and too delicate a regard for her father's happiness, to suffer the least intimation of a fault in his wife to escape her lips, as a good opinion of her was so necessary to his ease; but as she soon found out these visits were made by stealth, they gave her great pleasure as a plain proof of his affection. Lady Melvyn thought her daughter's coming abroad would be as hurtful as her being visited at home, and therefore very seldom sent for her to her house; and when she did, took care to have her carried home before the hour that she expected company, on pretence of preserving the regularity of hours, which she knew would be agreeable to Mademoiselle d'Avaux.

The true reason of this great caution was an unwillingness to be seen with one whose person all her vanity could not prevent her from being sensible was more attractive than her own. Miss Melvyn was very pretty, had an engaging sweetness in her countenance, and all the bloom which belongs to youth, though it does not always accompany it. Her person was elegant, and perfectly genteel.

Lady Melvyn was void of delicacy; she had a regular set of features but they wanted to be softened into effeminacy before they could have any just pretence to beauty. Her eyes were black and not void of vivacity, but they neither expressed penetration nor gentleness. Her person was well proportioned, but she was formed on too large a scale, and destitute of grace. She was not ill bred, but had none of that softness of manners which gives rise to all the sweet civilities of life. In short, Lady Melvyn was one who by herself and many others would be esteemed a fine woman, and by many more ranked only under the denomination of a shewey woman; like Mr Bayes's hero, she was unamiable, but she was great; she excited the admiration of some, but pleased none.

As soon as she appeared in the world as Lady Melvyn, she began to exercise what she thought only lively coquetry; but her entire want of grace and delicacy often made that appear like boldness, which she designed for vivacity. As her ambition to charm was as great as if she had been better qualified for success, it is not strange that she did not choose to give opportunities of comparison between herself and a daughter who, though not so striking at first sight, was filled with attractions.

The contempt which her ladyship thought she must in justice to her own understanding shew for her husband's, and the supercilious coldness with which she treated Miss Melvyn, made that young lady very glad that she was so seldom sent for to her father's house. But she wished to learn such accomplishments as whilst she lived in the country were out of her power, and therefore intimated to Lady Melvyn her desire of being taught music and drawing, with the better hope of success, as the necessity of completing her education had been made the excuse for sending her to a boarding school; but this request was denied her on frivolous pretences, the real cause, when she perceived the very extravagant turn of her step-mother, she soon understood was to avoid expense.

She had flattered herself she might obtain permission to have her books sent to her; but upon enquiry found that Lady Melvyn had removed them to her dressing room, and intermixed them with china, in so ornamental a manner, so truly expressive of the turn of her mind, where a pretended love of reading was blended with a real fondness for trifles, that she had no chance for this indulgence.

While Miss Melvyn was suffering all these mortifications from a parent, Miss Mancel was receiving every proof of the most tender affection from one bound to her by no paternal ties. Mr Hintman, as soon as the season of the year brought him to town, visited his little charge, and was charmed with the vivacity which was now restored to her. He called upon her frequently, and seldom without some present, or a proposal of some pleasure. He would continually entreat her to make him some request, that he might have the pleasure of gratifying her. He frequently gave Mademoiselle d'Avaux tickets for the play and the opera, that the young Louisa might have somebody to accompany her; but as Miss Melvyn did not think it proper at her age to go often with only her schoolmistress, or, according to the language of schools, her governess, Miss Mancel frequently declined being of the party, rather than leave her amiable friend and instructor.

There was no one who shewed any particular civility to Miss Mancel, but received some return from Mr Hintman. Miss Melvyn was very deservedly the chief object of his gratitude;

but as she declined accepting the presents he offered her, he chose a way more agreeable to himself, as it would make his little Louisa the rewarder of the favours she received. He therefore was lavish of his money to her, and intreated her to lay it out in such manner as would be most agreeable to herself and Miss Melvyn; at the same time asking her by what means she could most gratify that young lady.

Miss Mancel said she knew nothing that would be so acceptable to Miss Melvyn as books. To this Mr Hintman replied that since that was the case, he could very easily accommodate them, for he had by him a very pretty library left him by his sister about a year before, which he had never unpacked, having most of the same books in his own study.

This accordingly he sent to Miss Mancel, with proper bookcases to contain them, which they immediately put up in their apartments. This was the most agreeable acquisition imaginable; for Miss Hintman having been a very sensible young lady, the collection was extremely valuable.

Mr Hintman's great indulgence could not fail of receiving from Miss Mancel the wished-for return of affection and gratitude; whenever he came she flew to him with delight, caressed him with all the fondness so enchanting at that age, and parted from him with the extremest reluctance. Her great obligations to him were the frequent subjects of her discourse with Miss Melvyn, who had the highest admiration of his generosity.

His allowance to Miss Mancel was sufficient to have defrayed all her expenses, but those were to be the care of Mademoiselle d'Avaux, for the money he gave Louisa was for no other purpose than her gratifications; necessity, or even usefulness, was out of the question; every thing of that kind being provided for her. Nor was he more sparing in what concerned her education, she learnt dancing, music, and drawing; besides other things generally taught at schools; but her greatest improvement was from reading with Miss Melvyn, who instructed her in geography, and in such parts of philosophy of which her age was capable: but above all, she was most attentive to inculcate into her mind the principles of true religion.

Thus her understanding opened in a surprising degree, and while the beauty and graces of her person, and her great progress in genteel accomplishments, charmed every eye, the nice discernment, and uncommon strength of reason which appeared in her conversation, astonished every judicious observer; but her most admirable qualities were her humility and modesty; which, notwithstanding her great internal and external excellencies, rendered her diffident, mild, bashful, and tractable; her heart seemed as free from defects as her understanding was from the follies which in a degree are incident to almost every other person.

Miss Melvyn and her little companion received a considerable increase of happiness from the present of books Mr Hintman had made them; the latter had no wish but that Miss Melvyn might receive equal indulgence from parents that she enjoyed from one who bore no relation to her. The first desire that occurred to her on Mr Hintman's profuse presents of money was to treat her friend with masters for music and drawing, and such other things as she knew she had an inclination to learn; but as she was not unacquainted with her delicacy on that subject, as soon as Mr Hintman left her, she ran to Miss Melvyn with some of the impatience in her countenance, though she endeavoured to conceal it, with which her heart was filled, and tried every tender caress, every fond and humble petition, to obtain a promise from that young lady, that she would grant her a request she had to make. She hung round her neck, and endeavoured to prevail by a thousand engaging infantine arts; and when she found they would not succeed, she knelt down before her, and with all the grace and importunity of the most amiable suppliant, tried to win her to compliance. Nothing would avail, for Miss Melvyn was convinced by her earnestness that her design was to confer some favour; she knew the generosity of her youthful mind too well to believe she so ardently aimed at any thing that was for her own private gratification.

Thus Louisa found herself reduced to explain the use she

intended to have made of the promise she wanted to obtain; and having acquainted Miss Melvyn with Mr Hintman's generous allowance, and of the payment she had received of the first quarter, she in explicit terms told her, 'Mr Hintman has indeed given me money, but it depends on you to make that money yield me pleasure, by suffering me to apply it to such uses as will procure me the inexpressible joy of contributing in some degree to the pleasure of one who renders my life so very happy.'

Miss Melvyn was so pleased with the generosity of her little pupil that she gave her as many caresses as the other had lavished on her in order to obtain the promise she so much wished for; but she could not be induced to grant her request. Miss Melvyn was void of that pride which often conceals itself under the name of spirit and greatness of soul; and makes people averse to receiving an obligation because they feel themselves too proud to be grateful, and think that to be obliged implies an inferiority which their pride cannot support. Had Louisa been of the same age with herself, she would have felt a kind of property in all she possessed; friendship, the tenure by which she held it; for where hearts are strictly united, she had no notion of any distinction in things of less import- ance, the adventitious goods of fortune. The boundaries and barriers raised by those two watchful and suspicious enemies, Meum and Tuum, were in her opinion broke down by true friendship; and all property laid in one undistinguished common; but to accept Miss Mancel's money, especially in so great a proportion, appeared to her like taking advantage of her youth; and as she did not think her old enough to be a sufficient judge of the value of it, she did not look upon her as capable of being a party in so perfect a friendship, as was requisite to constitute that unity of property.

Poor Louisa by this disappointment of the first wish of her heart found what older people often experience, that her riches instead of pleasure procured her only mortification. She could scarcely refrain from tears at a refusal which she thought must arise from want of affection, and told Miss Melvyn she saw that she loved her but imperfectly; for, added she, 'Could we change places, with how much pleasure should I have accepted it from you! And the satisfaction that learning these things now gives me would be turned into delight by reflecting on the gratification you would receive in having been the means of procuring them for me. I should not envy you the joy of giving, because I as receiver should not have the less share of that satisfaction, since by reflecting on yours I must partake of it, and so increase my own.'

Miss Melvyn could not forbear blushing at finding a superior degree of delicacy, and a generosity much more exalted, in one so young, than she had felt in herself. She plainly saw that the greatest proof of a noble mind is to feel a joy in gratitude; for those who know all the pleasures of conferring an obligation will be sensible that by accepting it they give the highest delight the human mind can feel, when employed on human objects; and therefore while they receive a benefit, they will taste not only the comforts arising from it to themselves, but share the gratification of a benefactor, from reflecting on the joy they give to those who have conferred it: thus the receiver of a favour from a truly generous person, 'by owing owes not, and is at once indebted and discharged.'

As Miss Melvyn felt her little friend's reproach, and saw that she had done her injustice in thinking her youth rendered her incapable of that perfection of friendship, which might justify the accepting of her offer; she acknowledged her error, and assured her she would comply if she had no other means of obtaining the instruction she proposed to purchase for her; but that was not the case, for she found she could very well learn from seeing the masters teach her, and practising in their absence.

Mr Hintman expressed a desire that Miss Mancel should learn Italian, if she had no objection to it; for he never dictated to her, but offered any advice he had to give, or any inclination which he chose to intimate, with the humility of a dependant, rather than the authority of a benefactor; and indeed it was sufficient; for the slightest hint that any thing would be agreeable to him, met with the most impatient desire in Miss Mancel to perform it: actuated by sincere affection, and the strongest gratitude, nothing made her so happy as an opportunity to shew him the readiness of her obedience.

But as they were at a loss for a master to teach her that language, Miss Melvyn told them she knew an Italian gentleman, who had been at Sir Charles's house near two months before she had the misfortune of losing the best of mothers. Lady Melvyn had begun to teach her daughter Italian, but desirous that she should speak it with great propriety, she invited this gentleman to her house who was reduced to great distress of circumstances, and whose person, as well as his many virtues, she had known from her childhood. He had been a friend of her father's and she was glad of this excuse for making him a handsome present, which otherwise it was not easy to induce him to accept.

Mr Hintman was not long before he procured this Italian master for Miss Mancel; nor did she delay making use of his instructions; but I shall not describe her progress in the acquisition of this, any more than her other accomplishments, in all of which she excelled to a surprising degree; nor did Miss Melvyn fall very short of her, though she was at such disadvantage in her method of learning many of them, not having the assistance of a master. Their time was so entirely engrossed by these employments, that they had little leisure, and still less desire, to keep company with the rest of the school; but they saved themselves from the dislike which might naturally have arisen in the minds of the other scholars, from being thus neglected, by little presents which Miss Mancel frequently made them.

These two young ladies were very early risers, and the time which was not taken up by Miss Mancel's masters, and that wherein it was requisite to practise what they taught her, they employed in reading, wherein Mr d'Avora, their Italian master, often accompanied them.

Mr d'Avora was a man of excellent understanding, and had an incomparable heart. Misfortunes had softened common humanity into a most tender disposition; and had given him a thorough knowledge of mankind without lessening his benevolence for individuals; though such as learn it by adversity, the surest school for that science, seldom see them in an amiable light.

Mr d'Avora was not less acquainted with particular nations than with mankind in general; he had travelled through all the countries in Europe, some parts of Asia and Africa, and having traversed them with discernment and the curiosity of wisdom, not of impertinence, he received such improvement of understanding, as few travellers can boast.

He had an affection for Miss Melvyn, both for her own merits and the obligations he had to her family, and a very short acquaintance with Miss Mancel made him extremely fond of her. He took great pleasure in assisting them in the improvement they so industriously laboured for, and as he was a man of universal knowledge, he was capable of being very useful to them in that respect. For this purpose he often read with them, and by explaining many books on abstruse subjects, rendered several authors intelligible to them, who, without his assistance, would have been too obscure for persons of their age. He had very few scholars, therefore had much leisure, and with great satisfaction dedicated part of it to our young ladies, as he saw he thereby gave them a very sincere pleasure; and he was much gratified with thinking that by his care and instruction of Miss Melvyn, he made some return for the friendship he had received from her family; and that could her mother be sensible of his attendance on her much-loved and now neglected daughter, it would be highly agreeable to her.

In the manner I have mentioned, these two young ladies passed their time, till Miss Mancel reached her fifteenth year, with little alteration, except the increase of her charms, and her great improvement in every accomplishment. Her appearance began to grow womanly, she was indeed

'In the bloom of beauty's pride'.

Dazzlingly handsome at first view; but such numerous and

various charms appeared on a more intimate acquaintance that people forgot how much they had been struck by the first sight of her, lost in wonder at her increasing attractions, to the force of which she was the only person that was insensible. Humble piety rendered her indifferent to circumstances which she looked upon rather as snares than blessings, and like a person on the brink of a precipice could not enjoy the beauty of the prospect, overawed by the dangers of her situation.

She had indeed too much of human nature in her not to feel sometimes a little flush of vanity on seeing herself admired; but she immediately corrected the foible, by reflecting that whatever advantages of mind or form had fallen to her share, they were given her by one who expected she should not suffer her thoughts or attention to be withdrawn thereby from him, who was the perfection of all excellence, while she at best could but flatter herself with being less imperfect than many of her fellow creatures.

She considered flattery and admiration as the rocks on which young people, who are at all superior to the multitude, are apt to be wrecked; deprived of quiet happiness in this world, and exalted felicity in the next; and as she was really convinced that she had only a few obvious external advantages over others, she opposed to the praises lavished on her reflections of her imper-fections, which, though not apparent to any one but herself, she verily believed were uncommonly great, as she beheld them with very scrutinizing and rigid eyes, while she looked on those of others with the greatest lenity. But of all the means she used to preserve her humility, she was the most assiduous in praying to him who made her heart, to preserve it humble.

Though the degree of piety I mention may sound in the ears of many too grave for so young a person, yet it by no means rendered her so; she had great vivacity; a lively imagination; an uncommon share of wit; and a very happy manner of express-ing herself. She had all the amiable gaiety of youth, without the least tendency to imprudence; and when she talked most, and, in appearance, let fancy assume the reins, said nothing to repent of. Her heart was all purity, universal benevolence and good-nature; and as out of its abundance her mouth spake, she was in little danger of offending with her tongue.

It is not strange that Mr Hintman's fondness should increase with Miss Mancel's excellencies, but the caresses which suited her earlier years were now become improper; and Mr Hintman, by appearing insensible of the necessary change of behaviour, reduced her to great difficulties; she could not reconcile herself to receiving them; and yet to inform him of the impropriety implied a forward consciousness which she was not able to assume.

She communicated the vexation of her mind to Miss Melvyn, who was still more alarmed as her superior age and experience rendered her more apprehensive; but she knew not what to advise.

In this dilemma Miss Melvyn had recourse to their good friend, whose knowledge of mankind, his integrity and prudence, rendered him the safest guide. Accordingly one day when Louisa was called from them to Mr Hintman, who came to make her a visit, Miss Melvyn informed Mr d'Avora of the reason why her friend obeyed the summons with less joy than he had observed in her on the like occasion the year before.

Mr d'Avora was much disturbed at this information; but not choosing to increase the uneasiness the young ladies seemed to be under till he had more certain foundation for his opinion, he only intimated, that customs were hard to break, but he should hope, that when Mr Hintman reflected on the impropriety of behaving to a young woman as if she was still a child, he would alter it, and if he was not immediately sensible of the difference a small addition of age makes, yet her behaviour would lead him to recollect it.

Although Mr d'Avora seemed to pay little regard to what Miss Melvyn said, yet it made great impression on him, and as soon as he left her, he took all proper measures to enquire into the character, and usual conduct of Mr Hintman.

This scrutiny did not turn out at all to his satisfaction, every account he received was the same; he had not the pleasure of

finding what is usually asserted, that 'all men have two characters'; for Mr Hintman had but one, and that the most alarming
that could be for Miss Mancel. Every person told him that Mr
Hintman had a very great fortune, which he spent entirely in the
gratification of his favourite vice, the love of women; on whom
his profuseness was boundless. That as he was easily captivated,
so he was soon tired; and seldom kept a woman long after he
had obtained the free possession of her; but generally was
more bountiful than is customary with men of his debauched
principles at parting with them.

This, Mr d'Avora was assured, was Mr Hintman's only vice;
that he was good-natured, and generous on all occasions. From
this account he saw too great reason to fear, that all the care
which had been taken to improve Miss Mancel arose only from
a sort of epicurism in his predominant vice, but yet this was too
doubtful a circumstance to be the ground-work of any plan of
action. A man of acknowledged generosity and good-nature,
however vicious, might do a noble action without having any
criminal design. In this uncertainty of mind he knew not what
to advise her, and was unwilling to excite such fears in the
breasts of these two young friends, as might be groundless; but
yet would entirely destroy their peace; therefore, he only told
Miss Melvyn in general terms, that Mr Hintman's character was
such, as rendered it very necessary that Louisa should be much
on her guard; but that whether more than prudent caution, and
decent reserve were requisite, her own observation must
discover, for no one else could determine that point, since he
had the reputation of being generous as well as debauched;
therefore his actions towards her might be, and he hoped were,
the result of his greatest virtue, rather than of his pre dominant
vice.

Miss Melvyn made a faithful report of what Mr d'Avora had
said to her, which filled both herself and her friend with
inexpressible uneasiness.

Louisa was in great difficulty how to act, between gratitude
and affection on the one side, and necessary caution and
reserve on the other. She was almost as much afraid of appear-

ing ungrateful, as of being imprudent. She found little assistance from the advice of her friends, who declared themselves incapable of directing her, therefore she was obliged to lay aside all dependence on her own care, and to trust in that of heaven, convinced that her innocence would be guarded by that power who knew the integrity and purity of her heart; and that while she preserved it unblemished, even in thought and inclination, her prayers for his protection would not be unavailing.

The remainder of the winter passed like the former part, only that the increase of her apprehensions so far lessened her easy vivacity, that Mr Hintman observed the alteration, and complained of the constraint and awe which damped her conversation.

As the school broke up at Easter, he intreated her to accompany him that short time into the country, from which she would gladly have excused herself, both on account of her fears, and of her unwillingness to leave Miss Melvyn, of whose conversation she was now more particularly tenacious, as Lady Melvyn had determined to suffer her to return home in a short time, not knowing how to excuse her remaining longer at school, as she was entered into her one and twentieth year. Miss Melvyn would have been glad that her ladyship had not shewn this token of regard to popular opinion; for since she had enjoyed Miss Mancel's company, and been in possession of so good a collection of books, she was grown perfectly contented with her situation.

Louisa, to make Mr Hintman desist from the request he urged with so much importunity, tried every means that did not appear like a total disinclination to accompany him, for any thing that bore the air of ingratitude could not be supported by her, whose heart was so void of it, and who thought she could never feel enough for her benefactor, if his designs were not so criminal as she feared, but scarcely could suffer herself to suspect.

Mr Hintman was too ardent in his purposes to give up his favourite scheme, and Louisa beheld with inexpressible concern the day approach, when she must either accompany him into the country, or disoblige him for ever, and make herself appear extremely ungrateful in the eyes of a man whom she loved and honoured like a father. Her addresses to heaven for protection now became more vehement and continual, and the greatest part of her time was spent on her knees in praying to that power in whom she trusted. Miss Melvyn and Mr d'Avora were scarcely less anxious, or under fewer apprehensions than herself, but could see no resource except in the protection of the Almighty, to whom we seldom apply with entire faith and resignation while we have any hopes in human assistance.

Two days before that fixed on for the purposed journey, when Louisa's anxiety was risen to the utmost height, the schoolmistress entered the room, with a countenance so melancholy, as was more suitable to the situation of mind in which the two young friends were then in, than to any reason they apprehended she could have for an air of so much sorrow. She soon began a discourse, which they immediately apprehended was preparatory to the opening of some fatal event, and which, as is usual in such cases, was, if possible, more alarming than any misfortune it could precede. The ladies expressed their fears, and begged to be acquainted with what had befallen them. After considerable efforts to deliver her of the secret with which she was pregnant, they learnt that a gentleman was in the parlour, who came to inform Miss Mancel that Mr Hintman died the day before in a fit of an apoplexy.

All Louisa's fears and suspicions vanished at once, and grief alone took possession of her heart. The shock so entirely overcame her, that she was not able to see the fatal messenger of such melancholy tidings as the death of her benefactor, and second father. Miss Melvyn was obliged to undertake this office, and learnt from the gentleman that Mr Hintman died without a will, and therefore left the poor Louisa as destitute, except being enriched by various accomplishments, as he found her, and at a much more dangerous time, when her beauty would scarcely suffer compassion to arise unaccompanied with softer sentiments. This gentleman proceeded to inform Miss Melvyn, that his father and another person of equal relation to Mr Hintman were heirs at law. He expressed great concern for Miss Mancel, and wished he had his father's power of repairing Mr Hintman's neglect, but that his influence extended no farther than to obtain a commission to pay the expenses of another year at that school, that the young lady might have time to recollect herself after so fatal a change, and determine at leisure on her future course of life.

Miss Melvyn was so sensibly touched at the prospect of the approaching distress with which her friend was threatened, that she burst into tears and uttered some exclamations concerning 'the inconsistency of that affection, which could suffer a man to rest a moment without securing a provision in case of death, to a young woman he seemed to love with the greatest excess of tenderness'. 'Believe me, madam,' said the young gentleman, 'Mr Hintman was capable of no love that was not entirely sensual, and consequently selfish; all who knew him lamented the fate of a young woman, who by every account is so superiorly lovely. Among his friends he made no secret of his designs in all he had done for her, and boasted frequently of the extraordinary charms which were ripening for his possession. It was but two days ago, that he was exulting in the presence of some of them, that the time was now approaching, when he should be rewarded for long expectation, and boundless expense; for he should then, he said, be sure of her person, and had long secured her heart. He knew he had strong prejudices and strange scruples to combat; but was prepared, and should not find them difficult to conquer; at worst, his steward in a parson's habit would lull them all to sleep.'

'Good heaven!' cried Miss Melvyn, 'could there be such a wretch, and were there men who would keep company with him, who would bear the disgrace of being called his friends?'

'Your notions, madam,' replied the gentleman, 'are too refined for persons who live in the world: should a man insist on strict morals in all his acquaintance, he might enjoy a solitude in the most populous city; though, I confess, nothing but ties of kindred could have made me intimate with one of Mr Hintman's character, which I should not thus have exposed to you, but as I imagined a better knowledge of the man might alleviate the affliction you seemed to feel for Miss Mancel's having lost one whom you esteemed so sincere a friend. I should have been glad,' continued he, 'could I have seen the young lady, of whom Mr Hintman told such wonders; but I will not presume to press it, time may offer me some opportunity for satisfying my curiosity without paining her, I therefore take my leave, with only requesting your permission to remit the money of which I was made the bearer.'

Miss Melvyn was so much affected with her friend's situation, that she took the paper the gentleman offered her, without having power to reflect whether she ought to accept it, or being able to make him any acknowledgement; and he retired directly. She was obliged to stay some time to compose her spirits before she went to her friend, that she might be the better able to comfort her. On examining the paper, she found it a bank-note of an hundred pounds, which was now become all Miss Mancel's fortune.

Lamont could not forbear interrupting Mrs Maynard in this place, by some very severe reflections on Mr Hintman's having neglected to make a provision for Miss Mancel in case of his death, which I believe was the part of his conduct that to Lamont appeared most inexcusable; for though he is too fashionable to think intriguing very criminal, yet he is naturally generous, as far as money is concerned. 'I cannot think,' replied my cousin, 'that Mr Hintman's behaviour in that particular can be much wondered at. Death to such a man must be so dreadful an event, that he will naturally endeavour to banish it from his mind, whenever it attempts to intrude, and when a person takes so little care to make provision for his own happiness after death, is it strange he should be unmindful of what shall befall another after that fatal period? When a man neglects his own soul, and deprives himself of all hope of everlasting felicity, can we expect he should take any trouble to provide for the temporal convenience of another person?

'Besides, could he, who aimed at reducing an innocent and amiable young woman to guilt and infamy in this world, and eternal perdition in the next, be under any concern lest she should fall into the lesser miseries of poverty? It would have been an inconsistency in such a character.'

'You see gallantry in a very serious light, madam,' said Lamont.

'I do indeed, sir,' answered Mrs Maynard, 'I look on it as the most dangerous of vices, it destroys truth, honour, humanity, it is directly contrary to the laws of God, is the destruction of society, and almost as inconsistent with morality as with religion.'

'I beg pardon, madam,' interrupted Lamont (who felt himself a little touched with what she said), 'for breaking into your narrative, and must beg you will continue it.'

Miss Melvyn, resumed Mrs Maynard, was too well acquainted with the strength of Louisa's mind to think it necessary to conceal from her any part of what had passed between herself and Mr Hintman's relation.

Louisa, much affected by Mr Hintman's dying, with a heart so unfit to appear at the tribunal before which he was so suddenly summoned, thought not immediately of herself; but when she reflected on the dangers she had escaped, she blessed her poverty, since it was the consequence of an event which delivered her from so much greater evils, and sent up many sincere and ardent thanksgivings to heaven, for so signal a preservation. These thoughts possessed our young friends for the first three or four days after Mr Hintman's death; but then they began to think it requisite to consult with Mr d'Avora, on what course of life it was most advisable for Miss Mancel to enter. This was a difficult point to determine; though her understanding and attainments were far superior to her years, yet they were sensible her youth would be a great impediment to her in any undertaking. Mr d'Avora therefore advised that she should continue a little longer at the school, and then fix in the most private manner imaginable for three or four years, by which time he hoped to be able to establish her in some widow's family, as governess to her children; for he told her she must not expect, while her person continued such as it then was, that a married woman would receive her in any capacity that fixed her in the same house with her husband.

As Miss Mancel had many jewels and trinkets of value, she had no doubt but that with economy she might support herself for the term Mr d'Avora mentioned, and even longer if requisite, as she could add to her little fund by the produce of her industry. As Miss Melvyn's return home drew near, it was agreed that she should seek out some place in Sir Charles's neighbourhood where Louisa might lodge cheaply and reputably; and in the mean time Mr d'Avora should dispose of whatever she had of value, except her books and her harpsichord; these she resolved not to part with till the produce of her other things, and the money she had by her, was spent, as they would not only amuse her in the country, but afford her the power of improving herself in those accomplishments which were to be her future provision.

This plan softened the pangs of separation when the time of Miss Melvyn's departure arrived. It was not long before she found out an apartment at a reputable farmer's, where Miss Mancel might lodge conveniently. Had it been a less tolerable place, its vicinity to Sir Charles's house, from which it was but a quarter of a mile distant, would have made it a very delightful abode to her, and she soon repaired thither.

Great was the joy of the two friends at meeting. Miss Melvyn's situation at home was rendered as irksome as possible by Lady Melvyn's behaviour both to her and Sir Charles who, notwithstanding her ill treatment, was extremely fond of, and totally guided by her. His mind was so entirely enslaved that he beheld nothing but in the light wherein she pleased to represent it, and was so easy a dupe, that she could scarcely feel the joys of self triumph in her superior art, which was on no subject so constantly exerted, as in keeping up a coldness in Sir Charles towards his daughter; this she had with tolerable facility effected in her absence, and was assiduously careful to preserve now she was present. To those who know not the power an artful woman can obtain over a weak man, it would appear incredible that any father could be prejudiced against a daughter whose whole attention was to please him. She had so perfect a command over her temper that she never appeared to take offence at any thing Lady Melvyn said or did, though that lady endeavoured by every provocation to throw her off her guard. This behaviour only increased her hatred, which was not in the least abated by Miss Melvyn's taking every opportunity of being serviceable to her half-brothers and sisters. Lady Melvyn persuaded Sir Charles that his daughter's calmness was only assumed in his presence, and continually complained of her insolence when he was not by. If he ever appeared to doubt the truth of her report, she would burst into tears, complain of his want of love and little confidence in her, and sometimes thought proper to shew her grief at such treatment by a pretended hysteric fit, always ready at call to come to her assistance, though really so unnecessarily lavished on one easily duped without those laborious means, that it appeared a wantonness of cunning, which was thus exerted only for its own indulgence. She soon perceived that Miss Melvyn rather chose to submit to any aspersions, than to render her father unhappy by undeceiving him; and taking advantage of this generosity, would sometimes, to establish his opinion of her veracity, accuse Miss Melvyn to her face of offences which she had never committed, and things she had never said.

In such a situation the arrival of a friend, into whose sympathetic bosom she could pour all her griefs, and in whose delightful society she could forget them, was the highest blessing. But Lady Melvyn contrived to make her feel mortifications even in this tenderest particular, for though she was in her heart glad to have her out of the house, that she might not be witness of much improper behaviour, yet she would sometimes mortify herself in order to tease Miss Melvyn, by preventing her from going to her beloved friend; and continually alleged her spending so much time with Louisa as a proof of the aversion she had made Sir Charles believe Miss Melvyn had to her.

Louisa felt deeply her friend's uneasiness, but when they

were together they could not be unhappy. They seldom passed a day without seeing each other, but as Lady Melvyn had taken no notice of Louisa, she could not go to her house, therefore their meetings were at her lodgings, where they often read together, and at other times would apply to music to drive away melancholy reflections. As Louisa wished to remain near her friend as long as possible, she endeavoured, by taking in plainwork, to provide for some part of her current expenses, the less to diminish the little fund she had by her. She likewise employed part of her time in painting, having reason to hope that if she could find a means of offering her pictures to sale, she might from them raise a very convenient sum. While she was thus contriving to enable herself to enjoy for many years the conversation of her friend, Lady Melvyn was as industriously laying schemes that, if successful, must disappoint all the young ladies' hopes.

Towards the end of the autumn, Mr Morgan, a man of fortune who had spent above half a year in a fruitless pursuit after health, made a visit to a gentleman in the neighbourhood. Unfortunately Miss Melvyn's charms made a conquest of this gentleman, in whom age had not gained a victory over passion. Miss Melvyn's humility occasioned her being the last person who perceived the impression she had made on his heart, and his age would scarcely suffer her to believe her senses when the symptoms became most apparent. A girl may find some amusement in a young lover, though she feels no disposition in herself to return his passion, her vanity is flattered by his addresses, and a woman must be very little disposed to be pleased, who receives no pleasure from one who is continually endeavouring to oblige and amuse her; but the most whimsical of the poets never fancied a grey-bearded Cupid, or represented Hymen with a torch in one hand, and a crutch in the other. I allow that

> 'Oft the matrimonial Cupid,
> Lash'd on by time grows tir'd and stupid,'

and does not always wear that blooming joyous countenance,

which the painters give him; but should any capricious artist take the sickle out of the hand of old Time, and in its place put Hymen's torch, the picture might be thought very unnatural, yet would represent a proper hymeneal Cupid to attend Mr Morgan to the altar.

Such a lover could excite no emotion in his mistress's heart but disgust. Miss Melvyn's principles were too delicate to suffer her to think she had any title to ridicule a man for his partiality to her, however ill-suited to himself; but no consideration could prevent his addresses from being extremely disagreeable: however, she could without any great difficulty have so far commanded herself, as to have treated him with complaisance, till he gave her an opportunity of rejecting his courtship, had she not been apprehensive that this affair would give Lady Melvyn a new subject for persecution. She was pretty certain that lady would be glad to settle her in another county; and that her averseness to so ill-suited a marriage would only serve as an additional recommendation to her mother. She was indeed determined in justice to Mr Morgan and compassion to herself, not to be induced by any solicitations to marry a man whom she could not hope that even the strongest attachment to duty could render so well as indifferent to her, but she dreaded the means that might be taken to oblige her to accept Mr Morgan's proposal.

Little did she guess what those means would be. She expected to be attacked alternately with all the violence of passion, the affected softness of dissimulation, and every art that cunning could devise, to force Sir Charles to concur in her persecution. These indeed were employed as soon as Mr Morgan made his proposals; but her ladyship had too many resources in her fertile brain to persevere long in a course she found unavailing. The farmer where Miss Mancel lodged had a son, who was in treaty with Lady Melvyn for a farm, which at the end of the year would become vacant. This person she thought fit for her purpose, as Miss Melvyn's going so frequently to Miss Mancel might give some colour to her invention. She therefore took care to be found by Sir Charles drowned in tears; he pressed to know the occasion of her grief, but she resisted his importunity in such a manner as could not fail to increase it, still she declared, that she loved him to that excess she could not communicate a secret which she knew must afflict him, even though the suppression and inward preyings of her sorrow should prove fatal to her life.

Sir Charles now on his knees intreated her to acquaint him with the misfortune she endeavoured to conceal, assuring her, that nothing could give him so much concern as seeing her in that condition. She told him she was sensible, that as his wife it was her duty to obey him (a duty newly discovered, or at least newly performed by her ladyship); but she feared she had not strength left to give it utterance. The endeavour threw her into a hysteric fit, which was succeeded by so many others that Sir Charles was almost frantic with his fears for so tender a wife, who was thus reduced to the last agonies by her affectionate apprehensions of giving him pain.

After rubbing her hands and feet till they were sore, suffocating her with burnt feathers, and half poisoning her with medicines, Sir Charles and her servants so far brought her to life that after sending her attendants out of the room, she had just power to tell him she had discovered an intrigue between his daughter and Simon the young farmer, and then immediately sunk into another fit, which however did not last so long; for as she had removed the heavy burden off her mind, she soon began to recover.

Sir Charles was very much shocked at what Lady Melvyn told him, but could not doubt the reality of the fact when he had seen the very violent effect it had had on his tender wife. He asked her advice how to proceed; and it was soon determined that it was necessary, either to oblige Miss Melvyn to marry Mr Morgan directly, or to disclaim her for ever, and remove the disgrace of so infamous a conduct as far from themselves as possible. With this resolution she was to be immediately acquainted.

Miss Melvyn was accordingly called in, and bitterly reproached by Sir Charles; to which my lady added frequent lamentations that she should so far forget herself, and disgrace so worthy a family, interspersing with them many expressions of the undeserved tenderness she had always had for her, and her great confidence in Miss Melvyn's prudence and virtue, shedding tears for her having so unhappily swerved from them.

As all this passed for some time in general terms, Miss Melvyn was in doubt whether she or her parents had lost their senses; convinced there must be distraction on one side or the other. As soon as she could recover her surprise, she begged to know what crime she had committed. Her astonishment was still increased by the answer she received, which was an accusation of this strange intrigue; and her frequent visits to Miss Mancel were brought as proofs of it. The submissive and mild temper which had hitherto most strongly characterized her, vanished at so injurious a charge and she denied the fact with that true spirit which innocence inspires. She told Lady Melvyn, that though she had hitherto silently submitted to all her ill usage, yet it was her duty to repel an injury like this, and when her reputation was so cruelly aspersed, it would be criminal to suffer the vile inventors to pass unexposed. She insisted on being confronted with her accusers, a privilege allowed to the greatest criminals, and by the severest judges, therefore surely could not be refused by a father to a daughter, on a charge so highly improbable, and for which no lightness in her conduct ever gave the least ground.

As Mrs Maynard was in this part of her narrative a bell rang, which informed us that dinner was ready, and we were unwillingly obliged to postpone the continuation of the history of the two young friends, till a more convenient opportunity.

In the afternoon before we rose from table, four ladies came to drink tea with this admirable society. No addition was necessary to render the conversation amusing; but the strangers seemed to look on the ladies of the house with such gratitude and veneration, and were treated by them with so much friendly politeness, as gave me pleasure. I found by the various enquiries after different persons that these visitors likewise lived in a large society. When they rose up to take leave Miss Trentham proposed to walk part of the way home with them. No one objected to it, for the evening was inviting, and they had designed to spend it in the park, through which these ladies were to pass; for Lady Mary observed, that after having shewn us the beauties of the place, they ought to exhibit the riches of it.

The park is close to one side of the house; it is not quite three miles round; the inequality of the ground much increases its beauty, and the timber is remarkably fine. We could plainly perceive it had been many years in the possession of good economists, who unprompted by necessity, did not think the profit that might arise from the sale a sufficient inducement to deprive it of some fine trees, which are now decaying, but so happily placed, that they are made more venerable and not less beautiful by their declining age. This park is much ornamented by two or three fine pieces of water; one of them is a very noble canal, so artfully terminated by an elegant bridge, beyond which is a wood, that it there appears like a fine river vanishing from the eye.

Mrs Morgan stopped us in one spot, saying, from hence, as Lady Mary observed, you may behold our riches, that building (pointing to what we thought a pretty temple) which perhaps you imagine designed only for ornament or pleasure, is a very large pidgeon house, that affords a sufficient supply to our family, and many of our neighbours. That hill on your right-hand is a warren, prodigiously stocked with rabbits; this canal, and these other pieces of water, as well as the river you saw this morning, furnish our table with a great profusion of fish. You will easily believe from the great number of deer you see around us, that we have as much venison as we can use, either in presents to our friends, or our own family. Hares and all sorts of game likewise abound here; so that with the help of a good dairy, perhaps no situation ever more amply afforded all the necessaries of life. These are indeed our riches; here we have almost every thing we can want, for a very small proportion of that expense which others are at to procure them. 'Such a situation,' said I, 'would be dangerous to many people, for if, as some have supposed, and, in regard to a great part of the world, I fear with truth, mutual wants are the great bands of society, a person thus placed, would be in danger of feeling himself so independent a being as might tempt him to disclaim all commerce with mankind, since he could not be benefited by them. He would look on himself in the light of a rich man gaming with sharpers, with a great probability of losing, and a certainty of never being a gainer.'

'I do not think the danger,' replied Lady Mary, 'so great as you imagine, even though we allow that society arises from the motive you mention. However fortune may have set us above any bodily wants, the mind will still have many which would drive us into society. Reason wishes for communication and improvement; benevolence longs for objects on which to exert itself; the social comforts of friendship are so necessary to our happiness that it would be impossible not to endeavour to enjoy them. In sickness the langour of our minds makes us wish for the amusements of conversation; in health the vivacity of our spirits leads us to desire it. To avoid pain we seek after corporeal conveniencies, to procure pleasure we aim at mental enjoyments; and I believe, if we observe the general course of men's actions, we shall see them at least as strongly actuated by the desire of pleasure, as by the fear of pain; though philosophers, who have formed their judgements more on reason than the knowledge of mankind, may have thought otherwise.'

'I think,' said Mrs Morgan, 'somebody has asserted that he who could live without society must be more than a God, or less than a man; the latter part of this assertion would have held good had he carried it farther, and said lower than a brute, for there is no creature in the universe that is not linked into some society, except we allow the existence of that exploded and unsociable bird the Phoenix.'

'I am surprised,' interrupted Lamont, 'to hear ladies, who seclude themselves from the world in this solitary though beautiful place, so strongly plead for society.'

'Do you then,' replied Miss Mancel, 'mistake a crowd for society? I know not two things more opposite. How little society is there to be found in what you call the world? It might more properly be compared to that state of war, which Hobbes supposes the first condition of mankind. The same vanities, the same passions, the same ambition, reign in almost every breast; a constant desire to supplant, and a continual fear of being supplanted, keep the minds of those who have any views at all in a state of unremitted tumult and envy; and those who have no aim in their actions are too irrational to have a notion of social comforts. The love, as well as the pleasures, of society, is founded in reason, and cannot exist in those minds which are filled with irrational pursuits. Such indeed might claim a place in the society of birds and beasts, though few would deserve to be admitted amongst them, but that of reasonable beings must be founded in reason. What I understand by society is a state of mutual confidence, reciprocal services, and correspondent affections; where numbers are thus united, there will be a free communication of sentiments, and we shall then find speech, that peculiar blessing given to man, a valuable gift indeed; but when we see it restrained by suspicion, or contaminated by detraction, we rather wonder that so dangerous a power was trusted with a race of beings who seldom make a proper use of it.

'You will pity us perhaps because we have no cards, no assemblies, no plays, no masquerades, in this solitary place. The first we might have if we chose it, nor are they totally disclaimed by us; but while we can with safety speak our own thoughts, and with pleasure read those of wiser persons, we are not likely to be often reduced to them. We wish not for large assemblies, because we do not desire to drown conversation in noise; the amusing fictions of dramatic writers are not necessary where nature affords us so many real delights; and as we are not afraid of shewing our hearts, we have no occasion to conceal our persons, in order to obtain either liberty of speech or action.'

'What a serious world should we have, madam,' replied

Lamont, 'if you were to regulate our conduct!'

'By no means, sir,' answered Miss Mancel, 'I wish to make only these alterations, to change noise for real mirth, flutter for settled cheerfulness, affected wit for rational conversation; and would but have that degree of dissipation banished which deprives people of time for reflection on the motives for, and consequences of, their actions, that their pleasures may be real and permanent, and followed neither by repentance nor punishment. I would wish them to have leisure to consider by whom they were sent into the world, and for what purpose, and to learn that their happiness consists in fulfilling the design of their Maker, in providing for their own greatest felicity, and contributing all that is in their power to the convenience of others.'

'You seem, madam,' answered Lamont, 'to choose to make us all slaves to each other.'

'No, sir,' replied Miss Mancel, 'I would only make you friends. Those who are really such are continually endeavouring to serve and oblige each other; this reciprocal communication of benefits should be universal, and then we might with reason be fond of this world.'

'But,' said Lamont, 'this reciprocal communication is impossible; what service can a poor man do me? I may relieve him, but how can he return the obligation?'

'It is he,' answered Miss Mancel, 'who first conferred it, in giving you an opportunity of relieving him. The pleasure he has afforded you, is as far superior to the gratification you have procured him, as it is more blessed to give than to receive. You will perhaps say of him, as the apothecary in *Romeo and Juliet* does of himself and tell me that,

> "His poverty and not his will consents."

'So let it be, and do you

> "Pay his poverty and not his will."

'But certainly the highest satisfaction is on your side, and much obliged you are to that poverty, which enables you to obtain so great a gratification. But do not think the poor can made no adequate return. The greatest pleasure this world can give us is that of being beloved, but how should we expect to obtain love without deserving it? Did you ever see any one that was not fond of a dog that fondled him? Is it then possible to be insensible to the affection of a rational being?'

'If Mr Lamont,' said one of the visitors, 'has not so high a sense of the pleasure of being gratefully loved and esteemed, we ought not to blame him; he, perhaps, like the greatest part of the world, has not sufficiently tried it, to be a proper judge; Miss Mancel is certainly very deep in this knowledge, and her opinion may be received as almost an infallible decision, since it is founded on long experience; and how nobly does she calm the eager wishes of impotent gratitude, in declaring herself to be the most benefited when she confers obligations.'

This was uttered with so much warmth, and accompanied by looks so expressive of affection and grateful sensibility, that I plainly saw it proceeded from something more than mere speculative approbation. Lamont declared, that he was well convinced of the justness of what Miss Mancel had said; at first it appeared rather a sentiment uttered in sport than an opinion which could be proved by argument; but that a little reflection on one's own sensations would afford sufficient conviction of the truth of her assertion, and that the general errors in the conduct of mankind plainly evinced they were of the same opinion, though they often mistook the means; for what, continued he, do people ruin themselves by pomp and splendour, hazard their lives in the pursuits of ambition, and, as Shakespeare says,

'Seek the bubble reputation even in the cannon's mouth.'

But to gain popular applause and esteem? For what do others throw away their time in useless civilities, and politely flatter all they meet, but in hopes of pleasing? Even those who make it their business to slander merit, and exaggerate the faults of others, do it from a desire of raising themselves in the opinion of mankind, by lowering those who may be brought into comparison with them.

During this conversation we had advanced within a field of the house, and the ladies stopped to take their leave, saying, as the evening was too far advanced to suffer them to make any stay with their good friends, they would not disturb them by just entering their doors. But as some parley ensued, several ladies who had seen us from the windows ran out, just to pay their compliments to the worthy inhabitants of Millenium Hall. The pleasure of this short meeting seemed reciprocal, and both sides appeared unwilling to part, but the setting sun admonished us to return.

The house to which we had so nearly approached was a very large old mansion, and its inhabitants so numerous, that I was curious to know how so many became assembled together. Mrs Maynard said that if she did not satisfy my inquiries, I was in great danger of remaining ignorant of the nature of that society, as her friends would not be easily prevailed with to break silence on that subject.

'These ladies,' said she, 'long beheld with compassion the wretched fate of those women, who from scantiness of fortune, and pride of family, are reduced to become dependent, and to bear all the insolence of wealth from such as will receive them into their families; these, though in some measure voluntary slaves, yet suffer all the evils of the severest servitude, and are, I believe, the most unhappy part of the creation. Sometimes they are unqualified to gain a maintenance, educated as is called, genteelly, or in other words idly, they are ignorant of every thing that might give them superior abilities to the lower rank of people, and their birth renders them less acceptable servants to many, who have not generosity enough to treat them as they ought, and yet do not choose while they are acting the mistress, perhaps too haughtily, to feel the secret reproaches of their own hearts. Possibly pride may still oftener reduce these indigent gentlewomen into this wretched state of dependence, and therefore the world is less inclined to pity them; but my friends see human weakness in another light.

'They imagine themselves too far from perfection to have any title to expect it in others, and think that there are none in whom pride is so excusable as in the poor; for if there is the smallest spark of it in their compositions, and who is entirely free from it, the frequent neglects and indignities they meet with must keep it continually alive. If we are despised for casual deficiencies, we naturally seek in ourselves for some merit, to restore us to that dignity in our own eyes which those humiliating mortifications would otherwise debase. Thus we learn to set too great a value on what we still possess, whether advantages of birth, education, or natural talents; any thing will serve for a resource to mortified pride; and as every thing grows by opposition and persecution, we cannot wonder if the opinion of ourselves increases by the same means.

'To persons in this way of thinking, the pride which reduces many to be, what is called with too little humanity, toad-eaters, does not render them unworthy of compassion. Therefore for the relief of this race they bought that large mansion.

'They drew up several regulations, to secure the peace and good order of the society they designed to form, and sending a copy of it to all their acquaintance, told them that any gentleman's daughter, whose character was unblemished, might, if she desired it, on those terms be received into that society.'

I begged, if it was not too much trouble, to know what the regulations were.

'The first rule,' continued Mrs Maynard, 'was that whoever chose to take the benefit of this asylum, for such I may justly call it, should deposit in the hands of a person appointed for that purpose, whatever fortune she was mistress of, the security being approved by her and her friends, and remaining in her possession. Whenever she leaves the society, her fortune should be repaid her, the interest in the mean time being appropriated to the use of the community. The great design of this was to preserve an exact equality between them; for it was not expected that the interest of any of their fortunes should pay the allowance they were to have for their clothes. If any appeared to have secreted part of her fortune she should be expelled from the society.

'Secondly, each person to have a bed-chamber to herself, but the eating-parlour and drawing-room in common.

'Thirdly, all things for rational amusement shall be provided for the society; musical instruments, of whatever sort they shall choose, books, tents for work, and in short conveniences for every kind of employment.

'Fourthly, they must conform to very regular hours.

'Fifthly, a housekeeper will be appointed to manage the household affairs, and a sufficient number of servants provided.

'Sixthly, each person shall alternately, a week at a time, preside at the table, and give what family orders may be requisite.

'Seventhly, twenty-five pounds a year shall be allowed to each person for her clothes and pocket expenses.

'Eighthly, their dress shall be quite plain and neat, but not particular nor uniform.

'Ninthly, the expenses of sickness shall be discharged by the patronesses of this society.

'Tenthly, if any one of the ladies behaves with imprudence she shall be dismissed, and her fortune returned; likewise if any should by turbulence or pettishness of temper disturb the society, it shall be in the power of the rest of them to expel her; a majority of three parts of the community being for the expulsion, and this to be performed by ballotting.

'Eleventhly, a good table and every thing suitable to the convenience of a gentlewoman, shall be provided.

'These were the principal articles; and in less than two months a dozen persons of different ages were established in the house, who seemed thoroughly delighted with their situation. At the request of one of them, who had a friend that wished to be admitted, an order was soon added, by the consent of all, that gave leave for any person who would conform exactly to the rules of the house, to board there for such length of time as should be agreeable to herself and the society, for the price of a hundred pounds a year, fifty for any child she might have, twenty for a maidservant, and thirty for a man.

'The number of this society is now increased to thirty, four ladies board there, one of whom has two children, and there are five young ladies, the eldest not above twelve years old, whose mothers being dead, and their families related to some of the society, their kinswomen have undertaken their education; these likewise pay a hundred pounds a year each. It has frequently happened, that widow ladies have come into this society, till their year of deep mourning was expired.

'With these assistances the society now subsists with the utmost plenty and convenience, without any additional expense to my good friends, except a communication of what this park affords; as our steward provides them with every thing, and has the entire direction of the household affairs, which he executes with the most sensible economy.'

I should imagine, said I, it were very difficult to preserve a comfortable harmony among so many persons, and consequently such variety of tempers?

'Certainly,' answered Mrs Maynard, 'it is not without its difficulties. For the first year of this establishment my friends dedicated most of their time and attention to this new community, who were every day either at the hall, or these ladies with them, endeavouring to cultivate in this sisterhood that sort of disposition which is most productive of peace. By their example and suggestions (for it is difficult to give unreserved advice where you may be suspected of a design to dictate), by their examples and suggestions therefore, they led them to industry, and shewed it to be necessary to all stations, as the basis of almost every virtue. An idle mind, like fallow ground, is the soil for every weed to grow in; in it vice strengthens, the seed of every vanity flourishes unmolested and luxuriant; discontent, malignity, ill humour, spread far and wide, and the mind becomes a chaos which it is beyond human power to call into order and beauty. This therefore my good friends laboured to expel from their infant establishment. They taught them that it was the duty of every person to be of service to others. That those whose hands and minds were by the favours of fortune exempt from the necessary of labouring for their own support, ought to be employed for such as are destitute of these advantages. They got this sisterhood to join with them in working for the poor people, in visiting, in admonishing, in teaching them wherever their situations required these services. Where they found that any of these ladies had a taste for gardening, drawing, music, reading, or any manual or mental art, they cultivated it, assisted them in the pleasantest means, and by various little schemes have kept up these inclinations with all the spirit of pursuit which is requisite to preserve most minds from that state of languidness and inactivity whereby life is rendered wearisome to those who have never found it unfortunate.

'By some regulations made as occasions occurred, all burdensome forms are expelled. The whole society indeed must assemble at morning and evening prayers, and at meals, if sickness does not prevent, but every other ceremonious dependence is banished; they form into different parties of amusement as best suit their inclinations, and sometimes when we go to spend the afternoon there, we shall find a party at cards in one room, in another some at work, while one is reading aloud, and in a separate chamber a set joining in a little concert, though none of them are great proficients in music; while two or three shall be retired into their own rooms, some go out to take the air, for it has seldom happened to them to have less than two boarders at a time who each keep an equipage; while others shall be amusing themselves in the garden, or walking in the very pleasant meadows which surround their house.

'As no one is obliged to stay a minute longer in company than she chooses, she naturally retires as soon as it grows displeasing to her, and does not return till she is prompted by inclination, and consequently well disposed to amuse and be amused. They live in the very strict practice of all religious duties; and it is not to be imagined how much good they have done in the neighbourhood; how much by their care the manners of the poorer people are reformed, and their necessities relieved, though without the distribution of much money; I say much, because, small as their incomes are, there are many who impart out of that little to those who have much less.

'Their visits to us are frequent, and we are on such a footing that they never impede any of our employments. My friends always insisted when they waited on the community, that not one of the sisterhood should discontinue whatever they found her engaged in; this gave them the hint to do the same by us, and it is a rule that no book is thrown aside, no pen laid down at their entrance. There are always some of us manually employed, who are at leisure to converse, and if the visit is not very short, part of it is generally spent in hearing one of the girls read aloud, who take it by turns through a great part of the day; the only difference made for this addition to the company is a change of books, that they may not hear only part of a subject, and begin by a broken thread. Thus they give no interruption, and therefore neither trouble us, nor are themselves scrupulous about coming, so that few days pass without our seeing some of them, though frequently only time enough to accompany us in our walks, or partake of our music.'

'Have you not,' said Lamont, 'been obliged to expel many from the community? Since you do not allow petulancy of temper, nor any lightness of conduct, I should expect a continual revolution.'

'By no means,' answered Mrs Maynard, 'since the establishment of the community there has been but one expelled; and one finding she was in danger of incurring the same sentence, and I believe inwardly disgusted with a country life, retired of her own free choice. Some more have rendered themselves so disagreeable, that the question has been put to the ballot; but the fear of being dismissed made them so diligent to get the majority on their side, before the hour appointed for decision arrived, that it has been determined in their favour, and the earnest desire not to be brought into the same hazard again has induced them to mend their tempers, and some of these are now the most amiable people in the whole community.

'As for levity of conduct they are pretty well secured from it, by being exposed to few temptations in this retired place.

'Some, as in the course of nature must happen, have died, and most of them bequeathed what little they had towards constituting a fund for the continuation of the community. More of them have married; some to persons who knew them before, others to gentlemen in the neighbourhood, or such as happened to come into it; to whom their admirable conduct recommended them.'

I could not help exclaiming, 'In what a heaven do you live, thus surrounded by people who owe all their happiness to your goodness! This is, indeed, imitating your Creator, and in such proportion as your faculties will admit, partaking of his felicity, since you can no where cast your eyes without beholding numbers who derive every earthly good from your bounty and are indebted to your care and example for a reasonable hope of eternal happiness.'

'I will not,' said Mrs Maynard, 'give up my share of the felicity you so justly imagine these ladies must enjoy, though I have no part in what occasions it. When I reflect on all the blessings they impart, and see how happiness flows, as it were, in an uninterrupted current from their hands and lips, I am overwhelmed with gratitude to the Almighty disposer of my fate, for having so mercifully thrown me into such a scene of felicity, where every hour yields true heart-felt joy, and fills me with thanksgiving to him who enables them thus to dispense innumerable blessings, and so greatly rewards them already by the joyful consciousness of having obeyed him.'

The ladies at this time were at too great a distance to hear our conversation, for not choosing to be present while their actions were the subjects of discourse, they had gradually strayed from us. Upon enquiring of my cousin whether the persons in the large community we had been talking of brought any fortunes with them, she told me that most of them had a trifle, some not more than a hundred pounds. That in general the ladies chose to admit those who had least, as their necessities were greatest, except where some particular circumstances rendered protection more requisite to others. That the house not being large enough to contain more than were already established in it, they have been obliged to refuse admission to many, and especially some young women of near two thousand pounds fortune, the expensive turn of the world now being such that no gentlewoman can live genteelly on the interest of that sum, and they prefer this society to a retirement in a country town. Some who wished to board, have likewise been refused. As the expenses of the first community fall so far short of their expectation, and the sums appropriated for that purpose, they determined to hazard another of the same kind, and have just concluded a treaty for a still larger mansion, at about three miles distance, and by the persons now waiting for it, they have reason to believe it will not be less successful than the other, nor more expensive; but should they be mistaken in that particular, they have laid aside a fund sufficient to discharge it. Their scheme I find is to have some of the ladies down to Millenium Hall as soon as they have made the purchase, and there they are to remain, while the necessary repairs and additions are making to the house designed for their habitation, which they imagine will not be completed in less than half a year. They hope, by having the first admitted part of the community thus in the house with them for so long a time, to compensate, in a good degree, for the disadvantages of being settled so much farther from them. The sisterhood of the other society, likewise, in pity to those who are exposed to the same sufferings from which they have been delivered, have offered to crowd themselves for a few months, to leave vacant rooms for some who are destined to the other house, till they can be there accommodated. These also will be fitted for their new way of life, and taught to aim at the happiness enjoyed in this community, by the same means that they have attained to it.

Our subject ended with our walk. Supper was served as soon as we entered the house, and general conversation concluded the evening.

Had I not been led by several facts to repeat already so many conversations, I should be induced not to bury all that passed at this time in silence; but though I have taken the liberty, when the relation of facts naturally led to it, to communicate such discourses as were pertinent to the subject, it would be presuming too far on your time to repeat conversations which did not serve to illustrate any particular actions, however worthy they may be of recollection. I shall therefore only say that it was not with less reluctance I retired to my chamber, at the hour of bed-time, than the night before.

The next morning proved rainy, which prevented me from making any early excursion. But as it cleared up about eleven o'clock, Lamont and I went into the garden, to enjoy the fragrance which every herb and flower exhales at this time of the year, after the desirable refreshment of gentle showers. I conducted him to the flower garden, which had so much delighted me the morning before; and we had not paid due admiration to all the vegetable beauties there exhibited to our view when Mrs Maynard joined us.

I told her it was but a poor compliment to her conversation to say I longed for her company, since now my curiosity might occasion that impatience, which I should nevertheless have felt, had I not been left in painful suspense by the interruption we had received the day before, in the midst of her narrative.

'It would be unnatural,' said she, 'for a woman to quarrel with curiosity; so far from complaining of yours, I am come merely with a design to gratify it, and only expect you will judge of my desire to oblige you by my readiness in obeying your commands; were I myself the subject, the motive for my obedience might be equivocal.'

The History of Miss Mancel and Mrs Morgan continued

I think, continued Mrs Maynard, we left Miss Melvyn requiring to be confronted by her accuser, a request which her step-mother was not inclined to grant; for though in her dealings with young Simon she had perceived such a degree of solicitude for his own interest, and such flagrant proofs of want of integrity, that she did not doubt but that by promising him the farm on rather better terms than she had yet consented to he might be prevailed with to join so far in her scheme as to assert any thing to Sir Charles, yet she dared not venture to produce him face to face to Miss Melvyn, fearing lest his assurance should fail him on so severe a trial.

She replied, therefore, that the proofs were too strong to admit of doubt, but she could not think of exposing Miss Melvyn to the mortification of hearing her depravity witnessed by, perhaps, the last person whom she expected should acknowledge it. Besides, that by such an eclat the disgrace must infallibly become public, and she be deprived of the only means left her of rescuing her reputation from that infamy, to which, in a very short time, it must have been irrecoverably condemned; for it could not be supposed that Mr Morgan would accept as his wife a woman with a sullied character.

Miss Melvyn was almost distracted, at being both so injuriously accused and denied the liberty of defending herself; she begged, she intreated, on her knees, that Sir Charles would not suffer her to fall a prey to such undeserved malice. She asserted her innocence in the strongest and most persuasive terms, and insisted so warmly on her demand of being confronted with her accusers, that her father grew inclined to grant her just request. Lady Melvyn, perceiving he began to comply, repeated her refusal in the most peremptory manner; and declaring to Miss Melvyn that she had no other choice left her but either to resolve to marry Mr Morgan or to be exposed to shame in being publicly disclaimed by her parents, who would no longer suffer her to remain in their house, led Sir Charles out of the room; and he, though reluctant, dared not refuse to accompany her.

Miss Melvyn was now left to reflect on this dreadful alternative. Filled with horror at the shocking conduct of her stepmother, terrified with her threats, and sensible there was no villainy she was not capable of perpetrating rather than give up a point she was thus determined to carry, she was incapable of forming any resolution. She ran to her friend, to seek from her that advice and consolation which her own distracted thoughts could not afford her.

Miss Mancel was so struck with the terror and amazement which was still impressed on Miss Melvyn's countenance, that she had not for some time courage to ask the cause. Trembling with fears of she knew not what, she embraced her distressed friend with an air of such tender, though silent sympathy, as softened the horror of Miss Melvyn's mind, and brought a shower of tears to her relief, which at length enabled her to relate all that had passed between her and her parents. Louisa found it much easier to join in her friend's grief than to administer consolation. She knew not what to advise; two artless, virtuous young women were ill qualified to contend with Lady Melvyn, especially in an affair which could not be rendered public without hazarding Miss Melvyn's character; for reputation is so delicate a thing that the least surmise casts a blemish on it; the woman who is suspected is disgraced; and though Lady Melvyn did not stand high in the public opinion, yet it was scarcely possible for any one to believe she could be guilty of such flagrant wickedness.

Miss Melvyn had a very strong dislike to Mr Morgan, whose disposition appeared as ill suited to hers as his age; to enter into wedlock without any prospect of social happiness seemed to her one of the greatest misfortunes in life; but what was still of more weight in her estimation, she thought it the highest injustice to marry a man whom she could not love, as well as a very criminal mockery of the most solemn vows. On the other side she considered that to preserve her reputation was not only necessary to her own happiness, but a duty to society. 'It is true,' said she, 'I am not placed in a very conspicuous sphere of life, but I am far from being of a rank so obscure that my actions will affect no one but myself; nor indeed do I know any so low, but they have their equals who may copy after them, if they have no inferiors. The care of our virtue we owe to ourselves, the preservation of our characters is due to the world, and both are required by him who commands us to preserve ourself pure and unpolluted, and to contribute as far as we are able to the well-being of all his creatures. Example is the means given universally to all whereby to benefit society. I therefore look on it as one of our principal duties to avoid every imputation of evil; for vice appears more or less hateful as it becomes more or less familiar. Every vicious person abates the horror which it should naturally excite in a virtuous mind. There is nothing so odious to which custom will not in some degree reconcile us; can we expect then, that vice, which is not without its allurements, should alone retain all its deformity, when we are familiarized to its appearance. I should never therefore esteem myself innocent, however pure my actions, if I incurred the reputation of being otherwise, when it was in my power to avoid it. With this way of thinking, my Louisa, you may imagine that I might be brought to believe it my duty to sacrifice my ease of mind, to the preservation of my character; but in my case, there is no choice; I must either add to the contamination of a very profligate world, or, in the face of Heaven, enter into the most solemn vows to love a man, whom the most I can do is not to hate. This is wilful perjury. In such an alternative duty cannot direct me, and misery must follow my decision, let me determine as I will.'

In this irresolution, Miss Melvyn left her friend, but the vent she had given to her grief had greatly calmed her spirits and restored her to the power of reflection. At her entrance into the house, she met Lady Melvyn, who with a very stern countenance ordered her to go and entertain Mr Morgan, who waited for her in the parlour. She found him alone, and as he began to renew his addresses, which a repulse from her had not discouraged, since he hoped to succeed by the influence her parents had over her, she immediately formed the resolution of endeavouring to make him relinquish his pretensions, in hopes that if the refusal came from him, he might become the object of her mother's indignation, and her persecution might drop, at least for a time. She therefore frankly told him, that tho' her affections were entirely disengaged, yet he was so very repugnant to them that it was impossible she should ever feel that regard for him which he had a right to expect from his wife; and therefore intreated him, in consideration of his own happiness, if hers were indifferent to him, not to persist in a pursuit which, if successful, could not answer his hopes, nor reduce her to render herself wretched by becoming his wife, or to exasperate her parents by refusing him. She then added all her heart could suggest to flatter him into compliance with this request.

Mr Morgan's foible was not an excess of delicacy; he told her plainly, he admired her eloquence prodigiously, but that there was more rhetoric in her beauty than any composition of words could contain; which pleading in direct contradiction to all she had said, she must excuse him, if he was influenced by the more powerful oratory of her charms; and her good sense and unexceptionable conduct convinced him, that when it became her duty to love him, she would no longer remain indifferent.

All Miss Melvyn could urge to shew him this was but a very poor dependence, had no sort of weight, and he parted from her only more determined to hasten the conclusion of their marriage.

Lady Melvyn had not been idle all this time; she had prevailed on young Simon to acquiesce in the questions she put to him before Sir Charles, either by giving short answers, or by down cast eyes, which signified assent. With this Sir Charles acquainted Miss Melvyn, and insisted on her not thinking of exposing herself to the indignity of having the whole affair discussed in her presence. All the indignation that undeserved calumny can excite in an innocent mind could not have enabled Miss Melvyn to bear being charged before so low a creature, with a passion for him, and still less to have heard the suborned wretch pretend to confess it. She therefore found no difficulty in obeying her father in that particular, and rather chose to submit to the imputation than to undergo the shame which she must have suffered in endeavouring to confute it. She attempted to persuade Sir Charles to permit her to stay in the house under what restrictions he and his lady should think proper, till her conduct should sufficiently convince him of her innocence, and not to force her into a hated marriage, or unjustly expose her to disgrace and infamy. Her tears and intreaties would soon have softened his heart; and as far as he dared he shewed an inclination to comply with so reasonable a proposal; but his lady easily obliged him to retract and to deprive Miss Melvyn of all hopes of any mitigation of the sentence already pronounced against her.

Could she without the loss of reputation have fled to a remote part of the kingdom, and have hid herself in some obscure cottage, though reduced to labour for a subsistence, she would have thought it a state far more eligible than becoming Mr Morgan's wife; but if she thus turned fugitive and wanderer, in what light could she expect to be seen by the world; especially as Lady Melvyn would infallibly, to remove any blame from herself, be liberal in her aspersions? Where she should be unknown, whatever disgrace might be affixed to her name, she herself might escape censure; but yet she would not be less guilty of a violation of her duty to society, since she must appear very culpable to those who knew her, and contribute to the depravity of others, as far as was in her power, by an example which, her motives being unknown, would appear a very bad one.

This consideration determined her to sacrifice her peace to her character; for by having told Mr Morgan the true state of her heart, she had acquitted herself from any charge of attempting, by the gift of her hand, to deceive him into a belief that he was the object of her affections. She still had scruples about entering into the matrimonial state, on motives so different from those which ought to influence every one in a union of that kind: these were not to be removed, but she imagined this might in some measure be excused as the least culpable part she could act; and since man was herein neither her judge nor accuser, she hoped the integrity of her mind would be received as some alleviation of a fault she was thus forced to commit, since she was determined in the strictest manner to adhere to every duty of her station.

Having formed this resolution, she went to consult her friend upon it, who as a person less perplexed, though scarcely less concerned, as their affections were so strongly united, that one could not suffer without the other's feeling equal pain, might possibly be a calmer judge in so delicate a point. Louisa subscribed to her friend's sentiments on the occasion, only desired her to consider well, whether she should be able to bear all the trials she might meet with in the married state when she was entirely indifferent to her husband.

'My prospect,' said Miss Melvyn, 'I am sensible is extremely melancholy. All inclination must now be laid aside, and duty must become my sole guide and director. Happiness is beyond my view; I cannot even hope for ease, since I must keep a constant restraint on my very thoughts. Indifference will become criminal; and if I cannot conquer it, to conceal it at least will be a duty. I have learnt to suffer, but was never yet taught disguise and hypocrisy; herein will consist my greatest difficulty; I abhor deceit, and yet must not shew the real sentiments of my heart. Linked in society with a man I cannot love, the world can afford me no pleasure, indeed no comfort, for I am insensible to all joy but what arises from the social affections. The grave, I confess, appears to me far more eligible than this marriage, for I might there hope to be at peace. Mr Morgan's fortune is large, but his mind is narrow and ungenerous, and his temper plainly not good. If he really loved me, he could not suffer me to be forced into a marriage which he well knows I detest: a knowledge which will not mend my fate, most certainly.

'Could I enjoy the pleasures of self-approbation, it would be impossible to be very wretched, but the most exact performance of my duty will not yield me that gratification, since I cannot be perfectly satisfied that I do right in marrying a man so very disagreeable to me. I fear the pride of reputation influences me more than I imagine, and though it is as justifiable as any pride, yet still it is certainly no virtue.'

'When I reflect,' said she afterwards, 'on the step I am going to take, my terrors are inexpressible; how dreadful is it at my age, when nature seems to promise me so many years of life, to doom myself to a state of wretchedness which death alone can terminate, and wherein I must bury all my sorrows in silence, without even the melancholy relief of pouring them forth in the bosom of my friend, and seeking, from her tender participation, the only consolation I could receive! For after this dreaded union is completed, duty will forbid me to make my distresses known, even to my Louisa; I must not then expose the faults of him whose slightest failings I ought to conceal. One only hope remains, that you, my first and dearest friend, will not abandon me; that whatever cloud of melancholy may hang over my mind, yet you will still bear with me, and remove your abode to a place where I may have the consolation of your company. If it be in my power to make my house a comfortable habitation to my Louisa, I cannot be entirely wretched.'

Miss Mancel gave her the tenderest assurances of fixing at least in her neighbourhood, since a second paradise could not recompense her for the loss of her society; and that on no terms could she prevail on herself to continue in a house where she must see that wretched Simon, who had been a vile instrument in reducing her friend to that distressful situation. This gleam of comfort was a very seasonable relief to Miss Melvyn's dejected spirits, and gave some respite to her tears.

As soon as she returned home, she acquainted Sir Charles and Lady Melvyn with her resolution, who soon communicated it to Mr Morgan; and nothing was now thought of but hastening the wedding as much as possible.

'I wonder,' interrupted Lamont, 'how Miss Melvyn could bring herself to let her step-mother have such an opportunity of exulting in the success of her detestable arts.'

'That,' replied Mrs Maynard, 'was a consideration which had no weight with her, nor should it indeed be any mortification to our pride that deceit and cunning have triumphed over us. Wickedness serves itself by weapons which we would not use, and if we are wounded with them, we have no more reason to be mortified than a man would have to think his courage disgraced because when he lay sleeping in his bed he was taken prisoner by a body of armed men. To be circumvented by cunning must ever be the fate, but never the disgrace, of the artless.'

As Miss Melvyn's compliance procured her a greater degree of favour at home than she had ever before enjoyed, Miss Mancel was suffered to come to the house, and met with an obliging reception from the whole family. Her continual presence there was a great support to her friend in her very disagreeable situation, and after indulging her sorrow in their private conversation, and mingling their symphathetic tears, she was the better able to endure the restraint which she was obliged to undergo when any other person was present.

The dreaded day fixed on for this unhappy union soon came, and Miss Melvyn received Mr Morgan's hand and name with all the fortitude she could assume; but her distress was visible to all, even to Mr Morgan, who was so little touched with it that it proved no abatement to his joy; a symptom of such indelicacy of mind as increased his bride's grief and apprehensions.

The day after their marriage, Mrs Morgan asked his permission to invite Miss Mancel to his house, to which he answered, 'Madam, my wife must have no other companion or friend but her husband; I shall never be averse to your seeing company, but intimates I forbid; I shall not choose to have my faults discussed between you and your friend.'

Mrs Morgan was not much less stunned by this reply than if she had been struck with lightning. Practised as she had long been in commanding her passions and inclinations, a torrent of tears forced their way.

'I did not want this proof,' resumed Mr Morgan, 'that I have but a small share of your affections; and were I inclined to grant your request, you could not have found a better means of preventing it; for I will have no person in my house more beloved than myself. When you have no other friend,' added he with a malicious smile, 'I may hope for the honour of that title.'

Mrs Morgan was so well convinced before of the littleness of his mind that she was more afflicted than surprised at this instance of it, and wished he would not have rendered it more difficult to esteem him by so openly professing his ungenerous temper. However she silently acquiesced; but that her friend might not feel the pain of believing herself neglected, she was obliged to tell her what had passed.

The new married couple stayed but two days longer at Sir Charles's. Fortunately Mr Morgan spent the last day abroad in paying visits in the neighbourhood, which gave the two unhappy friends leisure to lament their ill fortune in this cruel separation, without giving the cause of it any new offence. They took a melancholy leave that night, fearing that even a correspondence between them might be considerably restrained by this arbitrary husband who seemed to think his wife's affections were to be won by force, not by gentleness and generous confidence.

This was the severest affliction they had ever yet experienced, or indeed were capable of feeling. United from their childhood, the connection of soul and body did not seem more indissoluble, nor were ever divided with greater pain. They foresaw no end to this cruel separation; for they could not expect that a husband's complaisance to his wife should increase after he ceased to be a bridegroom. Louisa indeed, who wished if possible to reconcile her friend to her fate, pretended to hope that her good conduct might in time enlarge his mind and cure him of that mean suspicious temper which then made him fear to have his faults exposed by a wife whose chief endeavour would be to conceal them.

But such distant views afforded no consolation to Mrs Morgan's affectionate heart; the present pain engaged her thoughts too much to suffer her to look so far off for comfort. She had flattered herself not only with the hopes of enjoying Miss Mancel's company, but of delivering her from all the difficulties of her situation, in offering her a protection from insult or poverty. To be disappointed of so delightful a prospect was her greatest affliction, and sat much heavier on her mind than the loss of her beloved society.

The evening was far spent when Lady Melvyn found them drowned in tears, anticipating the pangs of parting, the employment of that whole day; and as her ladyship's hatred for her step-daughter was much subsided, since she no longer feared the observation of her too-virtuous eye, her natural disposition inclined her to prevent the wife's discovering her real sentiments to her husband; she therefore reminded them that Mr Morgan must then be on his way home, and advised that by all means they should part before his return, lest he should be witness of a sorrow which he would take amiss. They were sensible that in this her ladyship judged well, and Louisa's fear of occasioning any additional uneasiness to her friend gave her resolution and strength to take a last farewell. Mrs Morgan's maid attended her home, as she was too much affected to be able to perform that little walk without some support. Mrs Morgan's condition was still more deplorable; more dead than alive, she followed Louisa's steps with eager eyes, till a turning in the road robbed her of the sight of her friend; and then, as if her eyes had no other employment worthy of them left, they were again overwhelmed in tears. Lady Melvyn found her incapable of consolation; but more successfully endeavoured to make her suppress the indulgence of her grief by alarming her fears with the approach of Mr Morgan. As soon as she was a little composed, she led her into the garden for air. The night was fine, and the moon shone very resplendent, the beauty of the scene and the freshness of the air a little revived her; and as Mr Morgan stayed out later than they expected she had time to acquire a sufficient command over herself to receive him with an air of tolerable cheerfulness.

The new married pair set out early the next morning, and arrived at Mr Morgan's seat the following day. The house was large and old, the furniture not much less ancient, the situation dreary, the roads everywhere bad, the soil a stiff clay, wet and dirty, except in the midst of summer; the country round it disagreeable, and in short, destitute of every thing that could afford any satisfaction to Mrs Morgan. Nature nowhere appears graced with fewer charms. Mrs Morgan however had vexations so superior that she paid little regard to external circumstances, and was so fully determined to acquit herself properly in her new sphere that she appeared pleased with every thing around her. Hypocrisy, as she observed, was now become a virtue, and the only one which she found it difficult to practise. They were received on their arrival by a maiden sister of Mr Morgan's, who till then had kept his house and he intended should still remain in it; for as through the partiality of an aunt who had bred her up she was possessed of a large fortune, her brother, in whom avarice was the ruling passion, was very desirous of keeping in her favour.

Miss Susanna Morgan had lived immaculate to the age of fifty-five. The state of virginity could not be laid to her charge as an offence against society, for it had not been voluntary. In her youth she was rather distinguished for sensibility. Her aunt's known riches gave the niece the reputation of a great fortune, an attraction to which she was indebted for many lovers, who constantly took their leave on finding the old lady would not advance any part of the money which she designed to bequeath her niece. Miss Susanna, extremely susceptible by nature, was favourably disposed to all her admirers, and imagining herself successively in love with each, lived in a course of disappointments. In reality, the impression was made only on her vanity, and her heart continued unengaged; but she felt such a train of mortifications very severely, and perhaps suffered more upon the whole than if she had been strongly impressed with one passion. In time the parsimony of her old aunt became generally known, and the young lady then was left free from the tender importunity of lovers, of which nothing else could probably have deprived her; for as she never had any natural attractions, she was not subject to a decay of charms; at near fifty-five her aunt departed this life, and left her in possession of twenty thousand pounds, a fortune which served to swell her pride, without increasing her happiness.

Nature had not originally bestowed upon her much sweetness of temper, and her frequent disappointments, each of which she termed being crossed in love, had completely soured it. Every pretty woman was the object of her envy, I might almost say every married woman. She despised all that were not as rich as herself, and hated every one who was superior or equal to her in fortune. Tormented inwardly with her own ill-nature, she was incapable of any satisfaction but what arose from teasing others; nothing could dispel the frown on her brow, except the satisfaction she felt when she had the good fortune to give pain to any of her dependants; a horrid grin then distorted her features, and her before lifeless eyes glistened with malice and rancorous joy. She had read just enough to make her pedantic, and too little to give her any improving knowledge. Her understanding was naturally small, and her self-conceit great. In her person she was tall and meagre, her hair black, and her complexion of the darkest brown, with an additional sallowness at her temples and round her eyes, which were dark, very large and prominent, and entirely without lustre; they had but one look, which was that of gloomy stupid ill-nature, except, as I have already said, when they were enlivened by the supreme satisfaction of having made somebody uneasy, then what before was but disagreeable became horrible. To complete the description of her face, she had a broad flat nose, a wide mouth, furnished with the worst set of teeth I ever saw, and her chin was long and pointed. She had heard primness so often mentioned as the characteristic of an old maid, that to avoid wearing that appearance she was slatternly and dirty to an excess; besides she had great addition of filthiness, from a load of Spanish snuff, with which her whole dress was covered, as if, by her profusion in that particular, she thought to compensate for her general parsimony.

This lady Mrs Morgan found in possession of her house, and was received by her with that air of superiority to which Miss Susanna thought herself entitled by her age and fortune. Mrs Morgan's charms, though drooping like a blighted flower, excited much envy in Susanna's breast, and she soon congratulated her on her extraordinary happiness in having captivated a gentleman of so large a fortune when her own was at present so very small.

At first she commended her for not being elated with so great an acquisition, but in a little time taxed her with ungrateful insensibility to so prodigious a blessing. She continually criticized her economy, accusing her of indolence; representing, how she used every morning to rouse the servants from their idleness, by giving each such a scold, as quickened their diligence for the whole day; nor could a family be well managed by any one who omitted this necessary duty. Mrs Morgan's desire that her servants should enjoy the comforts of plenty, and when sick, receive the indulgence which that condition requires, brought her continual admonitions against extravagance, wherein Mr Morgan readily joined; for his avarice was so great that he repined at the most necessary expenses.

His temper was a mixture of passion and peevishness, two things that seldom go together; but he would fret himself into a passion, and then through weariness of spirits cool into fretfulness, till he was sufficiently recovered to rise again into rage. This was the common course of his temper, which afforded variety, but no relief.

Sensible that his wife married him without affection, he seemed to think it impossible ever to gain her love, and therefore spared himself all fruitless endeavours. He was indeed fond of her person; he admired her beauty, but despised her understanding, which in truth was unavoidable; for his ideas and conversation were so low and sordid that he was not qualified to distinguish the charms of her elegant mind. Those who know Mrs Morgan best are convinced that she suffered less uneasiness from his ill-humour, brutal as it was, than from his nauseous fondness. But the account I give of him, I have received from others; Mrs Morgan never mentions his name, if it can possibly be avoided; and when she does, it is always with respect. In this situation, a victim to the ill-humour both of her husband and his sister, we will leave Mrs Morgan, and return to that friend whose letters were her only consolation.

Miss Mancel's person was so uncommonly fine, that she could not be long settled in the country without attracting general notice. Though the lower rank of people may be less refined in their ideas, yet her beauty was so very striking, that it did not escape their admiration, and the handsome lady, as they called her, became the general subject of discourse. As church was the only place where she exposed to public view, she had from the first endeavoured to elude observation, by mingling in the crowd, and sitting in the most obscure seat; but when fame had awakened the curiosity of those of higher rank, she was easily distinguished, and in a short time many inhabitants of the neighbouring parishes came to that church to see her. She more than answered every expectation; for such perfection of beauty scarcely ever came out of the hands of nature. Many ladies in the neighbourhood introduced themselves to her, and found her behaviour as enchanting as her person. She could not be insensible of the approbation which every eye significantly expressed; but she was abashed and in some degree more mortified than delighted by it. She well remembered what Mr d'Avora had said to her on that subject and saw that in her situation beauty was a disadvantage. He often repeated the same thing to her in letters (for she and Miss Melvyn keeping up a constant correspondence with him, the latter had acquainted him with the general admiration paid to Louisa) and told her that he feared the plan they had formed for her future way of life was at a still greater distance than they had hoped, since her beauty was the great obstacle to its being put in execution.

The ladies of the best fashion in the neighbourhood begged leave to visit her; and though she more than ever wished to have her time uninterrupted, since as she had no prospect of any other means of support, it was necessary, by such little additions as she could make to her small fund, to prevent its quick diminution, yet she could not decline the civilities so obligingly offered her, but avoided all intimacy with any of them as foreign to her plan, and hurtful to her interest. Thus was she circumstanced in respect to the neighbourhood when Miss Melvyn married.

As after this event Louisa was determined to change her habitation, she began to enquire for some family where she might be accommodated in the same manner as in that where she was then fixed. Among the persons who had taken most notice of her was Lady Lambton, a person of admirable understanding, polite, generous and good-natured; who had no fault but a considerable share of pride. She piqued herself upon the opulence of her family and a distinguished birth, but her good sense, and many virtues, so qualified this one blemish, that it did not prevent her being a very amiable woman.

When she found Miss Mancel designed to change her abode, she told her that at an honest farmer's near her house she might be accommodated, but that as some little alterations would be requisite to make the place fit for her, she, in the most obliging manner, desired her company till the apartment was ready; which would give her opportunity to see such things were done to it as would be most convenient and agreeable. Lady Lambton insisted so strongly on Miss Mancel's accepting this invitation that she could not without incivility refuse it; and as, after the loss of her friend, all places were alike to her, she had no reason to decline so obliging an offer.

No great preparations were required for this removal of abode. Lady Lambton came herself to fetch Miss Mancel home. The old lady was charmed with her new guest, many of whose accomplishments were unknown to her till she came under the same roof, and would not suffer any preparations to be made for another lodging, but insisted on her continuing much longer with her.

Lady Lambton behaved in so very obliging a manner, and Louisa found so much pleasure and improvement in the conversation of a woman whose admirable understanding and thorough knowledge of the world are seldom to be paralleled, that she could not be more agreeably placed; as she dared not go even into Mrs Morgan's neighbourhood, for fear of giving additional uneasiness to one whose situation she plainly perceived was by no means happy; for though Mrs Morgan suppressed all complaints, never hinted at the treatment she received, and endeavoured to represent her way of life in the best colours, to save her friend the sympathetic pangs of heart which she knew she would feel for her sufferings; yet the alteration in her style, the melancholy turn of mind which in spite of all her care was visible in her letters, could not escape the observation of one whose natural discernment was quickened by affection.

The full persuasion of Mrs Morgan's unhappiness, and that anxious solicitude which arose from her ignorance as to the degree of her wretchedness, was a source of continual grief to her mind, which Lady Lambton's sincere friendship could scarcely alleviate. But she knew too well how few people can bear the unhappy to suffer her uneasiness to appear. She stifled therefore every expression of that kind; for if Lady Lambton had generously sympathized in her affliction, it would have given her pain to know she had occasioned that lady's feeling any; and if she had been insensible to it, complaints would not fail to disgust her.

Lady Lambton was fond of music, and not void of taste for painting; Miss Mancel's excellence in these arts therefore afforded her the highest entertainment. Her ladyship was likewise a mistress of languages, and was pleased to find Louisa equally acquainted with them. In this house Miss Mancel had passed above a twelve month, when Sir Edward Lambton returned from his travels, in which he had spent four years. As soon as he arrived in the kingdom he came to wait on Lady Lambton, his grandmother, who was likewise his guardian, his father and mother being both dead. She had longed with impatience for his return, but thought herself well repaid for his absence by the great improvement which was very visible both in his manner and person.

Sir Edward was extremely handsome, his person fine and graceful, his conversation lively and entertaining, politeness adding charms to an excellent understanding. His behaviour, I have been told, was particularly engaging, his temper amiable, though somewhat too warm, and he had all his grandmother's generosity, without any of her pride.

It would have been strange if a man of three and twenty years old (for that was Sir Edward's age) had not been much charmed with so lovely a woman as Miss Mancel. That he was so, soon became visible, but she, as well as his grandmother, for some time imagined the attentions he paid her were only the natural result of the gallantry usual at his age, and improved into a softer address, by a manner acquired in travelling through countries where gallantry is publicly professed. Lady Lambton, however, knowing her own discernment, expressed some fears to Louisa, lest her grandson should become seriously in love with her, in order to discover by her countenance whether there was really any ground for her apprehensions, which she founded on the impossibility of his marrying a woman of small fortune, without reducing himself to the greatest inconvenience, as his estate was extremely incumbered, and he was by an intail deprived of the liberty of selling any part of it to discharge the debt. She was too polite to mention her chief objection to Miss Mancel, which was in reality the obscurity of her birth. Louisa, who sincerely believed Sir Edward had no real passion for her, answered with a frankness which entirely convinced Lady Lambton that she had received no serious address from him; but Louisa, who saw herself now in the situation which Mr d'Avora had warned her against, begged permission to leave Lady Lambton's, to prevent her ladyship's being under any uneasiness, and to avoid all danger of Sir Edward's receiving any strong impression in her favour.

Lady Lambton was unwilling to part with her amiable companion; and besides, thought if her grandson was really enamoured, she should increase the danger rather than lessen it by not keeping Louisa under her eye; she therefore told her she could not consent to lose her company, and was certain she might depend on her honour. Louisa thanked her for her good opinion, and assured her she would never do any thing to forfeit it.

Sir Edward was more captivated than either of the ladies imagined, and every day increased his passion. Louisa's beauty, her conversation and accomplishments were irresistible; but as he knew the great occasion he had to marry a woman of fortune, he long endeavoured to combat his inclinations. He might have conceived hopes of obtaining any other woman in her circumstances on easier terms; but there was such dignity and virtue shone forth in her, and he was so truly in love, that such a thought never entered his imagination. He reverenced and respected her like a divinity, but hoped that prudence might enable him to conquer his passion, at the same time that it had not force enough to determine him to fly her presence, the only possible means of lessening the impression which every hour engraved more deeply on his heart by bringing some new attractions to his view. He little considered that the man who has not power to fly from temptation will never be able to resist it by standing his ground.

Louisa was not long before she grew sensible that what she had offered to Lady Lambton for the ease of her ladyship's mind, was advisable to secure the peace of her own. Sir Edward's merit, his sincere respect for her, which certainly is the most powerful charm to a woman of delicacy, could scarcely fail to make an impression on a heart so tender, so generous as hers. She kept so strict a watch over herself that she soon perceived her sensibility, and endeavoured to prevail on Lady Lambton to part with her; but the old lady, imagining it was only in order to quiet her apprehensions, would not consent; and the difficulty in finding a place where she could be properly received, strongly discouraged her from insisting on it. If she continued in the neighbourhood, her purpose would not be answered; for she could not avoid Sir Edward's visits; her only friend was denied the liberty of protecting her, and to go into a place where she was unknown would subject a young woman of her age and beauty to a thousand dangers.

These difficulties detained her, though unwillingly, at Lady Lambton's for above half a year after Sir Edward's return; who, at length, unable to confine in silence a passion which had long been obvious to every observer, took an opportunity, when alone with Louisa, to declare his attachment in the most affecting manner. She received it not with surprise, but with real sorrow. She had no tincture of coquetry in her composition; but if she had been capable of it, her affections were too deeply engaged to have suffered her to retain it. Her sensibility was never so strongly awakened; all her endeavours to restrain it were no longer of force, her heart returned his passion, and would have conquered every thing but her justice and her honour; these were deeply engaged to Lady Lambton; and she would have detested herself if she could have entertained a thought of making that lady's goodness to her the occasion of the greatest vexation she could receive. She therefore never hesitated on the part she should act on this trying occasion; but the victories which honour gains over the tender affections are not to be obtained without the severest pangs. Thus tormented by the struggles between duty and affection, she was not immediately capable of giving him an answer; but finding that her difficulties were increasing by his repeated professions, and animated by the necessity of silencing a love which too successfully solicited a return of affection, she assumed a sufficient command over herself to conceal her sentiments, and with averted eyes, lest her heart should through them contradict her words, she told him, he distressed her to the greatest degree; that the respect she had for him on account of his own merit, and not less for the relation he bore to Lady Lambton, made her extremely concerned that he should have conceived a passion for her, which it was not in her power to return; nor could she listen to it in justice to Lady Lambton, to whom she was bound in all the ties of gratitude; neither should anything ever prevail with her to do any thing prejudicial to the interests of a family into which she had been so kindly received.

Sir Edward was too much in love to acquiesce in so nice a point of honour; but Louisa would not wait to hear arguments which it was so painful to her to refute, and retired into her own chamber, to lament in secret her unhappy fate in being obliged to reject the addresses of a man whose affections, were she at liberty, she would think no sacrifice too great to obtain.

Miss Mancel endeavoured as much as possible to avoid giving Sir Edward any opportunity of renewing his addresses; but his vigilance found the means of seeing her alone more than once, when he warmly urged the partiality of her behaviour, representing how much more his happiness was concerned in the success of a passion which possessed his whole soul, than his grandmother's could be in disappointing it. She, he observed, was actuated only by pride, he by the sincerest love that ever took place in a human heart. In accepting his addresses Louisa could only mortify Lady Lambton; in rejecting them, she must render him miserable. Which, he asked, had the best title to her regard, the woman who could ungenerously and injudiciously set a higher value on riches and birth than on her very superior excellencies, or the man who would gladly sacrifice fortune and every other enjoyment the world could afford, to the possession of her; of her who alone could render life desirable to him? By these, and many other arguments, and what was more prevalent than all the arguments that could be deduced from reason, by the tenderest intreaties that the most ardent passion could dictate, Sir Edward endeavoured to persuade Louisa to consent to marry him, but all proved unavailing. She sometimes thought what he said was just, but aware of her partiality, she could not believe herself an unprejudiced judge, and feared that she might mistake the sophistry of love for the voice of reason. She was sure while honour, truth and gratitude pleaded against inclination they must be in the right, though their remonstrances were hushed into a whisper by the louder solicitations of passion. Convinced that she could not be to blame while she acted in contradiction to her secret choice, since the sincerity of her intentions were thereby plainly, though painfully evinced, she persisted in refusing to become Sir Edward's wife, and told him, that if he did not discontinue his addresses, he would force her to leave the house, and retire to any place that would afford her a quiet refuge from his importunity.

A hint of this sort was sufficient to drive Sir Edward almost to distraction, and Louisa dared not pursue the subject. When he found she could not be induced to consent to an immediate marriage, he endeavoured to obtain a promise of her hand after Lady Lambton's decease; though to a man of his impatient and strong passions such a delay was worse than death; but Miss Mancel told him, by such an engagement she should be guilty of a mean evasion, and that she should think it as great a breach of honour as marrying him directly.

The despair to which Louisa's conduct reduced Sir Edward, whose love seemed to increase with the abatement of his hopes, was very visible to his grandmother, but her pride was invincible; neither her affection for him, nor her great esteem for Miss Mancel's merit, could conquer her aversion to their union. She saw them both unhappy, but was convinced the pangs they felt would not be of very long continuance, trusting to the usual inconstancy of young persons, while the inconveniencies attending an incumbered fortune, and the disgrace which she imagined must be the consequence of Sir Edward's marrying a woman of obscure birth, would be permanent and influence the whole course of his life.

Louisa, unable to support so hard a conflict, continually resisting both her lover and her love, was determined to seek some relief from absence. She wrote Mr d'Avora a faithful account of all the difficulties of her situation, and intreated him to receive her into his house, till he could find some proper place wherein to fix her abode.

This worthy friend approved her conduct, while he grieved for her distress; his honest heart felt a secret indignation against Lady Lambton who could, by false pride, be blinded to the honour which he thought such a woman as Miss Mancel must reflect on any family into which she entered. He wrote that young lady word, that she might be assured of the best reception his house could afford, and every service that it was in his power to render her; desiring that she would let him know when she proposed setting out, that he might meet her on the road, not thinking it proper she should travel alone.

This letter gave Miss Mancel much satisfaction; she was now secure of an asylum; but the great difficulty still remained, she knew not how to get away from Lady Lambton's in a proper manner; for to go clandestinely was not suitable to her character, and might bring it into suspicion. In this dilemma she thought it best to apply to that lady, and with her usual frankness told her (what had not escaped her discernment) the affection Sir Edward had conceived for her, and the return her own heart made to it; only suppressing his solicitations, as her ladyship might be offended with his proceeding so far without her consent. She represented the imprudence of her continuing in the house with Sir Edward, whereby both his passion and her own must be increased; and yet she was at a loss how to depart privately, but was convinced it could not be affected with his knowledge, without such an eclat as must be very disagreeable to them all; nor could she answer for her own resolution when put to so severe a trial; as she should have more than her full measure of affliction in going from thence, without being witness to its effect on him.

One should have imagined that the generosity of Miss Mancel's conduct might have influenced Lady Lambton in her favour; but though it increased her esteem, it did not alter her resolution. With inexcusable insensibility she concerted measures with her, and engaged to procure Sir Edward's absence for a short time. Some very necessary business indeed demanded his presence in a neighbouring county where the greatest part of his estate lay, but he had not been able to prevail on himself to leave Lóuisa; too much enamoured to think any pecuniary advantage could compensate for the loss of her company. But as it was natural that an old grandmother should see the matter in another light; her pressing him to go and settle his affairs gave him no cause to suspect any latent meaning, and was too reasonable to be any longer opposed.

Though Sir Edward was resolved on so quick a dispatch of business as promised him a speedy return, yet any separation from Miss Mancel, however short, appeared a severe misfortune. The evening before the day of his departure, he contrived to see her alone and renewed his importunities with redoubled ardour, but with no better success than before. He lamented the necessity he was under of leaving her, though but for a little time, with an agony of mind better suited to an eternal separation. She, who saw it in that light, was overcome with the tender distress which a person must feel at taking a final leave of one who is extremely dear to her. Her own grief was more than she could have concealed; but when she anticipated in her thoughts what he would suffer when he knew he had lost her for ever, and judged from the pain he felt on the approach of what he thought so short an absence, how very great his distress would be, she was unable to support the scene with her usual steadiness. Tears insensibly stole down her face and bestowed on it still greater charms than it had ever yet worn, by giving her an air of tenderness, which led him to hope that she did not behold his passion with indifference. This thought afforded him a consolation which he had never before received; and though it increased his love, yet it abated his distress, and rendered him more able to leave her, since he flattered himself she would with pleasure see him return, which he was now more than ever resolved to do as speedily as possible.

The day of his departure she spent chiefly in her own room, to conceal, as far as she was able, a weakness she was ashamed of but could not conquer. She had written the day before to inform Mr d'Avora that she should set out for London four days after her letter. Accordingly at the time appointed, after having agreed with Lady Lambton that Sir Edward must be kept ignorant of the place to which she was gone, she set out with that lady, who carried her in her coach twelve miles of the way and then delivered her to Mr d'Avora, who was come thither to receive her. Lady Lambton could not part with her amiable companion without regret, and expressed her true sense of her merit in such strong terms to Mr d'Avora, who could not forgive that pride which had occasioned so much pain both to Louisa and Sir Edward, that he told her in plain terms how very happy and how much honoured any man must be who had her for his wife. Perhaps Lady Lambton would have subscribed to his opinion, had any one but her grandson been concerned; but the point was too tender, and it was no small command over herself that prevented her giving the good old man a hint that she thought him impertinent.

Our travellers arrived in town the next day, after a melancholy journey, for even the company of a friend she so much loved and esteemed could not restore Miss Mancel's natural vivacity, though in compassion to the good old man who sympathized tenderly in her distress she endeavoured to the utmost of her power to conceal how very deeply she was afflicted. It was some little time before her spirits were sufficiently composed to form any scheme for her future life, nor were they benefited by a letter from Lady Lambton which acquainted her that Sir Edward, at his return, finding she had left the place, that his grandmother had consented to her departure and refused to tell him where she was gone, was for some days frantic with rage and grief, and had just then left Lady Lambton with a determination to serve as volunteer in the army in Germany, in hopes, he said, to find there a release from his afflictions, which nothing but the hand of death could bestow.

The old lady was much shocked at this event, but hoped a little time would restore his reason and enable him to bear his disappointment with patience. There was room to believe, she said, that the rest of the campaign would pass over without a battle, and if so the change of scene might abate his passion.

Louisa's heart was too tenderly engaged to reason so philosophically, she was almost distracted with her fears, and was often inclined to blame her own scruples that had driven so worthy a man to such extremities. All Mr d'Avora could urge to reconcile her to herself and to calm her apprehensions for Sir Edward were scarcely sufficient to restore her to any ease of mind; but at length he brought her to submit patiently to her fate and to support her present trial with constancy.

They were still undetermined as to her future establishment when Mr d'Avora one day met an old acquaintance and countryman in the street. As this person had many years before returned to his native country, Mr d'Avora inquired what had again brought him into England? His friend replied that he was come in quality of factotum to a widow lady of fortune. In the course of their conversation he asked Mr d'Avora if he could recommend a waiting woman to his lady, hers having died on the road. The character this man gave of his mistress inclined Mr d'Avora to mention the place to Miss Mancel, who readily agreed that he should endeavour to obtain it for her.

Mr d'Avora had engaged the man to call on him the next day by telling him he believed he might be able to recommend a most valuable young person to his lady. He was punctual to his appointment and conducted Mr d'Avora and Louisa to Mrs Thornby's, that was the name of the lady in question.

Miss Mancel was dressed with care, but of a very different

sort from what is usually aimed at; all her endeavours had been to conceal her youth and beauty as much as possible under great gravity of dress, and to give her all the disadvantages consistent with neatness and cleanliness. But such art was too thin a veil to hide her charms. Mrs Thornby was immediately struck with her beauty, and made some scruple of taking a young person into her service whom she should look upon as a great charge, and she feared her maid might require more attention from her than she should think necessary for any servant to pay to herself. Mr d'Avora represented to her how cruel it was that beauty, which was looked upon as one of the most precious gifts of nature, should disqualify a young woman for obtaining a necessary provision. That this young person's prudence was so irreproachable as sufficiently secured her from any disadvantages which might naturally be feared from it. But still he allowed her person would justly deter a married woman from receiving her, and might make a cautious mother avoid it, since her good conduct would rather add to than diminish her attractions, therefore it was only with a single lady she could hope to be placed; and he was well convinced that such a one would have reason to think herself happy in so accomplished a servant; since her mind was still more amiable than her person.

Mrs Thornby allowed what he said to be reasonable and was so charmed with Louisa's appearance that she assured him she would receive her with pleasure. She was in haste for a servant, and Miss Mancel had no reason to delay her attendance, therefore it was agreed she should enter into her place the next day.

When Lady Lambton took leave of Louisa she would have forced her to receive a very handsome present; Louisa had accepted many while she lived with her ladyship, but at this time she said it would look like receiving a compensation for the loss of Sir Edward; and as she chose to sacrifice both her inclinations and happiness to her regard for Lady Lambton, she could not be induced to accept any thing that looked like a reward for an action which if she had not thought it her duty, nothing would have prevailed with her to perform. The tenderest affections of her heart were too much concerned in what she had done to leave her the power of feeling any apprehensions of poverty; all the evils that attend it then appeared to her so entirely external that she beheld them with the calm philosophy of a stoic and not from a very contrary motive; the insensibility of each arose from a ruling passion; the stoic's from pride, hers from love. But though she feared not poverty, she saw it was advisable to fix upon some establishment as soon as it could be obtained; and therefore received great satisfaction from being assured of Mrs Thornby's acceptance of her services. Mr d'Avora was not without hopes, that if Sir Edward continued constant till Lady Lambton's death, Louisa might then, without any breach of honour or gratitude, marry him; though to have engaged herself to do so, would, as she observed, have been scarcely less inexcusable than an immediate consent; therefore he advised her to assume another name, as Sir Edward might not choose, after she was his wife, to have it known that she had been reduced to servitude.

Louisa was accordingly received at Mrs Thornby's by the name of Menil. Her good sense and assiduity enabled her to acquit herself so well in her new place as greatly delighted her mistress; and though she concealed the greatest part of her accomplishments, sensible they could be of no assistance, and might on the contrary raise a prejudice against her; yet her behaviour and conversation so plainly indicated a superior education that before she had been there a week Mrs Thornby told her she was certain she had not been born for the station she was then in, and begged a particular account of her whole life.

Louisa, fearing that a compliance would render her less agreeable to her mistress, who already treated her with respect which seemed more than was due to her situation, and often appeared uneasy at seeing her perform the necessary duties of her place, intreated to be spared a task which, she said, was attended with some circumstances so melancholy as greatly affected her spirits on a particular recollection.

Mrs Thornby's curiosity was not abated by this insinuation, and she repeated her request in a manner so importunate, and at the same time so kind, that Louisa could no longer, without manifest disrespect, decline it.

She began then by acquainting her that she went by a borrowed name; but had proceeded no farther in her narration than to tell her that her real name was Mancel and that she had been left to the care of an aunt in her earliest infancy by parents who were obliged, for reasons she could never learn, to leave their country, when Mrs Thornby exclaimed, My child! my child! and sinking on her knees, with eyes and hands lifted up towards heaven, poured forth a most ardent thanksgiving, with an ecstasy of mind not to be described. Her first sensation was that of gratitude to the Almighty Power, who had reserved so great a blessing for her; maternal tenderness alone gave rise to the succeeding emotions of her heart; she threw her arms round Louisa, who on seeing her fall on her knees, and not comprehending the meaning of her action, ran to her; but struck with astonishment and reverence at the awful piety in her countenance and address, bent silent and motionless over her. Mrs Thornby, leaning her head on Louisa's bosom, burst into such a flood of tears, and was so oppressed with joy, that the power of speech totally failed her. Louisa raised her from the ground, crying, 'Dear madam, what can all this mean? What does this extreme agitation of your mind give me room to hope?'

'Every thing, my child! my angel! that a fond parent can bestow,' replied Mrs Thornby. 'I am that mother that was obliged to leave thee to another's care; and has Heaven preserved my daughter, and restored her to me so lovely, so amiable! Gracious Providence! Merciful beyond hope! Teach me to thank thee as I ought for this last instance of thy goodness!' And then her whole soul seemed again poured forth in grateful adoration.

Louisa could scarcely believe this event was real; thus unexpectedly to meet with a parent whom she supposed lost to her for ever almost stunned her; her thoughts were so engrossed by the raptures of her joyful mother that she did not feel half her good fortune; and the delight she received in seeing her mother's happiness robbed her of every other sensation.

It was some hours before Mrs Thornby's mind was sufficiently composed to enter into any connected conversation. From broken sentences Miss Mancel learnt that her father and mother, by the complicated distress of ruined fortune and the too fatal success of a duel in which Mr Mancel was unwillingly engaged, had been obliged to absent themselves from England. They went to one of the American colonies, in hopes of finding means to improve their circumstances, leaving the young Louisa, then in her cradle, with a sister of Mr Mancel's, who readily undertook the care of her. They were scarcely arrived in America when Mr Mancel was seized with a fever, of which he soon died, and with him all their hopes. Mrs Mancel was left entirely destitute, at a loss how to hazard the tedious passage home, without the protection of a husband and with hardly a sufficient sum remaining to discharge the expenses of it.

Her melancholy situation engaged some of the inhabitants of the place to offer her all necessary accommodations, till she could find a proper opportunity of returning to England. During this time, Mr Thornby, a gentleman who had acquired a fortune there, saw her, and was so well pleased with her person and conduct that he very warmly solicited her to marry him. Every person spoke in his favour, and urged her to consent; her poverty was no faint adviser, and with general approbation at the conclusion of the first year of her widowhood she became his wife.

His affairs soon called him into a more inland part of the country, to which she attributed her never having heard from her sister, to whom she wrote an account of her husband's death; but by what Miss Mancel told her she imagined her letter had not been received.

Mr and Mrs Thornby continued in the same place, till about two years before her arrival in England; but his health growing extremely bad, he was advised by his physicians to return to

Europe. He wished to re-visit his native country but was persuaded, for the re-establishment of his constitution, to spend some time in Italy. The climate at first seemed to relieve him, but his complaints returning with greater violence, he died in the latter part of the second year of his abode there.

His estate in the Indies he bequeathed to a nephew who lived upon the spot; but the money he had sent before him into England, which amounted to forty thousand pounds, he left to his widow. He had desired to be interred at Florence, where he died. As soon as the funeral was over, and some other necessary affairs settled, Mrs Thornby set out for England, where she no sooner arrived than she employed intelligent persons to find out her sister-in-law and daughter, but had not received any account from them, when her daughter was restored to her as the free gift of providence.

Mrs Thornby was now more desirous than ever to hear each minute particular that had befallen her Louisa; but Louisa begged that before she obeyed her orders she might have permission to communicate the happy event to Mr d'Avora, whose joy she knew would be nearly equal to her own. A messenger was dispatched for this purpose, and then she related circumstantially all the incidents in her short life, except her partial regard to Sir Edward Lambton, which filial awe induced her to suppress.

Mrs Thornby grew every day more delighted with her daughter, as her acquired accomplishments and natural excellencies became more conspicuous on longer acquaintance. Her maternal love seemed to glow with greater warmth for having been so long stifled, and Louisa found such delight in the tender affection of a mother that she was scarcely sensible of the agreeable change in her situation, which was now in every circumstance the most desirable. All that fortune could give she had it in her power to enjoy, and that esteem which money cannot purchase her own merit secured her, besides all the gratification a young woman can receive from general admiration. But still Louisa was not happy, her fears for Sir Edward's life, while in so dangerous a situation, would not suffer her mind to be at peace. She might hope every thing from her mother's indulgence, but had not courage to confess her weakness, nor to intimate a wish, which might occasion her separation from a parent whose joy in their reunion still rose to rapture. Chance, that deity which though blind is often a powerful friend, did what she could not prevail on herself to do.

One morning the news paper of the day being brought in, Mrs Thornby taking it up, read to her daughter a paragraph which contained an account of a battle in Germany wherein many of the English were said to be slain, but few of their names specified. Louisa immediately turned pale, her work dropped out of her hand and a universal trembling seized her. Mrs Thornby was too attentive not to observe her daughter's distress, and so kindly inquired the reason that Louisa ventured to tell her for whom she was so much interested; and gave an exact account of Sir Edward's address to her, her behaviour upon it, and the great regard she had for him.

Mrs Thornby affectionately chid her for having till then concealed a circumstance whereon so much of her happiness depended, and offered to write to Lady Lambton immediately, and acquaint her that if want of fortune was her only objection to Miss Mancel, it no longer subsisted, for that she was ready to answer any demands of that sort which her ladyship should choose to make, as she thought she should no way so well secure her daughter's happiness as by uniting her with a gentleman of Sir Edward's amiable character, and whose affection for her had so evidently appeared.

Louisa could not reject an offer which might rescue Sir Edward from the dangers that threatened him, and with pleasure thought of rewarding so generous and so sincere a passion. Perhaps she found some gratification in shewing that gratitude alone dictated her refusal. The letter was immediately dispatched, and received with great pleasure by Lady Lambton, whose esteem for Miss Mancel would have conquered any thing but her pride. She accepted the proposal in the politest manner, and that Sir Edward might be acquainted with his happiness as soon as possible, dispatched her steward into Germany, ordering him to travel with the utmost expedition, and gave him Mrs Thornby's letter, with one from herself, containing an account of the great change in Louisa's fortune.

The servant obeyed the directions given him and performed the journey in as short a time as possible; but as he entered the camp, he met Sir Edward indeed, but not as a future bridegroom. He was borne on men's shoulders, pale and almost breathless, just returned from an attack, where by his too great rashness he had received a mortal wound. He followed him with an aching heart to his tent, where Sir Edward recovering his senses, knew him, and asked what brought him there so opportunely, 'to close his eyes, and pay the last duties, to one of whose infancy he had been so careful?' for this servant lived in the family when Sir Edward was born, and loved him almost with paternal fondness, which occasioned his desire of being himself the messenger of such joyful news.

The poor man was scarcely able to answer a question expressed in such melancholy terms, and was doubtful whether he ought to acquaint him with a circumstance which might only increase his regret at losing a life which would have been blessed to his utmost wish, but incapable in that state of mind of inventing any plausible reason, he told him the truth, and gave him the two letters.

The pleasure Sir Edward received at the account of Louisa's good fortune, and the still greater joy he felt at so evident a proof of her regard for him, made him for a time forget his pains, and flattered the good old steward with hopes that his case was not so desperate as the surgeons represented it; but Sir Edward told him he knew all hope was vain. 'I must accuse myself,' said he, 'of losing that lovely generous woman what a treasure would have gladdened my future days had I not rashly, I fear criminally, shortened them, not by my own hand indeed, but how little different! Mad with despair, I have sought all means of obtaining what I imagined the only cure for my distempered mind. Weary of life, since I could not possess her in whom all my joys, all the wishes of my soul were centred, I seized every occasion of exposing myself to the enemy's sword.

Contrary to my hopes, I escaped many times, when death seemed unavoidable; but grown more desperate by disappointment, I this morning went on an attack where instead of attempting to conquer, all my endeavour was to be killed, and at last I succeeded, how fatally! Oh! my Louisa,' continued he, 'and do I then lose thee by my own impatience! Had I, like thee, submitted to the disposition of providence, had I waited, from its mighty power, that relief which it alone can give, I might now be expecting with rapture the hour that should have united us for ever, instead of preparing for that which shall summon me to the grave, where even thou shalt be forgotten, and the last traces of thy lovely image effaced from my too faithful remembrance. How just are the decrees of the Almighty! Thy patience, thy resignation and uncommon virtues are rewarded as they ought; my petulance, my impatience, which, as it were, flew in the face of my Maker, and fought to lose a life which he had entrusted to my keeping, and required me to preserve, is deservedly punished. I am deprived of that existence which I would now endure whole ages of pain to recall, were it to be done, but it is past and I submit to thy justice, thou all wise disposer of my fate.'

The agitation of Sir Edward's mind had given him a flow of false spirits, but at length they failed, leaving him only the more exhausted. He kept Mrs Thornby's letter on his pillow, and read it many times. Frequent were his expressions of regret for his own rashness, and he felt much concern from the fear that Louisa would be shocked with his death. Her mother's proceedings convinced him she was not void of regard for him; he now saw that he had not vainly flattered himself when he imagined, from many little circumstances, that her heart spoke in his favour; and the force she must have put on her affections raised his opinion of her almost to adoration. He often told his faithful attendant that in those moments he felt a joy beyond what he had ever yet experienced, in believing Louisa loved him; but these emotions were soon checked by reflecting, that if she did so, she could not hear of his death without suffering many heart-felt pangs.

He lingered for three days, without the least encouragement to hope for life, and on the last died with great resignation, receiving his death as a punishment justly due to his want of submission in the divine will, and that forward petulance which drove him to desperation in not succeeding to his wishes just at the time that to his impetuous passions, and short-sighted reason, appeared most desirable.

The afflicted steward wrote an account of this melancholy event to Lady Lambton, and stayed to attend Sir Edward's body home, that his last remains might be deposited in the family vault.

Lady Lambton received these mournful tidings with excessive grief, and communicated them to Mrs Thornby. Louisa, from the time of the messenger's setting out for Germany, had been pleasing herself with reflecting on the joyful reception he would meet with from Sir Edward, and had frequently anticipated, in imagination, the pleasures she and Sir Edward would receive at seeing each other after so melancholy a separation. She now every hour expected him, and when Mrs Thornby began to prepare her against surprise, she imagined he was arrived and that her kind mother was endeavouring to guard her against too sudden joy. She attempted to break through the delay which must arise from all this caution by begging to know if he was in the house, desiring her not to fear any ill effects from his sudden appearance, and rose from her seat, in order to attend her mother to Sir Edward. Mrs Thornby made her sit down again, and with a countenance which spoke very different things from what she expected, acquainted her with the fatal end of all her hopes.

Louisa was shocked in proportion to the degree to which she was before elated. She sunk lifeless in the arms of her mother, who had clasped her to her breast, and it was a considerable time before their cruel endeavours to bring her to her senses succeeded. Her first sensation was an agony of grief; she accused herself of being the occasion of Sir Edward's death, and from the unfortunate consequences of her actions, arraigned her motives for them. Mrs Thornby and Mr d'Avora, whom she had sent for on this occasion, endeavoured to convince her she was no way to blame, that what she had done was laudable, and she ought not to judge of an action by its consequences, which must always remain in the hands of the Almighty, to whom we are accountable for our motives, but who best knows when they ought to be crowned with success. When they had prevailed with her to exculpate herself, her piety and patience made it the more easy to persuade her calmly to submit to the decrees of providence. She soon saw that to suffer was her duty, and though she might grieve, she must not repine. The good advice of her two friends was some support to her mind, but her chief strength arose from her frequent petitions to him who tried her in sufferings to grant her patience to bear them with due resignation. Such addresses, fervently and sincerely made, can never be unavailing, and she found the consolation she asked for. Her affliction was deep, but silent and submissive, and in no part of her life did she ever appear more amiable than on this trying occasion when her extreme sensibility could never extort one word or thought which was not dictated by humble piety, and the most exemplary resignation. That Sir Edward had had so just a sense of his own error, and so properly repented his impatience was a great consolation, and she hoped to meet him whom she had so soon lost, in a state of happiness where they should never more be parted.

Mrs Morgan had borne a tender share in all Louisa's joys and sorrows; for in the frequency of her correspondence every circumstance that attended the latter was faithfully imparted, though the communication was less free on Mrs Morgan's side, who, contrary to her natural temper, acted with reserve on this particular; induced by a double motive, a belief that it was her duty to conceal her husband's faults, and a desire to spare her friend the pain of suffering participation in her vexations. She longed to attend Miss Mancel in her affliction, but dared not urge a request with which she knew Mr Morgan would not comply. He lived entirely in the country and seemed to be totally insensible to the pleasure of contributing to the happiness of others. All his tenderness was confined within the narrow circle of himself. Mrs Morgan daily beheld distress and poverty without the power of relieving it, for his parsimony would not let him trust her with the disposal of what money was necessary for her own expenses, his sister always brought what they in their wisdoms judged requisite, and Mrs Morgan was treated in those affairs like a little child.

In matters too trifling to come within Mr Morgan's notice, Miss Susanna, fearing her sister should enjoy a moment's ease, took care to perform her part in teasing, as if their joint business was only to keep that poor woman in a constant state of suffering. To complete her vexation, Mr Morgan, who had always drank hard, increased so much in that vice that few days passed wherein he was not totally intoxicated. Mrs Morgan saw no means of redress, and therefore thought it best to suffer without complaint; she considered that, by contention, she could not prevail over their ill temper, but must infallibly sour her own, and destroy that composure of mind necessary to enable every one to acquit herself well in all Christian duties. By this patient acquiescence her virtues were refined, though her health suffered, and she found some satisfaction in reflecting that him whom she most wished to please would graciously accept her endeavours, however unavailing they might be towards obtaining the favour of those on whom her earthly peace depended.

At this part of Mrs Maynard's narration we were again interrupted by dinner, but the arrival of some visitors in the afternoon afforded Lamont and myself an opportunity of begging her to give us the sequel, and for that purpose we chose a retired seat in the garden, when she thus proceeded.

The next six years of Miss Mancel's life passed in a perfect calm; this may appear too cold an expression, since her situation was such as would by most people have been thought consummate happiness. Mrs Thornby's ample fortune enabled them to live in great figure, and Miss Mancel's beauty and understanding rendered her the object of general admiration. Had her conduct been less admirable, she could not but have acquired many lovers; it is not strange then, such as she was, that she should be addressed by many men of distinguished rank and fortune. Wherever she appeared, she attracted all eyes and engrossed the whole attention. Mrs Thornby, more delighted with the admiration paid her daughter than she herself, carried her frequently into public and kept a great deal of company. Louisa could not be insensible to general approbation, but was hurt with the serious attachment of those who more particularly addressed her. As she was determined never to marry, thinking it a sort of infidelity to a man whose death was owing to his affection for her, she always took the first opportunity of discouraging every pursuit of that kind; and restrained the natural vivacity of her temper lest it should give rise to any hopes which could end only in disappointment. She endeavoured to make publicly known her fixed determination never to marry; but as those resolutions are seldom thought unalterable, many men flattered themselves that their rank and fortunes, with their personal merits, might conquer so strange an intention, and therefore would not desist without an express refusal.

In the seventh year after Mrs Thornby's return into England, she was taken off by a fever, and left Miss Mancel, at twenty-four years of age, in possession of forty thousand pounds, a fortune which could not afford her consolation for the loss of so tender a parent. Having nothing to attach her to any particular part of the kingdom, she more than ever longed to settle in Mrs Morgan's neighbourhood, but feared to occasion some new uneasiness to her friend, and was sensible that if, when vicinity favoured them, they should be denied the pleasure of each other's company, or very much restrained in it, the mortification would be still greater than when distance would not permit them to meet. She had the satisfaction of hearing from her friend that Mr Morgan seemed to esteem her more than for some years after their marriage, and often gave her reason to think he did not despise her understanding and was well pleased with her conduct. The truth was, this gentleman's eyes were at last opened to the merits of his wife's behaviour, the long trial he had made of her obedience, which was implicit and performed with apparent cheerfulness; if compared with his sister's conduct, could not fail of appearing in an amiable light, when he was no longer beset with the malicious insinuations of Susanna, who had bestowed herself on a young ensign whose small hopes of preferment in the army reduced him to accept that lady and her fortune as a melancholy resource, but his only certain provision. This alteration in Mr Morgan's temper gave Mrs Morgan and Louisa room to hope that he might not always continue averse to their becoming neighbours.

While they were flattering themselves with this agreeable prospect, Mr Morgan was seized with a paralytic disorder which at first attacked his limbs, but in a very short time affected his head so much as almost to deprive him of his senses. He was totally confined to his bed, and seemed not to know any one but his wife. He would take neither medicine nor nourishment except from her hands; as he was entirely lame, she was obliged to feed him, and he was not easy if she was out of the room. Even in the night he would frequently call to her; if she appeared at his bedside, he was then contented, being sure she was in the chamber, but would fall into violent passions which he had not words to express (for he was almost deprived of his speech) if she did not instantly appear.

When Miss Mancel heard of his deplorable situation, she was under the greatest apprehensions for her friend's health, from so close and so fatiguing an attendance, and begged she might come to her, as he was then incapable of taking umbrage at it. The offer was too agreeable to be rejected, and these ladies met after so long an enforced separation with a joy not to be imagined by any heart less susceptible than theirs of the tender and delicate sensations of friendship. Louisa was almost as constantly in Mr Morgan's room in the day time as his wife, though she kept out of his sight, and thus they had full opportunity of conversing together; for though the sick man often called Mrs Morgan, yet as soon as he saw she was in the chamber he sunk again into that state of stupefaction from which he never recovered. Mrs Morgan put a bed up in his room, and lay there constantly, but as he was as solicitious to know she was present in the night, as in the day, she could never quite undress herself the whole time of his sickness.

In this condition Mr Morgan lay for three months, when death released him from this world; and brought a seasonable relief to Mrs Morgan, whose health was so impaired by long confinement and want of quiet rest that she could not much longer have supported it; and vexation had before so far impaired her constitution that nothing could have enabled her to undergo so long a fatigue, but the infinite joy she received from Miss Mancel's company.

When Mr Morgan's will was opened, it appeared that he had left his wife an estate which fell to him about a month before the commencement of his illness, where we now live. The income of it is a thousand pounds a year; the land was thoroughly stocked and the house in good repair. Mr Morgan had at his marriage settled a jointure on his wife of four hundred pounds a year rent charge, and in a codicil made just after his sister's wedding, he bequeathed her two thousand pounds in ready money.

After Mrs Morgan had settled all her affairs, it was judged necessary that, for the recovery of her health, she should go to Tunbridge, to which place Miss Mancel accompanied her. As Mrs Morgan's dress confined her entirely at home, they were not in the way of making many acquaintances; but Lady Mary Jones being in the house, and having long been known to Miss Mancel, though no intimacy had subsisted between them, they now became much connected. The two friends had agreed to retire into the country, and though both of an age and fortune to enjoy all the pleasures which most people so eagerly pursue, they were desirous of fixing in a way of life where all their satisfactions might be rational and as conducive to eternal as to temporal happiness. They had laid the plan of many things, which they have since put into execution, and engaged Mr d'Avora to live with them, both as a valuable friend and a useful assistant in the management of their affairs.

Lady Mary was at that time so much in the same disposition,

and so charmed with such part of their scheme as they communicated to her, that she begged to live with them for half a year, by which time they would be able to see whether they chose her continuance there, and she should have experienced how far their way of life was agreeable to her. Lady Mary's merit was too apparent not to obtain their ready consent to her proposal, and when they had the satisfaction of seeing Mrs Morgan much recovered by the waters, and no farther benefit was expected, they came to this house.

They found it sufficiently furnished, and in such good order, that they settled in it without trouble. The condition of the poor soon drew their attention, and they instituted schools for the young and almshouses for the old. As they ordered everything in their own family with great economy, and thought themselves entitled only to a part of their fortunes, their large incomes allowed them full power to assist many whose situations differed very essentially from theirs. The next expense they undertook, after this establishment of schools and almshouses, was that of furnishing a house for every young couple that married in their neighbourhood, and providing them with some sort of stock, which by industry would prove very conducive towards their living in a comfortable degree of plenty. They have always paid nurses for the sick, sent them every proper refreshment, and allow the same sum weekly which the sick person could have gained, that the rest of the family may not lose any part of their support by the incapacity of one.

When they found their fortunes would still afford a larger communication, they began to receive the daughters of persons in office, or other life-incomes, who, by their parents' deaths, were left destitute of provision; and when, among the lower sort, they meet with an uncommon genius, they will admit her among the number. The girls you see sit in the room with us are all they have at present in that way; they are educated in such a manner as will render them acceptable where accomplished women of a humble rank and behaviour are wanted, either for the care of a house or children. These girls are never out of the room with us, except at breakfast and dinner, and after eight o'clock in the evening, at which times they are under the immediate care of the housekeeper, with whom they are allowed to walk out for an hour or two every fine day, lest their being always in our company should make them think their situation above a menial state; they attend us while we are dressing, and we endeavour that the time they are thus employed shall not pass without improvement. They are clad coarse and plain for the same reason, as nothing has a stronger influence on vanity than dress.

Each of us takes our week alternately of more particular inspection over the performances of these girls, and they all read by turns aloud to such of us as are employed about any thing that renders it not inconvenient to listen to them. By this sort of education my friends hope to do extensive good, for they will not only serve these poor orphans, but confer a great benefit on all who shall be committed to their care or have occasion for their service; and one can set no bounds to the advantages that may arise from persons of excellent principles, and enlarged understandings, in the situations wherein they are to be placed. In every thing their view is to be as beneficial to society as possible, and they are such economists even in their charities as to order them in a manner that as large a part of mankind as possible should feel the happy influence of their bounty.

In this place, and in this way of life, the three ladies already mentioned have lived upwards of twenty years; for Lady Mary Jones joined her fortune to those of the two friends, never choosing to quit them, and is too agreeable not to be very desirable in the society. Miss Mancel has often declared that she plainly sees the merciful hand of providence bringing good out of evil, in an event which she, at the time it happened, thought her greatest misfortune; for had she married Sir Edward Lambton, her sincere affection for him would have led her to conform implicitly to all his inclinations, her views would have been confined to this earth, and too strongly attached to human objects to have properly obeyed the giver of the blessings she so much valued, who is generally less thought of in proportion as he is more particularly bountiful. Her age, her fortune and compliant temper might have seduced her into dissipation and have made her lose all the heart-felt joys she now daily experiences, both when she reflects on the past, contemplates the present, or anticipates the future.

I think I ought to mention Mrs Morgan's behaviour to her half-sisters. Sir Charles died about five years ago, and through his wife's extravagance left his estate over-charged with debts and two daughters and a son unprovided for. Lady Melvyn's jointure was not great; Sir George, her eldest son, received but just sufficient out of his estate to maintain himself genteelly. By the first Lady Melvyn's marriage settlements, six thousand pounds were settled on her children, which, as Mrs Morgan was her only child, became her property; this she divided between her step-mother's three younger children, and has besides conferred several favours on that family and frequently makes them valuable presents. The young gentlemen and ladies often pass some time here; Lady Melvyn made us a visit in the first year of her widowhood, but our way of life is so ill suited to her taste that, except during that dull period of confinement, she has never favoured us with her company.

My cousin, I believe, was going to mention some other of the actions of these ladies, which seemed a favourite topic with her, when the rest of the company came into the garden, and we thought ourselves obliged to join them.

The afternoons, in this family, generally concluded with one of their delightful concerts; but as soon as the visitors were departed, the ladies said, they would amuse us that evening with an entertainment which might possibly be more new to us, a rustic ball. The occasion of it was the marriage of a young woman who had been brought up by them and had for three years been in service, but having for that whole time been courted by a young farmer of good character, she had been married in the morning, and that evening was dedicated to the celebration of their wedding.

We removed into the servants' hall, a neat room, and well lighted, where we found a very numerous assembly; sixteen couples were preparing to dance; the rest were only spectators. The bride was a pretty, genteel girl, dressed in a white calico gown, white ribbons, and in every particular neat to an excess. The bridegroom was a well looking young man, as clean and sprucely dressed as his bride, though not with such emblematic purity. This couple, contrary to the custom of finer people on such occasions, were to begin the ball together; but Lamont asked leave to be the bride's partner for two or three dances, a compliment not disagreeable to the ladies, and highly pleasing to the rest of the company, except the bride, whose vanity one might plainly see did not find gratification enough in having so genteel a partner to recompense her for the loss of her Colin; he, however, seemed well satisfied with the honour conferred on his wife.

That the bridegroom might not be without his share of civility, the ladies gave him leave to dance with the eldest of the young girls more particularly under their care, till his wife was restored to him.

We sat above an hour with this joyous company, whose mirth seemed as pure as it was sincere, and I never saw a ball managed with greater decorum. There is a coquetry and gallantry appropriated to all conditions, and to see the different manner in which it was expressed in this little set, from what one is accustomed to behold in higher life, afforded me great amusement; and the little arts used among these young people to captivate each other were accompanied with so much innocence as made it excessively pleasing. We stayed about an hour and half in this company, and then went to supper.

My cousin told me that Miss Mancel gave the young bride a fortune, and that she might have her share of employment and contribute to the provision for her family had stocked her dairy and furnished her with poultry. This, Mrs Maynard added, was what they did for all the young women they brought up, if they proved deserving; shewing, likewise, the same favour to any other girls in the parish who, during their single state, behaved with remarkable industry and sobriety. By this mark of distinction they were incited to a proper behaviour, and appeared more anxious for this benevolence on account of the honour that arose from it than for the pecuniary advantage.

As the ladies' conduct in this particular was uncommon, I could not forbear telling them, that I was surprised to find so great encouragement given to matrimony by persons whose choice shewed them little inclined in its favour.

'Does it surprise you,' answered Mrs Morgan smiling, 'to see people promote that in others which they themselves do not choose to practise? We consider matrimony as absolutely necessary to the good of society; it is a general duty; but as, according to all ancient tenures, those obliged to perform knight's service, might, if they chose to enjoy their own firesides, be excused by sending deputies to supply their places; so we, using the same privilege substitute many others, and certainly much more promote wedlock than we could do by entering into it ourselves. This may wear the appearance of some devout persons of a certain religion who, equally indolent and timorous, when they do not choose to say so many prayers as they think their duty, pay others for supplying their deficiencies.'

'In this case,' said I, 'your example is somewhat contradictory, and should it be entirely followed, it would confine matrimony to the lower rank of people, among whom it seems going out of fashion, as well as with their superiors; nor indeed can we wonder at it, for dissipation and extravagance are now become such universal vices that it requires great courage in any to enter into an indissoluble society. Instead of being surprised at the common disinclination to marriage, I am rather disposed to wonder when I see a man venture to render himself liable to the expenses of a woman who lavishes both her time and money on every fashionable folly, and still more, when one of your sex subjects herself to be reduced to poverty by a husband's love for gaming, and to neglect by his inconstancy.'

'I am of your opinion,' said Miss Trentham, 'to face the enemy's cannon appears to me a less effort of courage than to put our happiness into the hands of a person who perhaps will not once reflect on the importance of the trust committed to his or her care. For the case is pretty equal as to both sexes, each can destroy the other's peace. Ours seems to have found out the means of being on an equality with yours. Few fortunes are sufficient to stand a double expense. The husband must attend the gaming-table and horse-races; the wife must have a profusion of ornaments for her person, and cards for her entertainment. The care of the estate and family are left in the hands of servants who, in imitation of their masters and mistresses, will have their pleasures, and these must be supplied out of the fortunes of those they serve. Man and wife are often nothing better than assistants in each other's ruin; domestic virtues are exploded, and social happiness despised as dull and insipid.

'The example of the great infects the whole community. The honest tradesman who wishes for a wife to assist him in his business, and to take care of his family, dare not marry when every woman of his own rank, emulating her superiors, runs into such fashions of dress as require great part of his gains to supply, and the income which would have been thought sufficient some years ago for the wife of a gentleman of large estate will now scarcely serve to enable a tradesman's wife to appear like her neighbours. They too must have their evening parties, they must attend the places of public diversion, and must be allowed perpetual dissipation without control. The poor man sighs after the days when his father married; then cleanliness was a woman's chief personal ornament, half the quantity of silk sufficed for her clothes, variety of trumpery ornaments were not thought of, her husband's business employed her attention, and her children were the objects of her care. When he came home, wearied with the employment of the day, he found her ready to receive him, and was not afraid of being told she was gone to the play or opera, or of finding her engaged in a party at cards, while he was reduced to spend his evening alone. But in a world so changed, a man dare not venture on marriage which promises him no comfort, and may occasion his ruin, nor wishes for children whose mother's neglect may expose them to destruction.

'It is common to blame the lower sort of people for imitating their superiors; but it is equally the fault of every station, and therefore those of higher rank should consider it is their duty to set no examples that may hurt others. A degree of subordination is always acquiesced in, but while the nobleman lives like a prince, the gentleman will rise to the proper expenses of a nobleman, and the tradesman take that vacant rank which the gentleman has quitted; nor will he be ashamed of becoming a bankrupt when he sees the fortunes of his superiors mouldering away and knows them to be oppressed with debts. Whatever right people may have to make free with their own happiness, a beneficial example is a duty which they indispensably owe to society, and the profuse have the extravagance of their inferiors to answer for. The same may be said for those who contribute to the dissipation of others, by being dissipated themselves.'

'But, madam,' interrupted Lamont, 'do you think it incumbent on people of fashion to relinquish their pleasures, lest their example should lead others to neglect their business?'

'I should certainly,' replied Miss Trentham, 'answer you in the affirmative were the case as you put it, but much more so in the light I see it. Every station has its duties, those of the great are more various than those of their inferiors. They are not so confined to economical attentions, nor ought they to be totally without them; but their more extensive influence, their greater leisure to serve their Creator with all the powers of their minds, constitute many duties on their part to which dissipation is as great an enemy as it can be to those more entirely domestic; therefore on each side there is an equal neglect; and why should we expect that such as we imagine have fewer advantages of education should be more capable of resisting temptations and dedicating themselves solely to the performance of their duties, than persons whose minds are more improved?'

'I cannot deny,' answered Lamont, 'but what you say is just, yet I fear you have uttered truths that must continue entirely speculative; though if any people have a right to turn reformers, you ladies are best qualified, since you begin by reforming yourselves; you practise more than you preach, and therefore must always be listened to with attention.'

'We do not set up for reformers,' said Miss Mancel, 'we wish to regulate ourselves by the laws laid down to us, and as far as our influence can extend, endeavour to enforce them; beyond that small circle all is foreign to us; we have sufficient employment in improving ourselves; to mend the world requires much abler hands.'

'When you talk of laws, madam, by which you would regulate your actions,' said Lamont, 'you raise a just alarm; as for matter of opinion, every one may demand an equal power, but laws seem to require obedience; pray, from whence do you take those which you wish to make your rule of life?'

'From whence,' answered Miss Mancel, 'should a Christian take them, from the Alcoran, think you, or from the wiser Confucius, or would you seek in Coke on Littleton that you may escape the iron hand of the legislative power? No, surely, the Christian's law is written in the Bible, there, independent of the political regulations of particular communities, is to be found the law of the supreme Legislator. There, indeed, is contained the true and invariable law of nations; and according to our performance of it, we shall be tried by a Judge whose wisdom and impartiality secure him from error, and whose power is able to execute his own decrees. This is the law I meant, and whoever obeys it can never offend essentially against the private ordinances of any community. This all to whom it has been declared are bound to obey, my consent to receive it for the rule of my actions is not material; for as whoever lives in England must submit to the laws of the country, though he may be ignorant of many of the particulars of them, so whoever lives in a Christian land is obliged to obey the laws of the Gospel, or to suffer for infringing them; in both cases, therefore, it is prudent for every man to acquaint himself thoroughly with these ordinances, which he cannot break with impunity.'

'If such obedience be necessary,' said Lamont, 'what do you imagine will be the fate of most of the inhabitants of Christendom; for you will allow that they do not regulate their conduct by such severe commands?'

'What will be their fate,' replied Miss Mancel, 'I do not pretend even to suppose, my business is to take care of my own. The laws against robbery are not rendered either less just or less binding by the numbers that daily steal or who demand your purse on the highway. Laws are not abrogated by being infringed, nor does the disobedience of others make the observance of them less my duty. I am required to answer only for myself, and it is not man whom I am ordered to imitate. His failings will not excuse mine. Humility forbids me to censure others, and prudence obliges me to avoid copying them.'

Lamont thought Miss Mancel too severe in her doctrine; but there was something so respectable in her severity, that he forbore to contest it, and owned to me afterwards that, while she spoke and he contemplated that amiable society, his heart silently acquiesced in the justness of her sentiments.

We parted at our usual hour; and at the same time the company in the lower part of the house broke up, eleven o'clock being the stated hour for them on those occasions to return to their respective homes.

The next morning, as I went downstairs, I met the housekeeper and entered into conversation with her, for which the preceding night's festivity furnished me with topics. From her I learnt that since the ladies had been established in that house they had given fortunes from twenty to a hundred pounds, as merit and occasion directed, to above thirty young women, and that they had seldom celebrated fewer than two marriages in a year, sometimes more. Nor does their bounty cease on the wedding-day, for they are always ready to assist them on any emergency; and watch with so careful an eye over the conduct of these young people as proves of much greater service to them than the money they bestow. They kindly, but strongly, reprehend the first error, and guard them by the most prudent admonitions against a repetition of their fault. By little presents they shew their approbation of those who behave well, always proportioning their gifts to the merits of the person; which are therefore looked upon as the most honourable testimony of their conduct, and are treasured up as valuable marks of distinction. This encouragement has great influence, and makes them vie with each other in endeavours to excel in sobriety, cleanliness, meekness and industry. She told me also that the young women bred up at the schools these ladies support are so much esteemed for many miles round that it is not uncommon for young farmers, who want sober, good wives, to obtain them from thence, and prefer them to girls of much better fortunes, educated in a different manner, as there have been various instances wherein their industry and quickness of understanding, which in a great measure arises from the manner of their education, has proved more profitable to their husbands than a more ample dower.

She added that she keeps a register of all the boys and girls, which, by her good ladies' means, have been established in the world; whereby it appears that thirty have been apprenticed out to good trades, three score fixed in excellent places, and thirty married. And it seldom happens that any one takes an apprentice or servant till they have first sent to her ladies to know if they have any to recommend.

I expressed a desire to see the schools, which she obligingly offered to shew me, but feared we could not then have time to go thither, as breakfast was just ready. While I was talking with her, I observed that the fingers of one of her hands were contracted quite close to the palm. I took notice of it to her. 'Oh! sir,' said she, 'it was the luckiest accident that could possibly be; as I was obliged to work for my support, I was very much shocked at my recovery from a fever to find myself deprived of the use of a hand, but still tried if I could get myself received into service; as I was sensible I could, notwithstanding my infirmity, perform the business of a housekeeper; but no one would take me in this maimed condition. At last I was advised to apply to these ladies and found what had hitherto been an impediment was a stronger recommendation than the good character I had from my last place; and I am sure I have reason to value these distorted fingers, more than ever any one did the handsomest hands that ever nature made. But,' added she, smiling, 'few of my fellow-servants are better qualified; the cook cannot walk without crutches, the kitchen maid has but one eye, the dairy maid is almost stone deaf, and the housemaid has but one hand; and yet, perhaps, there is no family where the business is better done; for gratitude, and a conviction that this is the only house into which we can be received, makes us exert ourselves to the utmost; and most people fail not from a deficiency of power, but of inclination. Even their musicians, if you observed it, sir, are much in the same condition. The steward, indeed, must be excepted; he is one whom the good Mr d'Avora chose for the sake of his integrity some years before he died, as his successor in the care of the ladies' affairs, and employed him for some time under his own inspection, that he might be sure he was fit for the purpose, though he persuaded the ladies to receive their own rents and direct all the chief concerns of their estates, which they have done ever since, so that theirs is rather a household than a land steward. But, except this gentleman and the shepherd, there is not one of their musicians that is not under some natural disadvantage; the defects of two of them are so visible I need not point them out, but of the other two, one is subject to violent fits of the stone, and the other to the asthma. Thus disabled from hard labour, though they find some employment in the manufacture, yet the additional profit which accrues from their playing here adds much to their comfort, as their infirmities render greater expenses necessary to them than to others in their station.'

There was something so whimsically good in the conduct of the ladies in these particulars, as at first made me smile; but when I considered it more thoroughly, I perceived herein a refinement of charity which, though extremely uncommon, was entirely rational. I found that not contented with merely bestowing on the indigent as large a part of their fortunes as they can possibly spare, they carry the notion of their duty to the poor so far as to give continual attention to it, and endeavour so to apply all they spend as to make almost every shilling contribute towards the support of some person in real necessity; by this means every expense bears the merit of a donation in the sight of him who knows their motives; and their constant application is directed towards the relief of others, while to superficial observers they seem only providing for their own convenience. The fashionable tradesman is sure not to have them in the list of his customers; but should he, through the caprice of the multitude, be left without business, and see his elated hopes blasted, in all probability he will find these ladies his friends. Those whose youth renders them disregarded, or whose old age breeds neglect, will here meet with deserved encouragement. This sort of economy pleases me much, it is of the highest kind, since it regards those riches which neither moth nor rust can corrupt, nor thieves break through and steal; and is within the reach of every person's imitation, for the poorest may thus turn their necessary expenses into virtuous actions. In this they excel others, as much as the bee does the common butterfly; they both feed on the same flowers, but while the butterfly only gains a transient subsistence and flies and flutters in all its gaudy pride, the bee lays up a precious store for its future well-being, and may brave all the rigours of winter. Man, indeed, often encroaches on the labours of the bee and disappoints it of its reasonable hope; but no one without our own concurrence can despoil us of the treasures laid up in heaven.

As the good housekeeper foretold, the bell soon summoned me to breakfast; which, like every other hour spent in that society, was rendered delightful by their rational cheerfulness and polite freedom. We offered to take our leave, but should have been disappointed had we not been asked to prolong our visit; nor were we so insincere as to make much resistance to this agreeable invitation; we expressed some fears of interrupting their better employments; to which Mrs Morgan replied by assuring us that we did not do so in the least; but added, 'I will tell you plainly, gentlemen, the only alteration we shall wish to make, if you will favour us with your company a few days longer. Our family devotions are regular, as you were strangers we have not summoned you to them, but for the rest of your visit we must beg leave to alter that method; for we do not think it a proper example to our servants to suffer any one in this house to be excluded from them; though as your coming was sudden, and has been prolonged only, as it were, from hour to hour, we at first did not think it necessary to require your presence.'

You may imagine we expressed ourselves obliged by this frankness; and, for my own part, I was glad of what appeared to me like being received into a community of saints; but was forced to wait for it till night, the devotion of the morning having been paid before breakfast, as was usual in that family.

Mrs Maynard accompanied us that morning into the park, and having placed ourselves on a green bank under an elm, by the side of the canal, I called on her to perform her promise, and increase my acquaintance with the rest of the ladies, by giving some account of them.

'I shall not the less readily comply,' she answered, 'for being able to bring what I have to say of them into less compass, than I did my history of Mrs Morgan and Miss Mancel, of whom, when I begin to speak, I always find it difficult to leave off, and am led by my fondness for the subject into a detail, perhaps too circumstantial. Lady Mary Jones, by what I have already said, you may have perceived must come next in order.'

THE
HISTORY
OF
Lady MARY JONES

LADY Mary was daughter to the Earl of Brumpton by his second wife, who survived the birth of her child but a few hours. The earl died when his daughter was about ten years old, and having before his second marriage mortgaged to its full value all of his estate which was not settled on a son born of his first lady, his daughter was left entirely destitute of provision. But as she was too young to be much affected with this circumstance, so she had little reason to regret it, when an increase of years might have awakened a sensibility to that particular. Immediately on her father's death she was taken by her aunt, Lady Sheerness, who declared she should look upon her as her own child, and indeed her indulgence verified the truth of her declaration.

Lady Sheerness was a widow; her jointure considerable; and her lord at his decease left her some thousand pounds in ready money. When he died she was about twenty-five years old, with a good person and infinite vivacity. An unbridled imagination, ungovernable spirits, with a lively arch countenance and a certain quaintness of expression gained her the reputation of being possessed of a great deal of wit. Her lord, in the decline of life, had been captivated by her youthful charms, when she was but sixteen years old. His extreme fondness for her led him to indulge her vivacity in all its follies; and frequently while he was laid up at home in the gout her ladyship was the finest and gayest woman at every place of public resort. Often, when the acuteness of his pains obliged him to seek relief from the soporific influence of opium, she collected half the town, and though his rest was disturbed every moment by a succession of impetuous raps at the door, he was never offended; on the contrary, he thought himself obliged to her for staying at home, which she had assured him was because she could not bear to go abroad when he was so ill. This, as the greatest mark of her tenderness he ever received, he failed not to acknowledge with gratitude. She scarcely took more pleasure in having a train of admirers than his lordship felt from it; his vanity was flattered in seeing his wife the object of admiration and he fancied himself much envied for so valuable a possession. Her coquetry charmed him, as the follies of that vivacity of which he was so fond. He had no tincture of jealousy in his whole composition; and acknowledged as favours conferred on himself the attentions paid to his wife.

Though Lord Sheerness's conduct may appear rather uncommon, yet it seemed the result of some discernment, or at least his lady's disposition was such as justifies this opinion; she had received a genteel education; no external accomplishments had been neglected; but her understanding and principles were left to the imperfection of nature corrupted by custom. Religion was thought too serious a thing for so young a person. The opinion of the world was always represented to her as the true criterion by which to judge of everything, and fashion supplied the place of every more material consideration. With a mind thus formed, she entered the world at sixteen, surrounded with pomp and splendour, with every gratification at her command that an affluent fortune and an indulgent husband could bestow: by nature inclined to no vice, free from all dangerous passions, the charm of innocence accompanied her vivacity; undesigning and artless, her follies were originally the consequences of her situation, not constitutional, though habit engrafted them so strongly that at length they appeared natural to her. Surrounded with every snare that can entrap a youthful mind, she became a victim to dissipation and the love of fashionable pleasures; destitute of any stable principles, she was carried full sail down the stream of folly. In the love of coquetry and gaming few equalled her; no one could exceed her in the pursuit of every trifling amusement; she had neither leisure nor inclination to think, her life passed in an uninterrupted succession of engagements, without reflection on the past or consideration on the future consequences.

The lightness of her conduct exposed her to the addresses of many gay men during the life of her lord; but an attachment was too serious a thing for her; and while her giddiness and perpetual dissipation exposed her to suspicion, they preserved her from the vice of which she was suspected: she daily passed through the ordeal trial; every step she took was dangerous, but she came off unhurt. Her reputation was indeed doubtful, but her rank and fortune, and the continual amusements which her house yielded to her acquaintance, rendered her generally caressed.

Her lord's death made no alteration in her way of life; and as her mind was never fixed an hour on any subject, she thought not long enough of marriage to prepare for that state and therefore continued a widow. She was upwards of forty years old, unchanged in anything but her person, when she took Lady Mary Jones, I will not say into her care, for that word never entered into her vocabulary, but into her house. Lady Mary had naturally a very good understanding, and much vivacity; the latter met with everything that could assist in its increase in the company of Lady Sheerness, the other was never thought of: she was initiated into every diversion at an age when other girls are confined to their nursery. Her aunt was fond of her and therefore inclined to indulgence, besides she thought the knowledge of the world, which in her opinion was the most essential qualification for a woman of fashion, was no way to be learnt but by an early acquaintance with it.

Lady Mary's age and vivacity rendered this doctrine extremely agreeable; she was pretty and very lively and entertaining in her conversation, therefore at fifteen years of age she became the most caressed person in every company. She entered into all the fashionable tastes, was coquettish and extravagant; for Lady Sheerness very liberally furnished her with money and felt a sort of pride in having a niece distinguished by the fineness of her dress and her profusion in every expense, as it was well known to have no other source but in her ladyship's generosity. Though Lady Mary received much adulation, and was the object of general courtship, yet she had no serious love made to her till she was between sixteen and seventeen, when she accompanied her aunt to Scarborough: she was there very assiduously followed by a gentleman reputed of a large fortune in Wales. He was gay and well-bred, his person moderately agreeable, his understanding specious and his manner insinuating. There was nothing very engaging in the man, except the appearance of a very tender attachment. She had before found great pleasure in being admired; but her vanity was still more flattered in being loved: she knew herself capable of amusing; but till now had never been able to give either pleasure or pain, according to her sovereign decree. She grew partial to Mr Lenman (that was the name of her lover) because he raised her consequence in her own eyes: she played off a thousand airs of coquetry which she had never yet had an opportunity to exercise for want of a real lover. Sometimes she would elate him by encouragement; at others, freeze him into despair by her affected coldness: she was never two hours the same, because she delighted in seeing the variety of passions she could excite.

Mr Lenman was certainly sufficiently tormented; but so great a proficiency in coquetry at so early an age was no discouragement to his hopes. There are no people so often the dupe of their own arts as coquettes; especially when they become so very early in life; therefore, instead of being damped in his pursuit, he adapted his behaviour to her foible, vanity, and by assuming an air of indifference, could, when he pleased, put an end to her affected reserve; though he was not so unpolite a lover as quite to deny her the gratification she expected from her little arts. He found means, however, to command her attention by the very serious proposal of matrimony. She had no great inclination for the state, but the novelty pleased her. The pleasure she received from his addresses she mistook for love, and imagined herself deeply enamoured, when she was in reality only extremely flattered; the common error of her age. In the company she had kept matrimony appeared in no very formidable light; she did not see that it abridged a woman of any of the liberties she already enjoyed; it only afforded her an opportunity of choosing her own diversions; whereas her taste in those points sometimes differed from her aunt's, to whom, however, she was obliged to submit. Thus prepossessed, both in favour of her lover and his proposal, she listened to him with more attention than she chose he should perceive; but he was too well acquainted with the pretty arts of coquetry not to see through them. He therefore took courage to insinuate his desire of a private marriage, and ventured to persuade her to take a trip with him to the northern side of Berwick upon Tweed.

Lady Mary could not see, as Mr Lenman's fortune was considerable and hers entirely precarious, why he was so apprehensive of not being accepted by her aunt, but there was something spirited in those northern journeys that had always been the objects of her envy. An adventure was the supreme pleasure of life and these pretty flights gave marriage all the charms of romance. To be forced to fly into another kingdom to be married gave her an air of consequence; vulgar people might tie the knot at every parish church, but people of distinction should do everything with an eclat. She imagined it very probable that her aunt would consent to her union with Mr Lenman; for though he was not equal to her in birth, yet he was her superior in fortune; but yet she looked upon his fears of a refusal as meritorious, since he assured her they arose from his extreme affection, which filled him with terrors on the least prospect of losing her. Should Lady Sheerness, he urged, reject his proposal, she might then be extremely offended with their marrying, after they knew her disapprobation; but if they did it without her knowledge, she would not have room to complain of downright disobedience, and if it was displeasing to her, yet being done, and past remedy, she would be inclined to make the best of what was unavoidable, and forgive what she could not prevent.

These arguments were sufficiently solid for a girl of sixteen who never thought before and could scarcely be said to do so then. Lady Mary complied with his plan, and the day was fixed when they were to take this lively step; their several stages settled, and many more arts and contrivances to avoid discovery concerted, than they were likely to have any occasion for; but in that variety of little schemes and romantic expedients her chief pleasure in this intended marriage consisted.

The day before that on which Lady Mary and her lover were to set out for Scotland, she was airing with Lady Sheerness when one of the horses taking fright, they were overturned down a very steep declivity. Lady Sheerness was but very little hurt, but Lady Mary was extremely bruised; one side of her face received a blow which swelled it so violently that her eye was quite closed, and her body was all over contusions. She was taken up senseless, entirely stunned by the shock. As soon as she was carried home, she was put to bed; a fever ensued, and she lay a fortnight in a deplorable condition, though her life was not thought to be in danger. Her pain, for the greatest part of that time, was too acute to suffer her to reflect much on the different manner in which she had intended to employ that period; and when her mind became more at liberty, her disappointment did not sit too heavy on her spirits; for as her heart was not really touched, she considered the delay which this ill-timed accident had occasioned without any great concern, and rather pleased herself with thinking that she should give an uncommon proof of spirit, in undertaking a long journey, so soon after she was recovered from a very evident proof that travelling is not free from danger. As she had during this confinement more time to think than all her life had yet afforded her, a doubt would sometimes occur, whether she did right in entering into such an engagement without the consent of her aunt, to whom she was much obliged. But these scruples soon vanished, and she wondered how such odd notions came into her head, never having heard the word duty used, but to ridicule somebody who made it the rule of their conduct. By all she had been able to observe, pleasure was the only aim of persons of genius, whose thoughts never wandered but from one amusement to another, and, 'why should not she be guided by inclination as well as other people?' That one question decided the point, and all doubts were banished.

Before the blackness which succeeded the swelling was worn off her face, and consequently before she could appear abroad, a young lady of her acquaintance, who, out of charity, relinquished the diversions of the place to sit an afternoon with Lady Mary, told her as a whimsical piece of news she had just heard (and to tell which was the real motive for her kind visit, having long felt a secret envy of Lady Mary) that, her lover, Mr Lenman, had been married some years, to a young lady of small fortune, whom he treated on that account with so little ceremony that for a considerable time he did not own his marriage, and since he acknowledged it had kept her constantly at his house in Wales.

This was indeed news of consequence to Lady Mary, but she was little inclined to believe it and enquired what proof there was of this fact. The young lady replied that she had it from a relation of hers lately arrived at Scarborough who having been often in Mr Lenman's neighbourhood, was well acquainted both with him and his wife, and had in a pretty large company where she was present asked him after Mrs Lenman's health, to which he made as short an answer as he could, but such as shewed there was such a person, and his confusion on this question made her relation enquire what could be the meaning of it, which all the company could easily explain.

Lady Mary was prodigiously disconcerted with this intelligence; her informer imagined the visible agitation of her spirits proceeded from her attachment to Mr Lenman, but in reality it was the effect of terror. She was frighted to think how near she was becoming the object of general ridicule and disgrace, wedded to a married man and duped by his cunning; for she immediately perceived why her aunt was not to be let into the secret. How contemptible a figure must she afterwards have made in the world! There was something in this action of Mr Lenman's very uncommon, fashionable vices and follies had in her opinion received a sanction from custom, but this was of a different and a deeper dye; and little as she had been used to reflect on good and evil in any other light than as pleasant and unpleasant, she conceived a horror at this action.

After her visitor departed, she began to reflect on the luckiness of the overturn which had obstructed her rash design, and admiring her good fortune, would certainly have offered rich sacrifices on the shrine of Chance had there been a temple there erected to that deity.

While her mind was filled with these impressions, the nurse, who had attended her in her sickness, and was not yet dismissed, entered the room crying with joy and told her, that she had just received the news of the ship's being lost wherein her son was to have embarked, had he not been seized with a fit of sickness two days before it set sail, which made it impossible for him to go on board. The poor woman was profuse in her acknowledgements for God's great mercy, who had by this means prevented the destruction of her dear child. 'To be sure,' added she, 'I shall never again repine at any thing that happens to me. How vexed I was at this disappointment, and thought myself the most unfortunate creature in the world because my son missed of such a good post as he was to have had in this ship; I was continually fretting about it and fancied that so bad a setting out was a sign the poor boy would be unlucky all his life. How different things turn out from what we expect! Had not this misfortune, as I thought it, happened, he would now have been at the bottom of the sea, and my poor heart would have been broken. Well, to be sure God is very kind! I hope my boy will always be thankful for this providence and love the Lord who has thus preserved him.'

This poor woman spoke a new language to Lady Mary. She knew, indeed, that God had made the world, and had sent her into it, but she had never thought of his taking any further care about her. She had heard that he had forbidden murder and stealing and adultery and that, after death, he would judge people for those crimes, and this she supposed was the utmost extent of his attention. But the joy she felt for her own deliverance from a misfortune into which she was so near involving herself, and the resemblance there was in the means of her preservation to that for which her nurse was so thankful, communicated to her some of the same sensations, and she felt a gratitude to him who, she imagined, might possibly be more careful over his creatures than she had ever yet supposed.

These impressions, though pretty strong at the time, wore off after she got abroad. A renewal of the same dissipation scattered them with every other serious thought; and she again entered into the hurry of every trifling amusement. Mr Lenman, as soon as he found that his marriage was become public, despairing of the success of his scheme, left the place before Lady Mary was out of her confinement, afraid of meeting the reproachful glances of a woman whom he designed to injure; and whose innocence, notwithstanding her levity, gave her dignity in the eyes of a man who had really conceived an ardent passion for her.

Lady Sheerness and her niece stayed but a short time at Scarborough after the latter was perfectly recovered, the season being over. They returned to London and all the gaiety it affords; and though the town was at that time not full, yet they had so general an acquaintance, and Lady Sheerness rendered her house so agreeable, that she never wanted company. Every season has its different amusements, and these ladies had an equal taste for everything that bore the name of diversion. It is true, they were not always entertained; but they always expected to be so, and promised themselves amends the following day for the disappointment of the present. If they failed of pleasure, they had dissipation, and were in too continual a hurry to have time to ask themselves whether they were amused; if they saw others were so, they imagined themselves must be equally entertained; or if the dullness of the place was too great to be overlooked, they charged it on their own want of spirits, and complained of a languor which rendered them incapable of receiving pleasure.

Lady Mary fortunately had had no confidante in her design of running away with Mr Lenman, and the part he had acted was so dishonourable he could not wish to publish it; her imprudence was therefore known only to herself; and the fear of disobliging her aunt by letting her intended disobedience reach her ears induced her to conceal it; otherwise, most probably, in some unguarded hour, she would have amused her acquaintance with the relation, embellished with whatever circumstances would have rendered it amusing; for the love of being entertaining, and the vanity of being listened to with eagerness, will lead people of ungoverned vivacity to expose their greatest failings.

Lady Mary's levity encouraged her admirers to conceive hopes which her real innocence should have repressed. Among this number was Lord Robert St George. He was both in person and manner extremely pleasing; but what was a stronger charm to a young woman of Lady Mary's turn of mind, he was a very fashionable man, much caressed by the ladies, and supposed to have been successful in his addresses to many. This is always a great recommendation to the gay and giddy; and a circumstance which should make a man shunned by every woman of virtue, secures him a favourable reception from the most fashionable part of our sex.

Lady Mary would have accused herself of want of taste had she not liked a man whom so many others had loved. She saw his attachment to her in the light of a triumph over several of her acquaintance; and when a man raises a woman in her own esteem, it is seldom long before he gains a considerable share of it for himself. Vanity represented Lord Robert as a conquest of importance, and his qualifications rendered him a very pleasing dangler. Lady Mary liked him as well as her little leisure to attend to one person would permit. She felt that pleasure on his approach, that pain at his departure, that solicitude for his presence, and that jealousy at the civilities he paid any other woman, which girls look upon as the symptoms of a violent passion, whereas if they were to examine their hearts very nicely they would find that only a small part of it proceeded from love.

Lord Robert was too well skilled in these matters to remain ignorant of the impression he had made; and if he had been less quick-sighted, the frequent intelligence he received of it would not have suffered him long to remain in ignorance. Lady Mary, vain of her conquest and proud of being in love, as is usual at her age, let every intimate into her confidence, and by mutual communication they talked a moderate liking into a passion. Each of these young ladies were as ready to tell their friend's secrets as their own, till the circle of that confidence included all their acquaintance. From many of these Lord Robert heard of Lady Mary's great attachment to him, which served not a little to flatter his hopes. He imagined he should meet with an easy conquest of a giddy, thoughtless girl, entirely void of all fixed principles and violently in love with him; for his vanity exaggerated her passion. In this persuasion he supposed nothing was wanting to his success but opportunity, for which he took care not to wait long.

He was intimately acquainted with an old lady, whom he often met at Lady Sheerness's, whose disposition he knew well suited to his purpose; she had before proved convenient to him and others; not indeed by unrewarded assistance; for as her fortune was too small to supply the expenses of the genteel way of life she aimed at, she was glad to have that deficiency made up by presents which she was therefore very assiduous to deserve. This lady, as she was a woman of fashion and lived in figure, was politely received in all gay companies who were not disposed to take the trouble of examining scrupulously into her character. She had one material recommendation; she played high at cards, and omitted nothing to make her house agreeable; and few were more crowded.

This lady had often been visited by Lady Sheerness and her niece, though generally at the same time with the multitude; but one day, when she knew the former was confined at home by indisposition, she invited Lady Mary, whose aunt's complaisance would not suffer her to refuse the invitation on her account.

Lord Robert was there, and as it was only a private party, there were no card-tables but in the outward room. The mistress of the house drew Lady Mary into the inner, on pretence of having something particular to say to her; Lord Robert soon followed. The conversation grew lively between him and Lady Mary; and when the convenient gentlewoman saw them thoroughly engaged and animated in discourse, she quietly withdrew, returning to the company, whose attention was too much fixed on the cards to perceive that any one was missing; and to keep their thoughts more entirely engrossed, she betted with great spirit at every table.

Lady Mary did not perceive she was left alone with Lord Robert, till the growing freedom of his address made her observe it; but as prudence was not one of her virtues, she was not at all disconcerted with this tête-à-tête; nor did it lessen her vivacity. Lord Robert, encouraged by her easiness on the occasion, declared himself so plainly that she was no longer able to blind herself to his views and with surprise found seduction was his aim, if that word may be used for a man's designs against the honour of a woman who seems so careless of it. Her heart was entirely innocent of vice, and she could not imagine how his lordship could conceive it possible to succeed with her in intentions of that sort. She had always thought such imprudence in a woman a very great folly, for in a graver light she had never beheld it, and shewed herself offended at his supposing her capable of such a weakness; but without that honest indignation which a woman would have felt who had acted on better principles.

Lord Robert was not much discouraged; a woman is under great disadvantage when her lover knows himself to be so much beloved that she dare not let her anger continue long, for fear of losing him for ever. He was well convinced that mere worldly prudence could not make a lasting resistance against a strong passion, and such he flattered himself hers was. He therefore ventured to resume the subject; but his perseverance increased Lady Mary's surprise and she began to think herself affronted. Her partiality pleaded in his favour some time; but at length she thought it necessary to retire, notwithstanding his utmost endeavours to detain her. As she left him, she desired him to learn to believe better of her understanding: she perceived it no otherwise an insult; her education had deprived her of that delicacy which should have made her feel a severe mortification at the little share she had of the good opinion of a man she loved; on the contrary, she esteemed the affront she had received a proof of his affection. She had often indeed heard the name of virtue, but by the use she had known made of the word, it appeared to her to have no other signification than prudence. She was not at all shocked with Lord Robert's conduct; but resolved not to concur in his views, because she had no inclination to do so, that overbalanced her very moderate degree of prudence. On this account she determined to avoid being again alone with him.

Lady Mary's natural sense gave rise to some doubts, whether the very open professions of gallantry which Lord Robert had made to her were common; she had been frequently addressed with freedom, but his behaviour seemed more than commonly presuming. In order to find what others would think of it, she often turned the conversation to those sort of subjects, and was a good deal startled one day by a lively, but amiable and modest young lady who said she believed no man that was not an absolute fool, or at the time intoxicated, ever insulted a woman with improper behaviour or discourse; if he had not from some impropriety in her conduct seen reason to imagine it would not be ill received; and I am sure, added she, 'if such a thing was ever to befall me, it would convert me into a starched prude, for fear that hereafter innocent vivacity might be mistaken for vicious levity: I should take myself very severely to task, convinced the offence was grounded on my conduct; for I am well persuaded there is something so respectable in virtue that no man will dare to insult it, except when a great disparity in circumstances encourages an abandoned wretch to take advantage of the necessity of the indigent.'

Lady Mary was greatly affected by this sentiment: she began to reflect on her own behaviour; and could not but see that Lord Robert might, without any great danger of offending, hazard the behaviour he had been guilty of; since in effect she had not conceived much anger against him, and though she had hitherto avoided being again alone with him, yet she had not shewn any very great marks of displeasure. She now watched with attention the conduct of other young ladies; many of them seemed to act on the same principles as herself; but she observed that she who had by her declaration first raised in her suspicions about her own behaviour, had a very different manner from hers. She was indeed gay and lively; but her vivacity seemed under the direction of modesty. In her greatest flow of spirits, she hazarded no improper expression, nor suffered others to do so without a manifest disgust: she saw that the gentlemen who conversed with her preserved an air of respect and deference, which they laid aside when they addressed women whose vivacity degenerated into levity. She now began to perceive some impropriety in her own behaviour, and endeavoured to correct it; but nothing is more difficult than to recover a dignity once lost. When she attempted to restrain her gaiety within proper bounds, she was laughed at for her affectation: if, when the conversation was improper, she assumed an air of gravity, she was accused of the vapours or received hints that she was out of humour.

These were great discouragements in her endeavours to correct the errors of her conduct, but gave her less pain than the difficulties she was under about Lord Robert St George. He still continued to address her with a freedom of manners which she now perceived was insulting; she wanted to discourage his insolence but feared giving a total offence to a man who had too great a share of her affections; she was apprehensive that if she quite deprived him of his hopes, she should entirely lose him and he would attach himself to some other woman. This situation was dangerous and Lord Robert knew the power he had over her. The dilemma she was in really abated the vivacity she wished to restrain, but it was immediately attributed to the anxiety of a love-sick mind, and she was exposed to continual raillery on that subject. Her lover secretly triumphed, flattering himself that her passion was now combating on his side.

In this situation she was unable to determine what part to act, and all her intimates were too much like herself to be capable of advising her. Thus distressed, she resolved to cultivate the acquaintance of the young lady who had opened her eyes to her own conduct, and try what relief she could obtain from her advice. This was easily effected; Lady Mary was too amiable not to have any advances she made answered with pleasure. An intimacy soon ensued.

Lady Mary communicated to her new friend all the difficulties of her situation and confessed to her the true state of her heart. That young lady was not void of compassion for her uneasiness; but told her that while she was encouraging Lord Robert's passion, she was losing his esteem, which alone was worth preserving. 'I allow,' said she, 'that by depriving him of his hopes, you may put an end to his addresses; but consider, my dear Lady Mary, what satisfaction they can afford you if they are only the result of a fondness for your person which would lose all its charms for him as soon as it became familiarized by possession. You would then at once find yourself both neglected and despised by the man for whose sake you had rendered yourself truly despicable. I know you are incapable of an action that would at the same time rid you of his esteem and of the more valuable consciousness of knowing yourself to be truly estimable. I am not of the opinion of those who think chastity the only virtue of consequence to our sex; but it is certainly so very essential to us that she who violates it seldom preserves any other. And how should she? For if there are others as great, greater there cannot be, there is none so necessary. But herein I know you are of my opinion; I only therefore intreat you to shew Lord Robert that you are so; do not let him mistake your real sentiments; nor in order to preserve his love, if custom will oblige me to call his passion by that name, leave him reason to flatter himself that you will fall a victim to his arts and your own weakness.

'Consider with yourself,' continued she, 'which is most desirable, his esteem or his courtship? If you really love him, you can make no comparison between them, for surely there cannot be a greater suffering than to stand low in the opinion of any person who has a great share of our affections. If he neglects you on finding that his criminal designs cannot succeed, he certainly does not deserve your love, and the consciousness of having raised yourself in his opinion and forced him to esteem you, together with the pleasure of reflecting that you have acted as you ought, will afford you consolation.'

These arguments had due weight with Lady Mary; she determined to follow her friend's advice and submit to the consequences. Lady Sheerness had company that evening and among the rest Lord Robert. He was, as usual, assiduous in his addresses to Lady Mary who, withdrawing to a little distance from the company, told him, that she had too long suffered his lordship to continue a courtship, which he had plainly acknowledged was made with such views as gave her great reason to blame herself for ever having listened to it. She acknowledged that the levity of her conduct had been such as lessened her right to reproach him. Encouraged by her errors, and presuming perhaps on a supposition that he was not unpleasing to her, he had ventured to insult her in a flagrant manner; but without complaining of what was past, she thought herself obliged to tell him his pursuit was in vain; that the errors in her conduct were the fault of education; nor might she so soon have been convinced of them if his behaviour had not awakened her to a sense of some impropriety in her own conduct, which, conscious of the innocence of her intentions, she had never suspected: she then told him that if he did not entirely desist from all addresses to her she should be obliged to acquaint her aunt with his behaviour, who could not suffer such an insult on her niece to pass unresented.

As soon as she had thus explained herself to Lord Robert, she mingled with the crowd, though with a mind little inclined to join in their conversation; but her young friend was there and endeavoured to support her spirits, which were overcome by the effort she had made. This young lady soon after went into the country and returned no more to London.

Lord Robert was so disconcerted that he left the room as soon as Lady Mary had thus given him his dismissal. As their acquaintance lay much in the same set, they frequently saw each other. Lord Robert endeavoured to conquer Lady Mary's resolution by sometimes exciting her jealousy and at others making her the object of his addresses; but she continued steady in her conduct, though with many secret pangs. He began at last to converse with her with greater ease to himself as his passion abated when no longer nourished by hope; and notwithstanding a remainder of pique, he could not forbear treating her with a respect which her conduct deserved; for he plainly saw she had acted in contradiction to her own heart. This alteration in his behaviour afforded her great satisfaction; and though her love was not extinguished, it ceased to be very painful when she was persuaded she had obtained some share of his esteem.

When Lady Mary was in her twentieth year, Lady Sheerness was seized with a lingering, but incurable disorder. It made little alteration in her mind. In this melancholy situation she applied to cards and company to keep up her spirits as assiduously as she had done during her better health. She was incapable indeed of going so much abroad, but her acquaintance, who still found her house agreeable, applauded their charity in attending her at home. Cards even employed the morning, for fear any intermission of visitors should leave her a moment's time for reflection. In this manner she passed the short remainder of her life, without one thought of that which was to come. Her acquaintance, for I cannot call them as they did themselves, friends, were particularly careful to avoid every subject that might remind her of death. At night she procured sleep by laudanum; and from the time she rose, she took care not to have leisure to think; even at meals she constantly engaged company, lest her niece's conversation should not prove sufficient to dissipate her thoughts. Every quack who proposed curing what was incurable was applied to, and she was buoyed up with successive hopes of approaching relief.

She grew at last so weak that, unable even to perform her part at the card-table, Lady Mary was obliged to deal, hold her cards and sort them for her, while she could just take them out one by one and drop them on the table. Whist and quadrille became too laborious to her weakened intellects, but loo supplied their places and continued her amusement to the last, as reason or memory were not necessary qualifications to play at it.

Her acquaintances she found at length began to absent themselves, but she re-animated their charity by making frequent entertainments for them, and was reduced to order genteel suppers to enliven the evening, when she herself was obliged to retire to her bed. Though it was for a considerable time doubtful whether she should live till morning, it was no damp to the spirits of any of the company from which she had withdrawn, except to Lady Mary, who, with an aching heart, was obliged to preside every evening at the table, and to share their unfeeling mirth, till two or three o'clock in the morning.

She was greatly afflicted with the thought of her aunt's approaching death, whose indulgence to her, however blameable, had made a deep impression on her heart; as this gave a more serious turn to her mind, she could not see Lady Sheerness's great insensibility to what must happen after death without much concern. The great care that was taken to rob her of leisure to reflect on matters of such high importance shocked her extremely; and she was disgusted with the behaviour of those she called her friends, who she plainly perceived would have fallen into total neglect of her had she not found means to render her house more amusing to them than any into which they could enter. She now saw that friendship existed not without esteem; and that pleasurable connections would break at the time they were most wanted.

This course of life continued, till one evening Lady Sheerness was seized with a fainting fit at the card-table; and being carried to her bed, in half an hour departed to a world of which she had never thought and for which she was totally unprepared.

As Lady Mary was not able to return to the company, they in decency, not in affliction, retired.

Having long expected this event, her grief was greater than her surprise. She sent for the gentleman who she knew was her aunt's executor, that her will might be opened and necessary directions given for the funeral. Lady Mary had no doubt of succeeding to an easy fortune, and when the will was read it confirmed her in that supposition by appointing her sole heiress. But the executor told her he feared she would find no inheritance. The will was made on her first coming to Lady Sheerness, when there was some remains of the money her lord had left her; but he was well convinced it had since been not only entirely expended, but considerable debts incurred.

This account was soon proved true by the demands of numerous creditors. Lady Mary gave up all her aunt's effects, which fell short of the debts, and remained herself in the same destitute condition from which Lady Sheerness had rescued her. This was a very severe shock; she had seen sufficient proof of the little real friendship to be found in such fashionable connections as she had been engaged in, to know that she had nothing to hope from any of her acquaintance. Her father had been at variance with most of his relations, and Lady Sheerness had kept up the quarrel. She had therefore little expectation of assistance from them in the only wish she could form, which was to obtain a pension from the government, whereto her rank seemed to entitle her. She saw no resource but in the pride of some insolent woman who would like to have a person of her quality dependent on her; a prospect far worse than death. Or possibly, good-nature might procure her a reception among some of her acquaintance; but as she had nothing even to answer her personal expenses, how soon would they grow weary of so chargeable a visitor?

While she was oppressed with these reflections, and had nothing before her eyes but the gloomy prospect of extreme distress, she received a message from Lady Brumpton, who waited in her equipage at the door, desiring to be admitted to see her, for Lady Mary had given a general order to be denied, being unfit to see company, and unwilling to be exposed to the insulting condolence of many whose envy at the splendour in which she had lived and the more than common regard that had usually been shewn her, would have come merely to enjoy the triumph they felt on her present humiliation.

Lady Brumpton was widow to Lady Mary's half-brother. She had been a private gentlewoman of good family but small fortune, by marrying whom her lord had given such offence to his father that he would never after admit him to his presence. Lady Sheerness had shewn the same resentment and there no longer subsisted any communication between the families. Lord Brumpton had been dead about three years and left no children.

His widow was still a fine woman. She was by nature generous and humane, her temper perfectly good, her understanding admirable. She had been educated with great care, was very accomplished, had read a great deal and with excellent taste; she had great quickness of parts and a very uncommon share of wit. Her beauty first gained her much admiration; but when she was better known, the charms of her understanding seemed to eclipse those of her person. Her conversation was generally courted, her wit and learning were the perpetual subjects of panegyric in verse and prose, which unhappily served to increase her only failing, vanity. She sought to be admired for various merits. To recommend her person she studied dress and went to considerable expense in ornaments. To shew her taste, she distinguished herself by the elegance of her house, furniture and equipage. To prove her fondness for literature, she collected a considerable library; and to shew that all her esteem was not engrossed by the learned dead, she caressed all living geniuses; all were welcome to her house, from the ragged philosopher to the rhyming peer; but while she only exchanged adulation with the latter, she generously relieved the necessities of the former. She aimed at making her house a little academy; all the arts and sciences were there discussed, and none dared to enter who did not think themselves qualified to shine and partake of the lustre which was diffused round this assembly.

Though encircled by science and flattery, Lady Mary's distress reached Lady Brumpton's ears and brought her to that young lady's door, who was surprised at the unexpected visit, but could not refuse her admittance. Lady Brumpton began by apologizing for her intrusion but excused herself on the great desire she had of being acquainted with so near a relation of her lord's, who, as she was too young to have any share in the unhappy divisions in the family, she was persuaded was free from those ill-grounded resentments which the malice and impertinence of tale-bearers are always watchful to improve; and when she considered herself as the first occasion of the quarrel, she thought it her duty, in regard to her deceased lord's memory, to offer that protection his sister might justly demand from her, and which her youth rendered necessary.

Lady Mary was charmed with the politeness of Lady Brumpton's address, but still more with the generosity of her behaviour in seeking her out, at a time when so many were diligent to avoid her. The acknowledgements she made for the favour done her spoke as much in her recommendation as her person. Lady Brumpton after some conversation told her she had a request to make to which she could not well suffer a denial; this was no other than that she would leave that melancholy house and make hers the place of her fixed abode; for as, by Lord Brumpton's will, he had bequeathed her his whole fortune, she should not enjoy it with peace of mind if his sister did not share in the possession.

This very agreeable invitation filled Lady Mary with joy and surprise. She made a proper return to Lady Brumpton for her generosity and they agreed that Lady Mary should remove to her house the next day.

When Lady Mary was left alone to reflect on this unexpected piece of good fortune, and considered the distress she had been in but two hours before, and from which she was now so happily delivered; when she reflected on the many calamities wherewith from her childhood she had been threatened and by what various means she had been saved so often from ruin, she could not forbear thinking that she was indeed the care of that Being who had hitherto employed so little of her thoughts. Such frequent mercies as she had received, sometimes in being preserved from the fatal consequences of her own follies, at others from the unavoidable distresses to which she had been exposed, awakened in her mind a lively gratitude to the supreme Disposer of all human events. The poor consolations to which her aunt had been reduced in the melancholy conclusion of her life shewed her that happiness did not consist in dissipation, nor in tumultuous pleasures, and could alone be found in something which every age and every condition might enjoy. Reason seemed this source of perpetual content and she fancied that alone would afford a satisfaction suitable to every state of mind and body. Some degree of religion she imagined necessary, and that to perform the duties it required was requisite to our peace. But the extent of true religion she had never considered, though her great good fortune told her that she ought to be thankful for the blessings conferred and not distrust the care of providence, of which she had received such signal proofs.

She had often heard Lady Brumpton ridiculed under the appellation of a genius and a learned lady; but when she recollected who those persons were, no other than the open professors of folly, it did not prejudice that lady in her opinion, but rather raised her expectation of being introduced into a superior race of beings for whose conversation she knew herself unqualified, but from whom she hoped for some improvement to her understanding, too long neglected.

In this disposition of mind Lady Brumpton found her at the hour that she had appointed to fetch her. They went directly into Lady Brumpton's dressing room, who presented Lady Mary with a settlement she had prepared of a hundred pounds a year which she begged her to accept for her clothes and desired that whenever she found it insufficient she would draw on her for more: she at the same time made her the first payment.

Lady Mary, now entered into a new set of company, frequently found herself entirely at a loss; for she was so totally unacquainted with the subjects of their discourse that she understood them almost as little as if they had talked another language; she told Lady Brumpton how much she was concerned at her own ignorance and begged she would give her some directions what she should read. That lady, whose chief aim was to shine, recommended to her the things most likely to fall into conversation, that she might be qualified to bear her part in it. Lady Mary took her advice and read some moral essays, just published; then a new play; after that the history of one short period; and ended with a volume of sermons then much in fashion. When she began to examine what she had acquired by her studies, she found such a confusion in her memory, where a historical anecdote was crowded by a moral sentiment and a scrap of a play interwoven into a sermon, that she determined to discontinue that miscellaneous reading and begin a regular and improving course, leaving to others the privilege of sitting in judgement on every new production.

In this situation Lady Mary continued some years, without any mortification, except what she felt from seeing the consequences of Lady Brumpton's too great vanity. It led her into expenses, which though they did not considerably impair her fortune, yet so far straitened it that she frequently had not power to indulge the generosity of her mind where it would have done her honour and have yielded her solid satisfaction. The adulation which she received with too much visible complacency inspired her with such an opinion of herself as led her to despise those of less shining qualities, and not to treat any with proper civility whom she had not some particular desire to please, which often gave severe pangs to bashful merit, and called her real superiority in question; for those who observed so great a weakness were tempted to believe her understanding rather glittering than solid. The desire of attracting to her house every person who had gained a reputation for genius occasioned many to be admitted whose acquaintance were a disgrace to her, and who artfully taking advantage of her weakness by excess of flattery found means of imposing on her to any degree they pleased.

The turn of conversation at her house was ridiculed in every other company by people who appeared most desirous of being in her parties. And indeed it was capable of being so; the extreme endeavour to shine took off from that ease in conversation which is its greatest charm. Every person was like a bent bow, ready to shoot forth an arrow which had no sooner darted to the other side of the room, than it fell to the ground and the next person picked it up and made a new shot with it. Like the brisk lightning in the Rehearsal, they gave flash for flash; and they were continually striving whose wit should go off with the greatest report. Lady Mary, who had naturally a great deal of vivacity and a sufficient share of wit, made no bad figure in the brilliant assembly; for though she perceived an absurdity in these mock skirmishes of genius, yet she thought proper to conform to her company; but saw plainly that a sprightly look and lively elocution made the chief merit of the best *bons mots* that were uttered among them.

After she had spent about five years with Lady Brumpton, this lady was seized with a nervous fever which all the art of her physicians could not entirely conquer. Her spirits were extremely affected and her friends decreased in their attentions as her vivacity decayed. She had indeed always been superior to her company in every requisite to please and entertain, therefore when she could not bear her part the conversations flagged; they dwindled from something like wit into oddity and then sunk into dullness. She was no longer equally qualified to please or to be pleased; her mind was not at unison with shallow jesters and therefore they could make no harmony.

Her disorder wore her extremely and turned to an atrophy. In that gradual decay she often told Lady Mary she was awakened from a dream of vanity; she saw how much a desire to gain the applause of a few people had made her forget the more necessary aim of obtaining the approbation of her Creator. She had indeed no criminal actions to lay to her charge; but how should she? Vanity preserved her from doing anything which she imagined would expose her to censure. She had done some things commendable, but she feared the desire of being commended was part of her motive. The humility and calmness of a true Christian disposition had appeared to her meanness of spirit or affectation, and a religious life as the extremest dullness; but now too late she saw her error, and was sensible she had never been in the path of happiness. She had not erred from want of knowledge, but from the strong impulse of vanity which led her to neglect it; but sickness, by lowering her spirits, had taken away the false glare which dazzled her eyes, and restored her to her sight.

Lady Brumpton was sensible of her approaching death some weeks before she expired, and was perfectly resigned. Lady Mary had a second time the melancholy office of closing the eyes of a benefactress and relation whom she sincerely loved. Lady Brumpton, to remove from her any anxiety on her own account, acquainted her, as soon as her disease became desperate, that she had bequeathed her ten thousand pounds, and all her plate and jewels.

Lady Mary found this information true, and received the sum. She was tenderly concerned for the loss of so good a friend; and by the various circumstances of her life and the many blessings bestowed on her, had a heart so touched with the greatness of divine mercy that her mind took a more serious turn than common; and tired of the multitude in which she had so long lived, she was seeking for a retirement when she met Mrs Morgan and Miss Mancel at Tunbridge; and as I have already told you, came hither with them.

Mrs Maynard was not a little wearied with so long a narrative, and therefore did not continue much longer with us; but Lamont and I remained in the park till dinner.

In the afternoon the ladies proposed we should go upon the

water, a scheme very agreeable to us all; some of the inhabitants of the other community were of the party. We got into a very neat boat, of a size sufficient to contain a large company, and which was rowed by the servants of the family. We went about three miles up the river, with great pleasure, and landed just by a neat house where we understood we were to drink tea. The mistress of it received us with great joy and told the ladies she had longed to see them, their young folks having quite finished her house, which she begged leave to shew us. Its extreme neatness rendered it an object worthy of observation; and I was particularly attentive as, its size suiting my plan of life, I determined to copy it.

The rooms were neither large nor numerous, but most of them hung with paper and prettily adorned. There were several very good drawings framed with shells, elegantly put together; and a couple of cabinets designed for use, but they became ornamental by being painted and seaweeds stuck thereon, which by their variety and the happy disposition of them rendered the doors and each of the drawers a distinct landscape. Many other little pieces of furniture were by the same art made very pretty and curious. I learnt in a whisper from Mrs Maynard that this gentlewoman was widow to the late minister of the parish and was left at his death with five small children in very bad circumstances. The ladies of Millenium Hall immediately raised her drooping spirits, settled an income upon her, took this house, furnished it and lent her some of their girls to assist in making up the furniture, and decorating it, according to the good woman's taste. She carried us into her little garden that was neat to an excess and filled with flowers, which we found some of her children tying up and putting in order while the younger were playing about, all dressed with the same exact neatness as herself.

When we had performed this little progress we found tea ready, and spent the afternoon with greater pleasure, for observing the high gratification which this visit seemed to afford the mistress of the house. In the room where we sat was a bookcase well stocked; my curiosity was great to see what it contained, and one of the ladies to whom I mentioned it indulged me by opening it herself and looking at some of the books. I found they consisted of some excellent treatises of divinity, several little things published for the use of children and calculated to instil piety and knowledge into their infant minds, with a collection of our best periodical papers for the amusement of lighter hours. Most of these books, I found, were Miss Mancel's presents.

The fineness of the evening made our return very delightful, and we had time for a little concert before supper.

The next morning I called up Lamont very early and reminded the housekeeper of her promise of shewing us the schools; which she readily performing, conducted us first to a very large cottage or rather five or six cottages laid together. Here we found about fifty girls, clad in a very neat uniform and perfectly clean, already seated at their respective businesses. Some writing, others casting accounts, some learning lessons by heart, several employed in various sorts of needlework, a few spinning and others knitting, with two schoolmistresses to inspect them. The schoolroom was very large and perfectly clean, the forms and chairs they sat on were of wood as white as possible; on shelves were wooden bowls and trenchers equally white, and shining pewter and brass seemed the ornaments of one side of the room; while pieces of the children's work of various kinds decorated the other; little samples of their performances being thus exhibited as encouragement to their ingenuity.

I asked many questions as to their education and learnt that they are bred up in the strictest piety; the ladies by various schemes and many little compositions of their own endeavour to inculcate the purest principles in their tender minds. They all by turns exercise themselves in the several employments which we saw going forward, that they may have various means of gaining their subsistence in case any accident should deprive them of the power of pursuing any particular part of their business. The ladies watch their geniuses with great care; and breed them up to those things which seem most suitable to the turn of their minds. When any are designed for service, they are taught the business of the place they are best fitted for by coming down to the hall and performing the necessary offices under the direction of the excellent servants there.

A very large kitchen garden belongs to the house, which is divided into as many parts as there are scholars; to weed and keep this in order is made their principal recreation; and by the notice taken of it they are taught to vie with each other which shall best acquit themselves, so that perhaps never was a garden so neat. They likewise have no small share in keeping those at the hall in order; and the grotto and seats are chiefly their workmanship.

I gave them due praise upon their performances at the clergyman's widow's, and delighted two of them very much by my admiration of a little arbour which they had there planted with woodbines and other sweet shrubs. In their own garden they are allowed the indulgence of any little whim which takes not up too much room; and it is pretty to see their little seats, their arbours and beds of flowers, according to their several tastes. As soon as school breaks up, they run with as much eagerness and joy to their garden, as other children do to their childish sports; and their highest pleasure is the approbation their patronesses give their performances. They likewise take it by turns to do the business of the house and emulation excites them to a cleanliness which could not by any other means be preserved.

From this school we went to one instituted for boys, which consisted of about half the number, and most of them small, as they are dismissed to labour as soon as they are able to perform any work, except incapacitated by ill health. This is instituted on much the same principles as the other, and every boy of five years old has his little spade and rake which he is taught to exercise.

We returned from our little tour in time enough for prayers, with minds well prepared for them, by the view of such noble fruits of real piety. Indeed the steward who reads them does it with such extreme propriety and such humble and sincere devotion as is alone sufficient to fix the attention and warm the hearts of his hearers.

After breakfast was over, we got Mrs Maynard to accompany us into the garden, she in complaisance to us abstaining while we were at the hall from her share in the daily visits the ladies pay to their several institutions, and to the poor and sick in their village. Their employments are great, but their days are proportionable; for they are always up by five o'clock, and by their example the people in the village rise equally early; at that hour one sees them all engaged in their several businesses with an assiduity which in other places is not awakened till much later.

I called on Mrs Maynard to continue her task, which without any previous ceremony she did as follows.

THE
HISTORY
OF
Miss SELVYN

Mr Selvyn, the younger brother of an ancient family, whose fortune was inferior to the rank it held in the country where it had long been fixed, was placed in trade in London; but his success not answering his hopes, he gave it up before it was too late to secure himself a small subsistence and retired into the country when Miss Selvyn was about five years old. His wife had been dead two years; thus his little girl's education devolved entirely on himself.

He bred her up genteelly, though his fortune was small, and as he was well qualified for the part became himself her tutor and executed that office so well that at twelve years old she excelled all the young ladies in the neighbourhood of her own age in French and writing, either for hand or style; and in the great propriety and grace with which she read English. She had no small knowledge of accounts and had made some progress in the study of history. Her person was elegant and pleasing and her temper and manner perfectly engaging; but yet these charms could not induce the neighbouring families to forgive her for excelling other girls in her accomplishments.

They censured Mr Selvyn for giving his daughter an education to which her fortune was so little suited, and thought he would have done better to have bred her up to housewifery and qualified her for the wife of an honest tradesman; for part of what he had was known to be a life income; a small sinecure having been procured him by his friends in town before he retired into the country.

The censures of those who love to shew their own wisdom by blaming others had little effect on Mr Selvyn; he continued his diligence in cultivating his little girl's mind; and even taught himself many things that he might be able to instruct her. If he did not breed her up in a manner to gain a subsistence by the most usual means, he however qualified her to subsist on little; he taught her true frugality without narrowness of mind, and made her see how few of all the expenses the world ran into were necessary to happiness. He deprived her of all temptation to purchase pleasures, by instructing her to seek only in herself for them; and by the various accomplishments he had given her, prevented that vanity of mind which leads people to seek external amusements. The day was not sufficient for her employments, therefore she could not be reduced to trifle away any part of it for fear of its lying heavy on her hands.

Thus Miss Selvyn was bred a philosopher from her cradle; but was better instructed in the doctrine of the ancient moralists than in the principles of Christianity. Mr Selvyn was not absolutely a free-thinker; he had no vices that made him an enemy to Christianity, nor that pride which tempts people to contradict a religion generally received; he did not apprehend that disbelief was a proof of wisdom, nor wished to lessen the faith of others, but was in himself sceptical; he doubted of what he could not entirely comprehend and seemed to think those things at least improbable which were not level to his understanding. He avoided the subject with Miss Selvyn; he could not teach her what he did not believe, but chose to leave her free to form that judgement which should in time seem most rational to her.

I could not forbear interrupting Mrs Maynard to signify my approbation of Mr Selvyn's conduct in this particular as the only instance I had ever met with of a candid mind in one who had a tendency towards infidelity; for 'I never knew any who were not angry with those that believed more than themselves, and who were not more eager to bring others over to their opinions than most foreign missionaries; yet surely nothing can be more absurd, for these men will not dare to say that the virtues which Christianity requires are not indispensable duties; on the contrary, they would have us imagine they are most sincerely attached to them; what advantage then can accrue to any one, from being deprived of the certainty of a reward for his obedience? If we deny revelation, we must acknowledge this point to be very uncertain; it was the subject of dispute and doubt among all the philosophers of antiquity; and we have but a poor dependence for so great a blessing if we rest our expectation where they did theirs. Can a man therefore be rendered happier by being deprived of this certainty? Or can we suppose he will be more virtuous, because we have removed all the motives that arise from hope and fear? And yet, what else can excuse an infidel's desire to make converts? Nothing. Nor can any thing occasion it but a secret consciousness that he is in the wrong, which tempts him to wish for the countenance of more associates in his error; this likewise can alone give rise to his rancour against those who believe more than himself; he feels them a tacit reproach to him, which to his pride is insupportable.'

'But,' said Lamont, 'do you imagine that a free-thinker may not be certain of a future state?'

'Not positively,' answered Mrs Maynard. 'If he is certain of that point, he is a believer without owning it; he must have had his certainty from Scripture; all the reason he boasts can only shew it probable, and that probability is loaded with so many difficulties as will much weaken hope. Where can reason say immortality shall stop? We must allow that Omnipotence may bestow it on such ranks of being as he pleases. But how can reason tell us to whom he has given it? Whether to all creation, or no part of it? Pride indeed makes man claim it for himself, but deny it to others; and yet the superior intelligence perceivable in some brutes, to what appears in some of his own species, should raise doubts in him who has nothing but the reasonings of his own weak brain to go upon. But to proceed with my subject.'

The minister of the parish wherein Mr Selvyn dwelt was a gentleman of great learning and strict probity. He had every virtue in the most amiable degree, and a gentleness and humility of mind which is the most agreeable characteristic of his profession. He had a strong sense of the duties of his function and dedicated his whole time to the performance of them. He did not think his instructions should be confined to the pulpit; but sensible that the ignorant were much more effectually taught in familiar conversation than by preaching, he visited frequently the very poorest of his parishioners; and by the humility of his behaviour as much as by his bounty (for he distributed a great part of his income among the necessitous) he gained the affections of the people so entirely that his advice was all-powerful with them.

This gentleman's great recreation was visiting Mr Selvyn, whose sense and knowledge rendered his conversation extremely entertaining, and Miss Selvyn's company was a great addition to the good minister's pleasure; he took delight in seeing her, as Hamlet says, 'bear her faculties so meekly'. She was entirely void of conceit and vanity, and did not seem to have found out that her knowledge exceeded 'that of most persons of her age, at least she looked upon it as a casual advantage which reflected no honour to herself but was entirely owing to Mr Selvyn. Her youthful cheerfulness enlivened the party without rendering the conversation less solid; and her amiable disposition made the good minister particularly anxious for her welfare.

He soon found out Mr Selvyn's scepticism and endeavoured to remove it. He represented to him that his not being able to understand the most mysterious parts of Christianity was no argument against the truth of them. That there were many things in nature whose certainty he by no means doubted, and yet was totally ignorant of the methods whereby many of them operated, and even of the use of some of them. Could he say what purpose the fiery comet answers? How is its motion produced, so regular in its period, so unequal in its motion, and so eccentric in its course? Of many other things man is in reality as ignorant, only being able to form a system which seems to suit in some particulars, he imagines he has discovered the whole, and will think so till some new system takes place, and the old one is exploded. He asked Mr Selvyn if they descended to the meanest objects in what manner could they account for the polypus's property of supplying that part of its body which shall be cut away? That insect alone, of all the creation, does not continue maimed by amputation, but multiplies by it. 'To what can we attribute this difference in an insect, which in all particulars beside, resembles so many others? Yet who doubts of the reality of these things? If we cannot comprehend the smallest works of almighty wisdom, can we expect to fathom that wisdom itself? And say that such things he cannot do, or cannot choose because the same effects could be produced by other means? Man no doubt might exert the same functions under another form, why then has he this he now wears? Who will not reply, because his Maker chose it, and chose it as seeing it best. Is not this the proper answer on all occasions, when the decrees of the Almighty are discussed? Facts only are obvious to our reason; we must judge of them by the evidence of their reality if that is sufficient to establish the facts; why, or how they were produced, is beyond our comprehension. Let us learn that finite minds cannot judge of infinite wisdom, and confine our reason within its proper sphere.' By these, and many other arguments, Mr Selvyn was brought to believe the possibility of what he did not comprehend; and by this worthy clergyman's care Miss Selvyn was early taught the truths of Christianity, which though the most necessary of all things, was at first the only one neglected.

In this retired situation they continued till Miss Selvyn was near seventeen years old; Mr Selvyn then determined to remove to London; and taking a small house in Park Street, fixed his abode there. Lady Emilia Reynolds lived next door and soon after their arrival made them a visit, a compliment she said, she looked upon as due to so near a neighbour. Some other ladies in the same street followed her example, and in a very short time Miss Selvyn was introduced into as large an acquaintance as was agreeable to her, for she was naturally averse to much dissipation.

Lady Emilia Reynolds was a single lady of very large fortune, her age upwards of thirty, her person fine, her manner gentle and pleasing, and an air of dejection did not render her countenance the less engaging. She was grave and sensible, and kept a great deal of good company, without entering into a gay way of life. Miss Selvyn's modesty and good sense seemed to have great charms for her; she cultivated a friendship with her, notwithstanding some disparity in their ages; and neither of them appeared so happy as when they were together.

Mr Selvyn could not be displeased at an intimacy so desirable; nor could Miss Selvyn be more properly introduced into the world than by a person of Lady Emilia's respectable character.

At her house Miss Selvyn saw a great deal of good company, and was so generally liked that many intreated Lady Emilia to bring her to them whenever her ladyship favoured them with a visit. These invitations were generally complied with, as under such a protectress Miss Selvyn might properly venture to any place. Lady Sheerness was one of this number, whose rank, and some degree of relationship, brought acquainted with Lady Emilia, though the different turn of their minds and their very opposite taste of life prevented any intimacy between them. Lady Emilia was not blind to Lady Sheerness's follies, but she esteemed them objects of her compassion, not of her censure; nicely circumspect in her own conduct, she judged with the extremest lenity of the behaviour of others, ready to attempt excusing them to the world, and not even suffering herself to blame what she could not approve; she sincerely pitied Lady Mary Jones, who seemed by fortune sacrificed to folly; and she was in continual fear lest she should fall a victim to that imprudence which in her case was almost unavoidable.

By this means Miss Selvyn became acquainted with Lady Mary and was the young woman I before mentioned as Lady Mary's adviser and conductor, in putting an end to Lord Robert St George's courtship.

Not long after she had the satisfaction of thus assisting a young lady whose failings gave her almost as many charms as they robbed her of, she had the misfortune to lose Mr Selvyn. All that a child could feel for the loss of a tender parent Miss Selvyn suffered. His death was not so sudden, but that it afforded him time to settle his affairs, and to give every direction to Miss Selvyn which he thought might save her from all embarrassment on the approaching event. He recommended to her, as her fortune would be but small, to attach herself as much as possible to Lady Emilia, since she now became still more necessary as a protectress, than she had before been desirable as a friend, and that interest as much as gratitude required her cultivating the affection that lady had already shewn her.

The latter motive was sufficient to influence Miss Selvyn, whose heart sincerely returned the regard Lady Emilia had for her; but at that time she was too much affected with Mr Selvyn's approaching dissolution to think of anything else. His care for her in his last moments still more endeared him who through life had made her happiness his principal study. Her affliction was extreme, nor could Lady Emilia by the tenderest care for some time afford her any consolation.

Miss Selvyn found herself heiress to three thousand pounds, a fortune which exceeded her expectation, though it was not sufficient to suffer her to live in London with convenience. Lady Emilia invited her to her house; and as the spring advanced, her ladyship inclining to pass the fine season in the country, hired a house about a hundred miles from London which she had formerly been fond of and was but just become empty. She had been but little out of town for some years and went to her new habitation with pleasure. Miss Selvyn bid adieu without regret to every thing but Lady Mary Jones, for whom she had conceived a real affection, which first took its rise from compassion and was strengthened by the great docility with which she followed her advice about Lord Robert, and the resolution with which she conquered her inclination. Lady Mary grieved to lose one whom she esteemed so prudent and faithful a friend, and considered her departure as a real misfortune; but they agreed to keep up a regular correspondence as the best substitute to conversation.

The country was perfectly agreeable to Lady Emilia and her young friend. The life they led was most suitable to their inclinations, and winter brought with it no desires to return to London; whereupon Lady Emilia disposed of her house there and settled quite in the country. They were both extremely fond of reading, and in this they spent most of their time. Their regular way of life, and the benefits of air and exercise, seemed to abate the dejection before so visible in Lady Emilia; and she never appeared to want any other conversation than that of Miss Selvyn, whom she loved with a tenderness so justly due to her merit.

After they had been settled about two years in the country, Lord Robert St George, who was colonel of a regiment quartered in a town not far from them, came to examine into the state of his regiment; and having at that time no other engagement, and the lodgings he had taken just out of the town being finely situated, he determined to make some stay there. Here he renewed his slight acquaintance with Lady Emilia and Miss Selvyn; and by favour of his vicinity saw them often. Lord Robert's heart was too susceptible of soft impressions not to feel the influence of Miss Selvyn's charms. He was strongly captivated by her excellent understanding and engaging manner; as for her person, he had known many more beautiful, though none more pleasing; but the uncommon turn of her mind, her gentleness and sensible modesty, had attractions that were irresistible.

Lord Robert's attachment soon became visible; but Miss Selvyn knew him too well to think his addresses very flattering, and by his behaviour to Lady Mary Jones feared some insulting declaration; but from these apprehensions he soon delivered her. Real affection conquering that assurance which nature had first given and success increased, he had not courage to declare his passion to her, but applied to Lady Emilia to acquaint her friend with his love, and begged her interest in his behalf, fearing that without it Miss Selvyn's reserve would not suffer her to listen to his addresses.

Lady Emilia promised to report all he had said, and accordingly gave Miss Selvyn a circumstantial account of the whole conversation, wherein Lord Robert had laid before her the state of his fortune, which was sufficient for a woman of her prudence; and she added that she did not see how Miss Selvyn could expect to be addressed by a man more eligible, whether she considered his birth, his fortune, or his person and accomplishments.

Miss Selvyn was a little surprised that so gay a man should take so serious a resolution. She allowed the justness of what Lady Emilia said in his favour and confessed that it was impossible Lord Robert could fail of pleasing; but added that it could not be advisable for her to marry: for enjoying perfect content, she had no benefit to expect from change; and happiness was so scarce a commodity in this life that whoever let it once slip, had little reason to expect to catch it again. For what reason then should she alter her state? The same disposition which would render Lord Robert's fortune sufficient made hers answer all her wishes, since if she had not the joy of living with her ladyship, it would still afford her every thing she desired.

Lady Emilia said some things in recommendation of marriage; and seemed to think it improbable Miss Selvyn should not be a little prejudiced in favour of so amiable a lover as Lord Robert, which tempted that young lady to tell her that though she allowed him excessively pleasing, yet by some particulars, which formerly came to her knowledge, she was convinced his principles were such as would not make her happy in a husband.

Lady Emilia allowed the force of such an objection, and did not press a marriage, for which she had pleaded only out of an apprehension lest Miss Selvyn's reserve might lead her to act contrary to her inclinations; and therefore she had endeavoured to facilitate her declaration in favour of Lord Robert, if she was in reality inclined to accept his proposals. She acquiesced then readily in her friend's determination; only desired she would herself acquaint Lord Robert with it, as he would not easily be silenced by a refusal which did not proceed from her own lips.

His lordship came in the evening to learn his fate, and Lady Emilia having contrived to be absent, he found Miss Selvyn alone. Though this was what he had wished, yet he was so disconcerted that Miss Selvyn was reduced to begin the subject herself, and to tell him that Lady Emilia had acquainted her with the honour he had done her, that she was much obliged to him for his good opinion and hoped he would be happy with some woman much more deserving than herself; but she could by no means accept the favour he intended her, being so entirely happy in her present situation that nothing in the world should induce her to change it.

This declaration gave rise to a very warm contest, Lord Robert soliciting her to accept his love with all the tenderness of the strongest passion, and she with equal perseverance persisting in her refusal. He could not be persuaded that her motive for doing so was really what she alleged but as she continued to affirm it, he begged however to know if she had not made so strange a resolution in favour of a single life, whether she should have had any particular objection to him?

Miss Selvyn shewed the uselessness of this question, since the reason of her refusing the honour he intended her would have made her reject the addresses of every other man in the world. Lord Robert could not believe this possible and therefore desisted not from urging a question so disagreeable to answer.

When Miss Selvyn found it impossible to avoid satisfying him in this particular, she told him that if he were entirely unexceptionable, she should be fixed in the same determination; but since he insisted on knowing if she had any objection to him, she was obliged to confess that had she been better inclined to enter into the matrimonial state, his lordship was not the man she should have chosen, not from any dislike to his person or understanding, but from disapprobation of his principles; that, in regard to her sex he had a lightness in his way of thinking and had been so criminal in his conduct that of all men she knew, she thought him most improper for a husband.

Lord Robert was surprised at so new an objection, and told her, that he did not apprehend himself more blamable in those respects than most young men. Gallantry was suitable to his age, and he never imagined that any woman would have reproached him with his regard for her sex, when he gave so strong a proof of an inclination to leave them all for her.

'I am sorry,' replied Miss Selvyn, 'that your lordship thinks me mean enough to take pleasure in such a triumph, or so vain as to imagine I can reform a man of dissolute manners, the last thing I should hope or endeavour to succeed in. Such a tincture or corruption will always remain the mind of what you are pleased to term a gallant man, to whom I should give the less polite appellation of vicious, that I could not be happy in his society. A reformed rake may be sober, but is never virtuous.'

Lord Robert growing very urgent to know what she had particularly to lay to his charge, she told him frankly, that his treatment of Lady Mary Jones had disgusted her, as she, and perhaps she only, had been acquainted with the whole.

Lord Robert endeavoured to excuse himself on the encouragement Lady Mary's levity had given to his hopes; observing that when a woman's behaviour was very light, his sex were not apt to imagine there was any great fund of virtue; nor could it be expected that any one else should guard that honour of which she herself was careless.

'I am sure,' replied Miss Selvyn, 'your lordship's hopes must have been founded on Lady Mary's folly, not her real want of innocence; a folly which arose from the giddiness of youth and the hurry of dissipation; for by nature Lady Mary's understanding is uncommonly good. By what you say, you imagined her honour was lawful prize, because she appeared careless of it;

would this way of arguing be allowed in any other case? If you observed a man who neglected to lock up his money, and seemed totally indifferent what became of it, should you think yourself thereby justified in robbing him? But how much more criminal would you be, were you to deprive him of his wealth because he was either so thoughtless or so weak as not to know its value? And yet surely the injury in this case would be much less than what you think so justifiable. If the world has but the least sense of real honour, in this light they must see it; and to that tribunal I imagine you only think yourself answerable; for did you reflect but one moment on another bar before which you will be summoned, you would see there can be no excuse for violating the laws by which you are there to be tried. If you could justify yourself to the world, or to the women of whose folly you take advantage, by the fallacious arguments which you have so ready for that purpose, such cobweb sophistry cannot weaken the force of an express command.'

'I will not pretend,' answered Lord Robert, 'to deny the truth of what you say, but must beg you will consider it more easy for you to urge these truths, than for those to obey them who are exposed to and susceptible of temptations. When a woman has no title to our respect, how difficult is it to consider her in the light you require! Levity of conduct we are apt to look upon as an invitation, which a man scarcely thinks it consistent with his politeness to neglect.'

'I wish,' replied Miss Selvyn, 'that women were better acquainted with the ways of thinking so common with your sex; for while they are ignorant of them, they act to a great disadvantage. They obtain by that levity which deprives them of your esteem, a degree of notice and pretended liking which they mistake for approbation; did they but know that you in your hearts despise those most to whom you are most assiduously and openly attached, it would occasion a great change in their behaviour; nor would they suffer an address to which they cannot listen without incurring your contempt. How criminally deceitful is this behaviour! And what real virtue can a man truly boast, who acts in this manner? What woman in her senses can enter into a union for life with such a man?'

'Why not, madam?' said Lord Robert. 'My behaviour to you shews that we yield to merit the homage it deserves; you would lose all your triumph were we to put you and the lighter part of your sex on an equality in our opinions. We are always ready to esteem a woman who will give us leave to do so; and can you require us to respect those who are not in the least respectable?'

'No,' answered Miss Selvyn, 'I only wish you would cease your endeavours to render those women objects of contempt, who deserve only to be neglected, and particularly not to deprive them of the very small portion of regard they are entitled to, by the fallacious appearance of an attachment of the tenderest kind; which in reality arises from contempt, not love. But,' added she, 'I have said more than I designed on the subject; I only meant to answer the question you put to me with so much importunity; and must now confirm what I have already declared, by telling you that were I inclined to marry, I would not on any account take a husband of your lordship's principles; but were you endowed with all the virtues that ever man possessed, I would not change my present happy situation for the uncertainties of wedlock.'

When Lord Robert found all his solicitations unavailing, he left the country and returned to London, where he hoped, by a series of diversions, to efface from his heart the real passion he had conceived for Miss Selvyn. She forbore informing Lady Mary Jones, though their correspondence was frequent, of Lord Robert's courtship; she did not doubt but her ladyship was sincere when she assured her she now beheld him with the indifference he deserved, but thought that to tell her she had received so very different an address from him would bear too much the air of a triumph, a meanness which her heart abhorred.

Lady Emilia and Miss Selvyn had lived several years in the country with great rational enjoyment, when the former was seized with a fever. All the skill of her physicians proved ineffectual, and her distemper increased daily. She was sensible of the danger which threatened her life, but insisted on their telling her, if they had any great hopes of her recovery, assuring them that it was of importance to her to know their opinions with the utmost frankness. Thus urged, they confessed they had but little hopes. She then returned them thanks for their care, but still more for their sincerity: and with the greatest composure took leave of them, desiring to be left alone with Miss Selvyn, who was in tears at her bedside. Every one else withdrew, when taking Miss Selvyn in her arms, and shedding a few silent tears, she afterwards thus addressed her.

'At the moment that I must bid you a long farewell, you will know that you have a mother in her whom you before thought only your friend. Yes, my dearest Harriot, I am your mother, ashamed of my weakness and shocked at my guilt, while your gentle but virtuous eyes could reproach your unhappy parent, I could not prevail on myself to discover this secret to you, but I cannot carry to my grave the knowledge of a circumstance which concerns you. Yes, you are my daughter, my child, ever most dear to me, though the evidence and continual remembrancer of my crime.'

Miss Selvyn imagined the distemper had now seized Lady Emilia's brain, which it had hitherto spared; and intreated her to compose herself, assuring her that what so much agitated her decaying frame was only the phantom of an overheated imagination; for her parents were well known, neither was there any mystery in her birth.

'Oh!' interrupted Lady Emilia, 'do not suspect me of delirium; it has pleased the Almighty to spare my senses throughout this severe disorder, with a gracious design of allowing me even the last moments of my life to complete my repentance. What I tell you is but true, Mr Selvyn knew it all and like a man of honour saved me from shame by concealing the fatal secret; and acted the part of a father to my Harriot, without having any share in my guilt. But I see you do not yet believe me; take this,' pulling a paper from under her pillow, 'herein you will find an account of the whole unfortunate affair, written a year ago; lest at the time of my death I should not be able to relate it; this will prove, by the nice connection of every circumstance, that the words therein contained are not the suggestions of madness.'

Miss Selvyn accordingly read as follows:

'When I was seventeen years old, Lord Peyton asked me of my father, but not till after he had secured my tenderest affections. His estate was sufficient to content a parent who was not regardless of fortune and splendour; and his proposals were accepted. But while the tediousness of the lawyers made us wait for the finishing of settlements, Lord Peyton, who was in the army, was commanded to repair immediately to his regiment, then stationed in Ireland. He endeavoured to prevail with my father to hasten our marriage, offering every kind of security he could desire, instead of the settlements so long delayed; my wishes concurred with his, rather than suffer him to go without me into a kingdom which I imagined would not prove very amusing to him. But my father, who was a very exact observer of forms, would not consent to any expedient. No security appeared to him equivalent to settlements; and many trifling circumstances requisite to the splendour of our first appearance were not ready; which to him seemed almost as important as the execution of the marriage writings.

'When Lord Peyton found my father inexorable, he attempted to persuade me to agree to a private marriage; only desiring, he said, to secure me entirely his before he left the kingdom; and proposed, that after his return, we should be publicly married, to prevent my father's suspecting that we had anticipated his consent. But this I rejected; disobedience to a parent, and other objections, were sufficient to make me refuse it; and we saw ourselves reduced to separate when we were so near being united. As Lord Peyton was an accepted lover, and our intended marriage was publicly known, and generally approved, he passed great part of his time with me. My father was obliged to go out of town on particular business, the day before that appointed for Lord Peyton's departure. It is natural to suppose we passed it entirely together. The concern we were both under made us wish to avoid being seen by others, and therefore I was denied to all visitors. Lord Peyton dined and supped with me; and by thus appropriating the day to the ceremony of taking leave, we rendered the approaching separation more afflicting than in reason it ought to have been, and indeed made it a lasting affliction; a grief never to be washed away.

'Lord Peyton left London at the appointed hour, but the next days, and almost every succeeding post, brought me the tenderest expressions of regret for this enforced absence, and the strongest assurances of the constancy of his affection. Mine could not with truth be written in a more indifferent strain, my love was the same, but my purpose was much altered; as soon as I had calmness of mind enough to reflect on what had passed, I resolved never to be Lord Peyton's wife. I saw my own misconduct in all its true colours. I despised myself, and could not hope for more partial treatment from my husband. A lover might in the height of his passion excuse my frailty, but when matrimony, and continued possession had restored him to his reason, I was sensible he must think of me as I was conscious I deserved. What confidence, what esteem could I hope from a husband who so well knew my weakness; or how could I support being hourly exposed to the sight of a man whose eyes would always seem to reproach me! I could scarcely bear to see myself; and I was determined not to depend on any one who was equally conscious of my guilt.

'I soon acquainted Lord Peyton with this resolution, which he combated with every argument love could dictate. He assured me in the most solemn manner of his entire esteem, insisted that he only was to blame, and that he should never forgive himself for the uneasiness he had already occasioned me; but intreated me not to punish him so severely as ever again to give the least intimation of a design not to confirm our marriage. As I resisted my own passion, it may be supposed that, although too late, I was able to resist his. I saw that a generous man must act as he did, but no generosity could restore me to the same place in his esteem I before possessed. His behaviour on this occasion fixed my good opinion of him, but could not restore my opinion of myself. All he could urge therefore was unavailing; the stronger my affection, the more determined I was in my purpose; since the more I valued his esteem, the greater would my suffering be at knowing that I had forfeited it. I acquainted my father with my resolution, alleging the best excuses I could make. He was at first angry with my inconstancy, charged me with capriciousness and want of honour; but at last was pacified by my assuring him I would never marry any man. As he had been sorry to part with me, the thought of my continuing with him as long as he lived, made my peace.

'Lord Peyton's impatience at being detained in Ireland increased with his desire of persuading me to relinquish a design so very grievous to my own heart, as well as to his; but he could not obtain leave to return into England before I found, to my inexpressible terror, that the misfortune I so sincerely lamented would have consequences that I little expected. In the agony of my mind I communicated my distress to Lord Peyton, the only person whom I dared trust with so important a secret.

'Instead of condoling with me on the subject of my affliction, he expressed no small joy in a circumstance which he said must reduce me to accept the only means of preserving my reputation; and added, that as every delay was now of so much importance, if the next packet did not bring him leave of absence, he should set out without it; and rather run the hazard of being called to account for disobedience, than of exposing me to one painful blush.

'I confess his delicacy charmed me; every letter I received increased my esteem and affection for him, but nothing could alter my purpose. I looked upon the execution of it as the only means of reinstating myself in his good opinion, or my own, in comparison of which even reputation seemed to lose its value. But severe was the trial I had to undergo upon his return into England, which was in a few days after his assurance of coming at any hazard. He used every means that the tenderest affection and the nicest honour could suggest to persuade me to marry him; and the conflict in my own heart very near reduced me to my grave; till at length pitying the condition into which I was reduced, without the least approach to a change of purpose, he promised to spare me any further solicitation and to bury his affliction in silence; after obtaining a promise from me that I would suffer him to contrive the means for concealing an event which must soon happen; as my unintriguing spirit made me very incapable of managing it with tolerable art and secrecy.

'Lord Peyton had maintained his former friendship with my father, who thought himself obliged to him for not resenting my behaviour in the manner he imagined it deserved. When the melancholy and much dreaded time approached, Lord Peyton gave me secret information that he would invite my father into the country, on pretence of assisting him by his advice in some alterations he was going to make there; and assured me of careful attendance, and the most secret reception, from a very worthy couple to whose house he gave me a direction if I could contrive, under colour of some intended visit, to leave my own.

'All was executed as he had planned it; and when my servants thought I was gone to visit a relation some miles distant from London, I went as directed, and was received with the greatest humanity imaginable by Mr and Mrs Selvyn; not at their own house, but at one taken for that purpose, where the affair might be more secretly managed. Lord Peyton had concealed my name even from them; and secured their care of me under a borrowed appellation.

'The day after I got to them I was delivered of you, my dearest child, whom I beheld with sorrow as well as affliction; considering you as the melancholy memorial and partner in my shame.

'Mr and Mrs Selvyn attended me with the greatest care, and were never both absent at a time; they acquainted Lord Peyton with the state of my health by every post; and I was enabled, by the necessity of the case, to write to my father as frequently as I usually did when absent from him. Within the fortnight from the time of my departure from my own house I returned to it again, after delivering my dear Harriot into the care of these good people, who promised to treat her as their own child. Under pretence of a cold I confined myself till I was perfectly recovered.

'Lord Peyton detained my father till he heard I was entirely well; and then went with impatience to see his little daughter, over whom he shed many tears, as Mr Selvyn afterwards informed me; telling it that it was a constant memorial of the greatest misfortune of his life, and could never afford him a pleasure that was not mingled with the deepest affliction.

'Mrs Selvyn had lain in about six weeks before I went to her, the child she brought into the world lived but a few months; upon its death, at Lord Peyton's desire, they took you from nurse, and pretending you their own, privately buried their child, who was likewise nursed abroad. Mr Selvyn was a merchant, but had never been successful, his wife died when you were about three years old. Having no children to provide for, and not being fond of trade, he was desirous of retiring into the country. Lord Peyton to facilitate the gratification of his wish, procured him a small sinecure; gave into his possession three thousand pounds, which he secured to you; and allowed him a hundred a year for the trouble of your education; with an unlimited commission to call on him for any sums he should want.

'The constant sense of my guilt, the continual regret at having by my own ill conduct forfeited the happiness which every action of Lord Peyton's proved that his wife might reasonably expect, fixed a degree of melancholy on my mind, which no time has been able to conquer. I lived with my father till his death, which happened not many years ago; at his decease, I found myself mistress of a large fortune, which enabled me to support the rank I had always enjoyed. Though Lord Peyton had provided sufficiently for Mr Selvyn's and your convenience, yet I constantly sent him a yearly present; till no longer able to deny myself the pleasure of seeing my dear child, I prevailed on him to remove to London and to fix in the same street with me, taking care to supply all that was requisite to enable him to appear there genteelly. You know with what appearance of accident I first cultivated a friendship with you, but you cannot imagine with how much difficulty I concealed the tenderness of a mother under the ceremonies of an acquaintance.

'Of late I have enjoyed a more easy state of mind: I have sometimes been inclined to flatter myself that your uncommon merit, and the great comfort I have received in your society, are signs that Heaven has forgiven my offence and accepted my penitence, which has been sincere and long, as an atonement for my crime; in which blessed hope I shall, I trust, meet death without terror, and submit, my dear daughter, whenever I am called hence, in full confidence to that Power whose mercy is over all his works. I ought to add a few words about your dear father, who seemed to think my extreme regular conduct and the punishment I had inflicted on myself, such an extenuation of my weakness that he ever behaved to me with the tenderest respect, I might almost say reverence, and till his death gave me every proof of the purest and the strongest friendship. By consent we avoided each other's presence for three years, by which time we hoped the violence of our mutual passion would be abated. He spent the greatest part of it abroad; and at the end of that period we met with the sincerer joy, from finding we were not deceived in our hopes. Our attachment was settled into the tenderest friendship; we forbore even the mention of your name, as it must have reminded us of our crime; and if Lord Peyton wanted to communicate any thing concerning you, he did it by letter; avoiding with the extremest delicacy ever to take notice that any such letters had passed between us; and even in them he consulted about his child, in the style of a man who was writing to a person that had no other connection with it than what her friendship for him must naturally occasion, in a point where he was interested by the tenderest ties of the most extreme paternal love.

'I have often with pleasure heard you mention his great fondness for you in your childhood, when he visited at your father's; your growing years increased it, though it obliged him to suppress the appearance of an affection which you would have thought improper. I need not tell you that I had the misfortune to lose this worthiest of friends, about half a year before you came to London, which determined me to send for you, that I might receive all the consolation the world could give me, and see the inheritor of her dear father's virtues. While he lived I dared not have taken the same step; your presence would have been too painful a testimony against me, and continually reminded my lord of a weakness which I hope time had almost effaced from his remembrance.'

Miss Selvyn was extremely affected with the perusal of this paper; she was frequently interrupted by her tears; grieved to the heart to think of how much uneasiness she had been the cause. As soon as she had concluded it, she threw herself on her knees at Lady Emilia's bedside, and taking one of her hands, which she bathed with her tears, 'Is it possible then,' said she, 'that I have thus long been ignorant of the best of parents? And must I lose you when so lately found? Oh! my dear mother, how much pleasure have I lost by not knowing that I might call you by that endearing name! What an example of virtue have you set me! How noble your resolution! How uniform and constant your penitence! Blest you must be supremely by him who loveth the contrite heart; and you and my father I doubt not will enjoy eternal felicity together, united never more to part. Oh! may your afflicted daughter be received into the same place, and partake of your happiness; may she behold your piety rewarded, and admire in you the blessed fruits of timely repentance; a repentance so immediately succeeding the offence, that your soul could not have received the black impression!'

'Can you, who have never erred,' said Lady Emilia, 'see my offence in so fair a light? What may I not then hope from infinite mercy? I do hope; it would be criminal to doubt, when such consolatory promises appear in almost every page of holy writ. With pleasure I go where I am called, for I leave my child safe in the Divine Protection, and her own virtue; I leave her, I hope, to a happy life, and a far more happy death; when joys immortal will bless her through all eternity. I have now, my love, discharged the burden from my mind; not many hours of life remain, let me not pass them in caressing my dear daughter, which, though most pleasing to my fond heart, can end only in making me regret the loss of a world which will soon pass from my sight. Let me spend this hour, as I hope to do those that will succeed it through all eternity. Join with me in prayers to, and praises of, him in whom consists all our lasting happiness.'

Miss Selvyn sent for the minister of the parish at Lady Emilia's desire, and the remainder of her life passed in religious exercises. She expired without a groan, in the midst of a fervent prayer, as if her soul was impatient to take its flight into the presence of him whom she was addressing with so much ardour.

Miss Selvyn's affliction was at first extreme, but when she reflected on her mother's well-spent life, and most happy death, it much abated the excess of her grief. By that lady's will, she found herself heir to twelve thousand pounds, and all her personal estate. She had been charmed with the account Lady Mary Jones had sent her of this society, and wished to increase her acquaintance with that lady, and therefore offered, if proper, to make her a short visit, as soon as her necessary affairs were settled. This met with the most welcome reception, and she came hither as a visitor. Her stay was gradually prolonged for near two months; when having reason, from the great regard shewn her, to think she should be no disagreeable addition, she asked leave to join her fortune to the common stock, and to fix entirely with them. Nothing could be more agreeable to the other three ladies than this offer, and with extreme satisfaction she settled here.

Upon this increase of income it was that my friends established the community of indigent gentlewomen, which gave you so much pleasure.

Lamont was much struck with the conduct of Lady Emilia; she had shewn, he said, a degree of delicacy and prudence which exceeded what he had a notion of; he never met with a woman who foresaw the little chance she had for happiness in marrying a man who could have no inducement to make her his wife but a nice, often a too nice, sense of honour; and who certainly could have no great opinion of her virtue. The folly of both men and women in these late unions was the subject of our conversation till we separated. In the afternoon the ladies asked us to accompany them to the house they had just taken for the new community, to which they were obliged to go that day, as they had set several persons to work there. They keep a post-coach and post-chaise, which with the help of ours, were sufficient to accommodate us all. A short time brought us to the house, a very old and formerly a very fine mansion, but now much fallen to decay. The outside is greatly out of repair, but the building seems strong. The inside is in a manner totally unfurnished; for though it is not empty, yet the rats and mice have made such considerable depredations on what time had before reduced to a very tattered condition that the melancholy remains can be reckoned little better than lumber.

The last inhabitant of this house we were informed was an old miser whose passion for accumulating wealth reduced him into almost as unfortunate a state as Midas, who, according to the fable, having obtained the long-desired power of turning every thing he touched to gold, was starved by the immediate transmutation of all food into that metal the instant it touched his lips. The late possessor of the house I am speaking of, when he was about fifty years old, turned away every servant but an old woman, who if she was not honest, was at least too weak to be able to put any dishonesty in practice. When he was about threescore, she died, and he never could venture to let any one supply her place. He fortified every door and window with such bars of iron that his house might have resisted the forcible attack of a whole army. Night and day growled before his inhospitable door a furious Dutch mastiff, whose natural ferocity was so increased by continual hunger, for his master fed him most sparingly, that no stranger could have entered the yard with impunity.

Every time this churlish beast barked, the old gentleman, with terror and dismay in his countenance, and quaking limbs, ran to the only window he ever ventured to unbar, to see what danger threatened him; nor could the sight of a barefoot child, or a decrepit old woman, immediately dispel his fears. As timorous as Falstaff, his imagination first multiplied and then clothed them in buckram; and his panic ceased not till they were out of view.

This wretched man upon the death of his only servant, agreed with an old woman to buy food for him, and bring it to the well defended door of his yard; where informing him of her arrival by a signal agreed upon between them, he ventured out of his house to receive it from her; and dressed it himself; till worn out by anxiety of mind he grew too weak to perform that office and ordered the woman to bring it ready prepared; this continued for a little time, till at last he appeared no more at his gate. After the old woman had knocked three days in vain, the neighbourhood began to think it necessary to take some measures thereupon; but not choosing to run the hazard of breaking open the house, they sent to the old gentleman's nephew, whose father had been suffered to languish in extreme poverty many years before his death; nor was the son in much better condition; but he had acquainted some of the neighbours with the place of his abode in hopes of the event which now induced them to send for him.

As soon as he arrived, he prepared to force his way into the house, but it was found so impracticable that at length they were obliged to untile part of the roof, from whence a person descended, and opened the door to those who did not choose so dangerous an entrance as that through which he had passed.

They found the old man dead on a great chest which contained his money, as if he had been desirous to take possession even in death.

His nephew was just of age, and having till then been exposed to all the evils of poverty, was almost distracted with joy at the sudden acquisition of a large fortune. He scarcely could be prevailed with to stay long enough in this house to pay the last duties to an uncle who had no right to anything more from him than just the decent ceremonies; and without giving himself time to look over his estate, hastened to London.

He hired a magnificent house in Grosvenor Square; bespoke the most elegant equipages; bought the finest set of horses he could hear of at double their real value; and launched into every expense the town afforded him. He soon became one of the most constant frequenters of Whites; kept several running horses; distinguished himself at Newmarket, and had the honour of playing deeper, and betting with more spirit, than any other young man of his age. There was not an occurrence in his life about which he had not some wager depending. The wind could not change or a shower fall without his either losing or gaining by it. He had not a dog or cat in his house on whose life he had not bought or sold an annuity. By these ingenious methods in one year was circulated through the kingdom the ready money which his uncle had been half his life starving himself and family to accumulate. The second year obliged him to mortgage great part of his land, and the third saw him reduced to sell a considerable portion of his estate, of which this house and the land belonging to it made a part.

I could not help observing the various fate of this mansion, originally the seat of ancient hospitality; then falling into the hands of a miser who had not spirit to enjoy it, nor sense enough to see that he was impairing so valuable a part of his possessions by grudging the necessary expenses of repairs; from him devolving to a young coxcomb who by neglect let it sink into ruin and was spending in extravagance what he inherited from avarice; as if one vice was to pay the debt to society which the other had incurred; and now it was purchased to be the seat of charity and benevolence. How directly were we led to admire the superior sense, as well as transcendent virtue of these ladies, when we compared the use they made of money with that to which the two late possessors had appropriated it! While we were in doubt which most to blame, he who had heaped it up without comfort, in sordid inhumanity, or he who squandered it in the gratification of gayer vices. Equally strangers to beneficence, self-indulgence was their sole view; alike criminal, though not equally unfashionable, one endeavoured to starve, the other to corrupt mankind; while the new owners of this house had no other view than to convenience and to reform all who came within their influence, themselves enjoying in a supreme degree the happiness they dispersed around them.

It was pleasing to see numbers at work to repair the building and cultivate the garden and to observe that at length from this inhospitable mansion. 'health to himself, and to his children bread, the labourer bears.' Within it were all the biggest schoolgirls, with one of their mistresses to direct them in mending such furniture as was not quite destroyed; and I was pleased to see with how much art they repaired the decays of time, in things which well deserved better care, having once been the richest part of the furniture belonging to the opulent possessors.

On our way home we called at a clergyman's house, which was placed in the finest situation imaginable and where we beheld that profusion of comforts which sense and economy will enable the possessors of narrow fortunes to enjoy. This gentleman and his wife have but a small living and still less paternal estate, but the neatness, prettiness and convenience of their habitation were enough to put one out of humour with riches, and I should certainly have breathed forth Agar's prayer with great ardour if I had not been stopped in the beginning by considering how great a blessing wealth may be when properly employed, of which I had then such hourly proof.

At our return to Millenium Hall we found some of the neighbouring society who were come to share the evening's concert and sup with us.

But at ten o'clock they departed, which I understood was somewhat later than usual, but they conformed to the alteration of hours our arrival had occasioned.

The next day being very hot, we were asked to breakfast in a delightful arbour in the flower garden. The morning dew, which still refreshed the flowers, increased their fragrance to as great an excess of sweetness as the senses could support. Till I went to this house, I knew not half the charms of the country. Few people have the art of making the most of nature's bounty;

these ladies are epicures in rural pleasures and enjoy them in the utmost excess to which they can be carried. All that romance ever represented in the plains of Arcadia are much inferior to the charms of Millenium Hall, except the want of shepherds be judged a deficiency that nothing else can compensate; there indeed they fall short of what romantic writers represent, and have formed a female Arcadia.

After breakfast all the ladies left us except Mrs Maynard. We were so charmed with the spot we were in that we agreed to remain there and I called on my cousin to continue the task she had undertaken, which she did in the following manner.

THE
HISTORY
OF
Miss TRENTHAM

MISS Trentham never knew the blessing of a mother's care, hers died the same month which gave her daughter birth; and Mr Trentham survived his wife but eight years. He left his little girl eleven thousand pounds, recommending both her person and fortune to his mother, Mrs Alworth.

Mrs Alworth was an old lady of good sense and merit. She had felt the most melancholy, but not unusual effect of long life, having outlived all her children. This misfortune she alleviated in the best manner she was able, by receiving her grandchildren into her family. Her son by her second husband left behind him a boy and girl, the former at the time I speak of about eleven years old, the latter ten. Her daughter had married Mr Denham and at her death left two girls. Mr Denham entering into wedlock a second time, very willingly complied with Mrs Alworth's desire of having his two daughters. The eldest of these was twelve years old, the youngest eleven.

These children had lived with the old lady some years, when she took home Harriot Trentham. As their grandmother was rich, there had been a strong contention among them for her favour, and they could not without great disgust see another rival brought to the house. Harriot was extremely handsome and engaging. The natural sweetness of her temper rendered her complying and observant; but having been bred under the care of a sensible and indulgent father, she had never been taught the little arts of behaviour which mothers too commonly inculcate with so much care that children are as void of simplicity at eight as at eight and twenty years old. The first thing a girl is taught is to hide her sentiments, to contradict the thoughts of her heart, and tell all the civil lies which custom has sanctified, with as much affectation and conceit as her mother; and when she has acquired all the folly and impertinence of a riper age, and apes the woman more ungracefully than a monkey does a fine gentleman, the parents congratulate themselves with the extremest complacency on the charming education they have given their daughter.

Harriot had been taught no such lessons. Her father had a strong dislike to prematurity, and feared that communication with the world would too soon teach her art and disguise, the last things he would have chosen to anticipate.

By teaching her humanity, he initiated her into civility of manners. She had learnt that to give pain was immoral; and could no more have borne to have shocked any person's mind than to have racked his body. Any thought therefore that could hurt she suppressed as an indispensable duty, and to please by her actions and not offend by her words was an essential part of the religion in which she was educated: but in every thing whereby no one could suffer she was innocence and simplicity itself; and in her nature shone pure and uncorrupted either by natural or acquired vices.

Mrs Alworth, though fond of all her grandchildren, could not conquer a degree of partiality for Harriot, whose attractions, both personal and mental, were very superior to those of her cousins. Her beauty secured her the particular attention of all strangers, she gained their favour at first sight, and secured it by her amiable disposition when they became more acquainted with her.

Envy is one of the first passions that appears in the human mind. Had Miss Alworth and the Miss Denhams been much younger, Harriot would not have passed unenvied. Every day increased their dislike to her as she grew daily more beloved by others, and they let no opportunity escape of making her feel the effects of their little malice. Their hatred to her produced a union among themselves; for the first time they found something in which they all agreed. They were continually laying little plots to lessen her in their grandmother's opinion; frequent were the accusations against her, but her innocence always triumphed, though it never discouraged them from repeating the same unsuccessful attempts. Mrs Alworth was extremely fond of them all, but yet she saw through their malice and their behaviour only served to endear Harriot the more, who defended herself without anger and retained no rancour in her mind. Free from resentment or suspicion she was ever open to their arts, and experience did not teach her to be on her guard against them, which often occasioned their having appearances on their side, and might have raised prejudices against her in Mrs Alworth's mind had she not found a defender in Master Alworth, who alone of all her cousins was free from envy. He was naturally of an honest and sweet disposition, and being fond of Harriot, for beauty has charms for all ages, felt great indignation at the treatment she received and would often express a resentment from which she was wholly free. Mrs Alworth's great fondness for her grandson and strong prejudices against schools, from a belief that boys acquire there more vice than learning, had determined on a private education. She therefore provided a tutor for him before he was seven years old; a man of learning and sense, with a great deal of religion and good humour and who was very attentive to the employment for which he had been chosen.

Master Alworth, by being thus kept at home, had frequent opportunities of observing the malice of his sister and Miss Denham against Harriot and never failed exposing their practices to his grandmother; who from thence learnt to suspect their reports about things which passed in his absence and consequently could not be cleared up by him. His fondness for Harriot soon made him beloved by her, and as she found little pleasure in the society of her other cousins, she sought his company, but as he was much engaged by his studies she seldom found him at leisure to play. The tutor, greatly delighted with her, tried to awaken in her mind a desire of improvement and found it an easy task; she was inclined to learn and capable of doing it with great quickness. Mrs Alworth readily entered into the good man's views, and was pleased with the eagerness of Harriot's application. Master Alworth was far enough advanced in learning to assist his favourite, and from him she received instruction with double pleasure and more easily comprehended his explanations than those of their tutor, who found it difficult to divest himself sufficiently of scientific terms, which greatly retard the increase of knowledge in a youthful mind.

Thus beloved by her grandmother and Mr Alworth, and hated and traduced by her female cousins, Harriot lived till she was sixteen. Years had still improved her person and she had made considerable progress in learning, when Mrs Alworth judged it proper that her grandson should go abroad to complete an education which she flattered herself was hitherto faultless. He had no objection to the scheme but what arose from his unwillingness to leave Harriot, who saw his departure approach with great concern. She loved and respected her grandmother, but Mr Alworth was the only person whom she could look upon in the tender and equal light of a friend. To be deprived of his society was losing the chief pleasure of her life and her best guardian against her enemies.

Mrs Alworth was pleased with the affection which so evidently appeared between these two young people, she hoped to see a happy union arise from it. Their fortunes and ages were properly suited, and a love which had taken root in childhood and grown with their increasing years seemed to promise a lasting harmony, of which the sweetness of their dispositions would be no bad security. These pleasing ideas amused this worthy woman, but the two friends themselves had not extended their views so far. Bred up like brother and sister, a tenderer degree of relation had not entered their thoughts, nor did any thing more appear necessary to their happiness than a constant enjoyment of each other's friendship. In this disposition they parted when Mr Alworth went abroad. His tutor thinking himself not properly qualified to conduct him in his travels, recommended another gentleman, and Mr Alworth, at Harriot's request, prevailed with their grandmother to detain his old tutor till Harriot's education was completed.

Mr Alworth continued abroad two years, during which time Harriot had applied with such unwearied diligence that she was perfect mistress of the living languages and no less acquainted with Greek and Latin. She was well instructed in the ancient and modern philosophy, and in almost every branch of learning.

Mr Alworth found his cousin not alone improved in understanding, her beauty was just then in its perfection and it was scarcely possible to conceive any thing handsomer. She had great elegance of manner, a point wherein her grandmother excelled, and was as far removed from conceit as from ignorance. Her situation was much mended by the marriage of the eldest Miss Denham; and Miss Alworth waited only for her brother's arrival and approbation to enter into the same state. The gentleman to whom she was going to be married had first made his address to Harriot but, as well as several others, was refused by her. She was not inclined to change her situation, or this gentleman's fortune, person and character were unexceptionable; however, one circumstance without any other objection would have been sufficient to have rendered his suit unsuccessful; she perceived that Miss Alworth was in love with him, and though she had little reason to have much regard for her, yet good nature made her anxious for the success of a passion which she saw was deeply rooted.

She therefore, while she discouraged his addresses, took

every means of recommending Miss Alworth, whose treatment of her she believed rather proceeded from compliance with Miss Denham's than from ill temper.

This gave her hopes that she might make a good wife to Mr Parnel, the object of her affections. He soon perceived that Miss Alworth did not behold him with indifference; but as he was much captivated by Harriot's charms, it at first had no other effect than leading him to indulge in complaints of her cruelty to Miss Alworth, who listened with compassion. Harriot often represented to him how little he ought to wish for her consent to marry him, which he so strongly solicited; for should she grant it, he would be miserable with a wife who did not love him. She told him that were he indifferent, her being so might do very well, and they live on together in that eternal ennui which must ever subsist between a married couple who have no affection for each other, and while natural good temper and prudence enabled them to dream away a dull life in peace and dead insensibility, the world might call them happy; but that if he really loved her, her indifference would render him more wretched than the most blamable conduct. She would then represent the advantages of marrying a woman whose sole affections he possessed, though at first he felt for her only esteem and gratitude; and advised him by all means to seek for one whose heart was in that situation, which he was well qualified to find.

Though Harriot forbore to mention Miss Alworth's name, Mr Parnel well understood to whom she alluded, but found it difficult to take her advice. At length, however, deprived of all hope of obtaining the woman he loved, and moved to compassion by the visible unhappiness of one who loved him, he began to listen to it and frankly told Harriot that he understood the aim of what she had said. She was not sorry to throw off all restraint as it gave her the power of speaking more to the purpose and at length brought him to say that he should not be unwilling to marry her. Harriot feared lest the belief of Mr Parnel's still retaining an affection for her might render Miss Alworth uneasy, and therefore advised him gradually to slacken his addresses to her and at the same time to increase in proportion his attentions for Miss Alworth, that he might appear to prefer her, since a symptom of inconstancy she knew would not so much affect her as any sign of indifference, and Harriot's generosity so far exceeded her vanity that she very sincerely desired to be thought neglected rather than give any alloy to the happiness of her cousin.

There was the more colour for this supposition as Mr Parnel had never been publicly discarded by her, since for the completion of her views she had found it necessary to preserve his acquaintance.

Miss Alworth was happy beyond expression when she found herself the object of Mr Parnel's addresses. Her wishes so far blinded her that she really believed Harriot was neglected for her; but yet knew she had long been endeavouring to serve her and was obliged to her for some instructions how to behave so to Mr Parnel as to secure his esteem and confidence, the best foundation for love. As her brother was then soon expected over, Mrs Alworth thought that to wait for his approbation was a proper compliment.

Mr Alworth was not at all inclined to object to so good a match, especially as it was much desired by his sister, and the marriage was celebrated soon after his return. This ceremony did not so engage his attention as to render him less sensible of the pleasure of renewing his friendship with Harriot, who received him with the sincerest joy. He found her greatly improved and every hour passed agreeably that was spent in her company. They were continually together and never happy but when they were so. Every one talked of their mutual passion; and they were so often told of it that they began to fancy it was true, but surprised to find that name should be given to an affection calm and rational as theirs, totally free from that turbulency and wildness which had always appeared to them the true characteristics of love. They were sensible, however, that nothing was so dear to them as each other, they were always sorry to part, uneasy asunder, and rejoiced to meet; a walk was doubly pleasing when they both shared it; a book became more entertaining if they read together; everything was insipid that they did not mutually enjoy. When they considered these symptoms, they were inclined to think the general opinion was just and that their affection, being free from passion, proceeded from some peculiarity of temper.

Mrs Alworth thought she should give them great satisfaction in proposing a speedy marriage; and rejoiced to see the first wish of her heart, which had been for their union, so nearly completed. The old lady's proposal made them a little thoughtful; they saw no very good reason for their marrying; they enjoyed each other's society already and did not wish for any more intimate tie. But neither knew how to refuse, since the other might take it for an affront, and they would not for the world have had the sincerity and tenderness of their affection brought into doubt. Besides they began to think that as their love was so generally looked upon as certain, it might become difficult to continue the same degree of intimacy without exposing themselves to censure. This thought was sufficient to determine them to marry; and their entire affection for and confidence in each other convinced them they ran no hazard in this step; and that they could not fail of being happy as man and wife who had so long enjoyed great felicity in the most intimate friendship.

In consequence of this resolution, lawyers were employed to draw up settlements and every thing requisite for a proper appearance on their marriage was ordered; but they were so very patient on the subject that the preparations went on slowly. Some who hoped to have their diligence quickened in a manner usual on such occasions, affected delays, but were surprised to find that no complaint ensued. They grew still more dilatory, but the only consequence that arose from it was a decent solicitation to dispatch, without any of those more effectual means being used, which impatient love or greedy avarice suggest.

These young people were perfectly happy and contented and therefore waited with composure for the conclusion of preparations, which however slowly did however proceed.

The old lady indeed was less patient, but a grandmother's solicitations have no very powerful effect on lawyers; therefore hers availed little.

During these delays Mrs Tonston, formerly the eldest Miss Denham, having been extremely ill, was sent to Buxton for the recovery of her health. As this place was but a day's journey from Mrs Alworth's house, she expressed a desire to see her grand-daughter, and Mr Alworth and Harriot, as well as Miss Denham, very readily accompanied her thither.

The accommodations at Buxton allow very little seclusion; and as Mrs Tonston was sufficiently recovered to conform to the customs of the place, they joined in the general society. The first day at dinner Mr Alworth's attention was much engrossed by Miss Melman, a very pretty woman. She was far from a perfect beauty, but her countenance expressed an engaging vivacity, and great good humour, though a wandering unfixed look indicated a light and unsteady mind. Her person was little but elegant; there was a sprightliness in her whole figure which was very attractive: her conversation was suitable to it, she had great life and spirit, all the common routine of discourse and a fashionable readiness to skim lightly over all subjects. Her understanding was sufficiently circumscribed, but what she wanted in real sense she made up in vivacity, no unsuccessful substitute in general estimation.

This young lady was almost a new character to Mr Alworth. He had lived constantly at his grandmother's till he went abroad, and as soon as he returned into the kingdom he went thither; from which, as it was the middle of summer and consequently London had no temptations, he had never stirred. He therefore had been little used to any woman but his sober and sensible grandmother; two cousins who were pretty enough, but had no great charms of understanding; a sister rather silly; and the incomparable Harriot, whose wit was as sound as her judgement solid and sterling, free from affectation and all little effeminate arts and airs. Reason governed her thoughts and actions, nor could the greatest flow of spirits make her for a moment forget propriety. Every thing in her was natural grace, she was always consistent and uniform, and a stranger to caprice.

Miss Melman was a complete coquette, capricious and fantastical. As Mr Alworth was the prettiest man at the place and known to have a good fortune, she soon singled him out as a conquest worthy of her and successfully played off all her arts. By appearing to like him, she enticed him to address her; and by a well managed capriciousness of behaviour kept up the spirit of a pursuit. She frequently gave him reason to believe her favourably disposed towards him, and as often, by obliging him to doubt of it, increased his desire to be certain it was true. She kept him in a state of constant anxiety, and made him know her consequence by the continual transition from pleasure to pain in which he lived.

He had not been much more than a fortnight at Buxton when his attachment to Miss Melman became apparent. Harriot saw an assiduity in his behaviour very different from what he had ever shewn to her. He felt that in the circumstances wherein he and Harriot then were, his conduct must appear injurious, and shame and the secret reproaches of his conscience made him take all possible opportunities of avoiding her presence: if he was obliged to converse with her, it was with an air so restrained and inattentive as made her fear his regard for her was entirely vanished. The sincere affection she had for him rendered this apprehension extremely painful. She would have been contented to have seen another woman his wife, but could not bear the thought of losing his friendship. At first she passed over this change in silence and appeared even not to observe it; but when they received an account that the marriage writings were finished, she thought an affected blindness highly unseasonable and told him, in the most friendly and generous manner, that nothing remained to be done but to cancel them, that she plainly perceived another had obtained the heart she never possessed; that the measures taken for their marriage were of no sort of consequence, and she flattered herself she might retain his friendship though he gave his hand to another.

Mr Alworth at first appeared confounded, but recovering himself, confessed to her frankly he never knew the weakness and folly of the human heart till his own convinced him of it; that he had always felt for her the most perfect esteem, joined with the tenderest affection, but his passions had had no share in his attachment. On the contrary, he found them strongly engaged on the side of Miss Melman, and felt an ardour for her which he had never before experienced. That he could not think of being her husband without rapture, though he saw plainly she was inferior to his Harriot both in beauty and understanding; and as for her principles, he was totally ignorant of them. He now, he said, perceived the difference between friendship and love, and was convinced that esteem and passion were totally independent, since she entirely possessed the one, while Miss Melman totally engrossed the other.

Harriot was pleased with the frankness of Mr Alworth's confession and wished only to be secure of his esteem, but she saw him so wholly taken up with Miss Melman that she was convinced passion had greater power over his sex than esteem, and that while his mind was under the tumultuous influence of love, she must expect very little satisfaction from his friendship.

She took upon herself the task of breaking off their treaty of marriage and acquainted her grandmother with her resolution, who saw too plainly the reason for her doing so to blame her conduct, though she grieved at the necessity for it and could not sincerely forgive her grandson's levity and want of judgement in preferring a wild fantastic girl to the extreme beauty and solid well-known merit of Harriot, an error for which she prophetically saw he would in time be severely punished.

Harriot, from the intended bride, now became the confidante of Mr Alworth, though with an aching heart; for she feared that after experiencing the more active sensations of a strong passion, friendship would appear too insipid to have any charms for him. She accompanied Mrs Alworth home before the lovers chose to leave Buxton, but not till she had prevailed with her grandmother to consent that the marriage between Miss Melman and Mr Alworth should be celebrated at her house.

When everything requisite for the ceremony was ready, they came to Mrs Alworth's, where the indissoluble knot was tied and in the bridegroom's opinion the most perfect happiness secured to his future years. They stayed but a few days after the marriage and then went to her father's house, till the approaching winter called them to London.

Harriot found a great loss of a friend she so sincerely loved, but she hoped he would be as happy as he expected and had the satisfaction of believing he retained a tender regard for her. They corresponded frequently and his letters assured her of his felicity. After he had been some time fixed in London, he grew indeed less eloquent on the subject, which did not surprise her as the variety of his engagements shortened his letters and denied him leisure to expatiate on the most pleasing topics.

Miss Denham had accompanied her sister home, and in the winter Mrs Alworth was informed by Mrs Tonston that Miss Denham had received a proposal from a gentleman of a good estate, but he insisted on a fortune of nine thousand pounds, which was two more than she was possessed of; and as they wished the old lady to make that addition, Mrs Tonston as an inducement added that the gentleman was extremely agreeable to her sister.

Mrs Alworth was not inclined to comply with their views, and made no other answer to all Harriot urged to prevail with her to give the requisite sum than that it was more than perhaps would at her death fall to Miss Denham's share and she saw no temptation to purchase so mercenary a man. When Harriot found that all she could say was unavailing, she told Mrs Alworth that if she would give her leave, she was determined to make the required addition out of her fortune; for she could not bear her cousin should be disappointed in a particular she thought essential to her happiness by the want of a sum of money which she could very well spare; adding that the treatment she had received from her cousins she attributed to childishness and folly and should be far worse than they were if she could remember it with resentment.

Mrs Alworth was greatly touched with this instance of Harriot's generosity, and finding that nothing but the exertion of her authority, which her grand-daughter acknowledged absolute and always obeyed implicitly, could prevent her from performing her purpose, she determined to take the most effectual means of hindering it by advancing the money herself, and invited Miss Denham and her lover to her house; where the marriage was performed, and they departed.

Mrs Alworth began to feel the infirmities of age, and now that she and Harriot were left to continual tête-à-tête, absolute quiet might have degenerated into something like dullness; but the disturbance they found not at home reached them from abroad. Mr Parnel was wearied with his wife's fondness, who not considering that he had married her more out of gratitude than affection, had disgusted him with the continual professions of a love to which his heart would not make an equal return. This fondness teased a temper naturally good into peevishness and was near converting indifference into dislike. Mrs Parnel, distressed beyond measure at an effect so contrary to what she intended, reproached him with ingratitude and tormented him with tears and complaints.

Harriot, who considered this match as in a great measure her own work, was particularly desirous of redressing these grievances and took great pains to persuade Mrs Parnel to restrain her fondness, and suppress her complaints, while she endeavoured to make her husband sensible that he ought, in consideration for the cause, to pardon the troublesome effects and not to suffer himself to be disgusted by that affection in his wife which to most husbands would appear a merit. Mrs Alworth joined to Harriot's persuasion the influence her age and respectable character gave her, and though not without great difficulty, they at last saw Mr and Mrs Parnel live in peace and amity, without any of the pleasures arising from strong and delicate affections or the sufferings occasioned by ill humour and hatred; and whatever void they might find in their hearts, they were so happy as to have well filled by two very fine children which Mrs Parnel brought her husband, who always treated her with great indulgence in hopes of fixing Harriot's good opinion; for though despair had damped his passion, yet he still loved her with the tenderest respect and reverence.

Towards the latter end of the second year of Mr Alworth's marriage, his grandmother died, much regretted by Harriot, whom she left mistress of her own fortune with the addition of four thousand pounds, part of it the accumulated interest of her paternal inheritance, the rest Mrs Alworth's legacy. Her grandson succeeded to her house and intreated Harriot that he might find her there when he came to take possession.

Their correspondence had been regular but they had never met since his marriage. Mrs Alworth was not fond of the conversation of an old lady; and from seeing herself not very agreeable to her grandmother, felt an uncommon awe in her presence. Harriot had received repeated invitations from them, but could not be prevailed with to leave old Mrs Alworth, who had no other companion.

The only relief she found in her affliction for the loss of so worthy a parent was putting the house, and all belonging to it, in order for the reception of her first friend, in whose society she expected to renew the happiness she had so long enjoyed from it. Nor was she disappointed in her hopes of finding him still her friend; they met with mutual joy, and Mrs Alworth seemed at first as much pleased with her new possession as they were with each other. But Harriot soon found her happiness considerably damped. Mr Alworth, unwilling to let his grandmother know the ill success of a union which he was sensible she disapproved, had been silent on that subject in his letters, but he was too well acquainted with the generosity of Harriot's temper to fear she would triumph at the natural consequence of his ill-grounded passion, and therefore concealed not from her any part of the uneasiness which his wife's disposition gave him. He too late saw the difference between sensible vivacity and animal spirits and found Mrs Alworth a giddy coquette, too volatile to think, too vain to love; pleased with admiration, insensible to affection, fond of flattery but indifferent to true praise; imprudently vivacious in mixed companies, lifeless when alone with him; and desirous of charming all mankind except her husband, who of his whole sex seemed the only person of no consequence to her. As her view was to captivate in public, she covered a very pretty complexion with pearl-powder and rouge because they made her more resplendent by candle-light and in public places. Mr Alworth had in strong terms expressed his abhorence of that practice; but she was surprised he should intermeddle in an affair that was no business of his, surely she might wear what complexion she pleased. The natural turn of his temper inclined him to rational society, but in that his wife could bear no part. The little time she was at home was employed in dressing and a multitude of coxcombs attended her toilet. Mr Alworth's extreme fondness for her made him at first very wretched; he soon found himself the most disregarded of all mankind and every man appeared his rival; but on nearer observation he perceived his jealousy was groundless and that she was too giddy to love any thing. This made his pride easy, but his tenderness still had much to endure, till at length contempt produced some degree of indifference and his sufferings became less acute, though he lived in continual grief at finding himself disappointed of all his airy hopes of happiness.

Harriot was scarcely less afflicted than himself, she endeavoured to render him more contented with his situation, and attempted to teach Mrs Alworth to think, but in both was equally unsuccessful. However, this was not all she had to endure. When Mr Alworth began with unprejudiced eyes to compare her he had lost with the woman for whom he relinquished her; when he saw how greatly Harriot's natural beauty eclipsed Mrs Alworth's notwithstanding the addition of all her borrowed charms, he wondered what magic had blinded him to her superiority. But when he drew a comparison between the admirable understanding of the one, her great fund of knowledge, the inexhaustible variety in her conversation, with the insipid dullness or unmeaning vivacity of the other, he was still more astonished and could not forgive his strange infatuation. This train of thought perhaps had no small share in giving rise to a passion for Harriot which he had never felt, while it might have been the source of much happiness to them both. In short, he became violently in love with her and fell a prey to the most cruel regret and despair, sensible that all he suffered was the consequence of his own folly.

Respect for Harriot made Mr Alworth endeavour to conceal his passion, but could not prevent its daily increase. At this time I became acquainted with her, during a visit I made in the neighbourhood; and as the natural openness both of her disposition and mine inclined us to converse with much freedom, I one day took the liberty to tell her how much Mr Alworth was in love with her. She had not the least suspicion of it, the entire affection which had always subsisted between them she imagined sufficient to lead me into that error but told me the thing was impossible; and to prove it, related all the circumstances of their intended union. Appearances were too strong to suffer me to be persuaded that I was mistaken; I acknowledged that what she urged seemed to contradict my opinion, but that it was no proof; for the perverseness of human nature was such that it did not appear to me at all improbable that the easiness of obtaining her, when they had both been, as it were, bred up with that view, might be the sole occasion of his indifference; and the impossibility of ever possessing her now would only serve to inflame his passion.

Harriot accused me of representing human nature more perverse and absurd than it really was, and continued firm in the persuasion of my being mistaken. Whatever glaring signs of Mr Alworth's love appeared, she set them all down to the account of friendship; till at length his mind was so torn with grief and despair that no longer able to conceal the cause of his greatest sufferings he begged her to teach him how to conquer a passion which, while it existed, must make him wretched; and with the greatest confusion told her how unaccountably unfortunate he was, both in not loving, and in loving, each equally out of season. Almost distracted with the distressful state of his mind, he was in the utmost horror lest this declaration should offend her; and throwing himself at her feet with a countenance and manner which shewed him almost frantic with despair, terrified her so much that she did not feel half the shock this declaration would have given her had it been made with more calmness.

She strove to silence him; she endeavoured to raise him from her feet, but to no purpose; she could not abate the agonies of his mind, without assuring him she forgave him. Her spirits were in extreme agitation till she saw him a little composed, for she feared his senses were affected; but when her alarm began to abate, the effect of her terrors and her grief appeared in a flood of tears; Mr Alworth found them infectious, and she was obliged to dry them up in order to comfort him. When he grew more composed, Harriot ventured, after expressing her concern for his having conceived so unfortunate a passion, to intimate that absence was the best remedy and that there was nothing to be done but for her to leave the house.

Mr Alworth was not able to support the mention of her going away and intreated her at least to give him time to arm himself against the greatest misfortune that could befall him, the loss of her society. She dared not control him in any thing material while his mind continued in that desperate situation and therefore consented to stay some time longer. She found it very difficult to make him think that there ever was a proper time for her to depart, though passion was much less tormenting since he had ventured to declare it; and what before arose nearly to distraction, sunk now into a soft melancholy. Mrs Alworth paid so little attention to her husband that she had not perceived the conflict in his mind. She was wearied with the country to the greatest degree, and made the tiresome days as short as she could by not rising till noon; from that time till dinner her toilet found her sufficient employment. As the neighbourhood was large, she very frequently contrived to make a party at cards; but as her company was not used to play high, this afforded her little relief except she could find somebody to bet with her, which was not very difficult as she was contented to do it to a disadvantage.

In this way she contrived, just, as she called it, to drag on life; and wondered how so fine a woman as Harriot could have so long buried herself in that place, scarcely more lively than the family vault.

When Harriot thought she had sufficiently convinced Mr Alworth of the necessity of her absence, she took her leave with much greater concern than she would suffer to appear, though she did not affect indifference; but the truth was, Mr Alworth's passionate tenderness for her had made an impression on her heart which without it all his merit could not effect. The melancholy languor which overspread his countenance gave it charms she had never before discovered in it; the soft accents in which he breathed the most delicate love penetrated to her very soul, and she no longer found that indifference which had been so remarkable a part of her character. But she carefully concealed these new sensations in hopes that he would more easily conquer his passion for not thinking it returned.

Though the winter was scarcely begun, yet having no inducement to go to any other place, she went to London; and as I had prolonged my stay in the country only to gratify my inclination for her company, I went with her to town. Mrs Alworth did not continue there a month after us; but her husband, whose health was by no means in a good state, went to Bath; and that he might not be quite destitute of pleasure, he carried his little boy with him, though but a year and a quarter old. His wife did not contend with him for this privilege, she would have seen little more of the babe had it been in London.

Harriot Trentham was at her first arrival in very low spirits, and every letter she received from Mr Alworth increased her dejection, as it painted his in very strong colours. As the town filled she began to try if dissipation could dispel her melancholy. Her beauty, the fineness of her person, and her being known to have a large fortune, which fame even exaggerated, procured her many lovers and she became the most admired woman in town. This was a new source of pleasure to her. She had lived where she saw not many single men, and though few of these who dared to flatter themselves with hopes, had failed paying their addresses to her, yet these successive courtships were very dull when compared with all the flutter of general admiration. Her books were now neglected, and to avoid thinking on a subject which constantly afflicted her, she forced herself into public and was glad to find that the idleness of the men and her own vanity could afford her entertainment.

She was not however so totally engrossed by this pleasing dissipation as to neglect any means of serving the distressed. Mrs Tonston, exerting the génius she had so early shewn for traducing others, set her husband and his family at variance, till at length the falsehoods by which she had effected it came to be discovered. Her husband and she had never lived well together, and this proof of her bad heart disgusted him so entirely that he turned her out of his house, allowing her a mere trifle for her support. In this distress she applied to Harriot, who she knew was ever ready to serve even those who had most injured her.

Her application was not unsuccessful. Harriot sent her a considerable present for her immediate convenience and then went into the country to Mr Tonston, to whom she represented so effectually his ungenerous treatment, since the fortune his wife brought him gave her a right to a decent maintenance, that he made a proper settlement upon her and gave the writings into Harriot's hands, who not only saw the money paid regularly, but took so much pains to convince Mrs Tonston of the malignity of her disposition that she brought her to a due sense of it, and by applying for his assistance to mend her heart, who best knew its defects, she became so altered in temper that five years after her separation from her husband Harriot effected a reconciliation, and they now live in great amity together, gratefully acknowledging their obligations to her.

I have anticipated this fact in order to render my narrative less tedious, or I should have stopped at Harriot's procuring a settlement for Mrs Tonston, and have told you that by lying in her return at an inn where the smallpox then was she caught that distemper, and soon after she arrived in London it appeared. I need not say that she had it to a very violent degree. Being then in town I had the good fortune to nurse her and flatter myself that my care was not useless; for in cases so dangerous, no one who does not feel all the tender solicitude of a friend can be a proper nurse.

Mrs Alworth wrote her husband word of Harriot's illness, who came post to London, filled with the extremest anxiety, and shared the fatigue of nursing with me; she was all the time delirious. When she came to her senses, she at first seemed mortified to think Mr Alworth had seen her in that disfigured condition; but on reflection told me she rejoiced in it, as she thought it must totally extinguish his passion; and her greatest solicitude was for his happiness. But she afterwards found her expectation was ill grounded.

When she recovered, she perceived that the smallpox had entirely destroyed her beauty. She acknowledged she was not insensible to this mortification; and to avoid the observation of the envious or even of the idly curious she retired, as soon as she was able to travel, to a country house which I hired for her.

In a very short time she became perfectly contented with the alteration this cruel distemper had made in her. Her love for reading returned, and she regained the quiet happiness of which flutter and dissipation had deprived her without substituting any thing so valuable in its place. She has often said she looks on this accident as a reward for the good she had done Mrs Tonston, and that few benevolent actions receive so immediate a recompense, or we should be less remiss in our duties though not more meritorious in performing them. She found retirement better calculated for overcoming a hopeless passion than noise and flutter. She had indeed by dissipation often chased Mr Alworth from her thoughts, but at the first moment of leisure his idea returned in as lively colours as if it had always kept possession of her mind. In the country she had time to reflect on the necessity of conquering this inclination if she wished to enjoy any tolerable happiness; and therefore took proper measures to combat it. Reason and piety, when united, are extremely prevalent, and with their assistance she restrained her affection once more within its ancient bounds of friendship. Her letters to Mr Alworth were filled with remonstrances against the indulgence of his love, and the same means she had found effectual she recommended to him and with satisfaction learnt that though they had not entirely succeeded, yet he had acquired such a command over his heart that he was as little wretched as a man can be who is a living monument of the too common folly of being captivated by a sudden glare of person and parts; and of the fatal error of those men who seek in marriage for an amusing trifler rather than a rational and amiable companion, and too late find that the vivacity which pleases in the mistress is often a fatal vice in a wife. He lives chiefly in the country, has generally a few friends in the house with him, and takes a great deal of pains in the education of his two sons; while their mother spends almost the whole year in town, immersed in folly and dissipation.

About fourteen years ago Harriot, who I ought to begin to call Miss Trentham, came to see a lady in this neighbourhood and thus was first known to the inhabitants of this mansion. They were much pleased with her acquaintance and when she had performed her visit, invited her to pass a little time with them. She required no solicitation, for it was the very thing she wished, and here she has remained ever since. When Mr Maynard died, leaving me but a small jointure, Miss Trentham was indulged in her inclination of asking me to spend the first part of my widowhood with her and her friends; and I have been fortunate enough to recommend myself so effectually that they have left me no room to doubt they choose I should continue with them, and indeed I think I could scarcely support life were I banished from this heavenly society. Miss Trentham and Mr Alworth keep up a constant correspondence by letters, but avoid meeting. His wife has brought him one daughter, and Miss Trentham's happiness has been rendered complete by obtaining from her permission to educate this child; a favour which contrary to what is usual is esteemed very small by her who granted and very great by the person that received it. This girl is now ten years old, and the most accomplished of her age of any one, perhaps, in the kingdom. Her person is fine, and her temper extremely engaging. She went about a week ago to her father, whom she visits for about three weeks twice in a year, and never returns unimproved.

As Miss Trentham's fortune made a good addition to the income of the society, they on this occasion established in the parish a manufacture of carpets and rugs which has succeeded so well as to enrich all the country round about.

As the morning was not very far advanced, I asked Mrs Maynard to conduct us to this manufacture, as in my opinion there is no sight so delightful as extensive industry. She readily complied, and led us to a sort of street, the most inhabited part of the village, above half a mile from Millenium Hall. Here we found several hundreds of people of all ages, from six years old to four score, employed in the various parts of the manufacture, some spinning, some weaving, others dying the worsted, and in short all busy, singing and whistling, with the appearance of general cheerfulness, and their neat dress shewed them in a condition of proper plenty.

The ladies, it seems, at first hired persons to instruct the neighbourhood, which was then burdened with poor and so over stocked with hands that only a small part of them could find work. But as they feared an enterprising undertaker might ruin their plan, they themselves undertook to be stewards; they stood the first expense, allowed a considerable profit to the directors, but kept the distribution of the money entirely in their own hands: thus they prevent the poor from being oppressed by their superiors, for they allow them great wages and by their very diligent inspection hinder any frauds. I never was more charmed than to see a manufacture so well ordered that scarcely any one is too young or too old to partake of its emoluments. As the ladies have the direction of the whole, they give more to the children and the aged, in proportion to the work they do, than to those who are more capable, as a proper encouragement and reward for industry in those seasons of life in which it is so uncommon.

We were so taken up with observing these people, that we got home but just as dinner was carrying in.

In the afternoon we informed the ladies how we had spent the latter part of the morning, and in the course of conversation Lamont told them that they were the first people he ever knew who lived entirely for others, without any regard to their own pleasure; and that were he a Roman Catholic, he should beg of them to confer on him the merit of some of their works of supererogation.

'I do not know where you could find them,' replied Miss Mancel, 'I believe we have not been able to discover any such; on the contrary, we are sensible of great deficiencies in the performance of our duty.'

'Can you imagine, Madam,' interrupted Lamont, 'that all you do here is a duty?'

'Indispensably so,' answered Miss Mancel, 'we are told by him who cannot err that our time, our money and our understandings are entrusted with us as so many talents for the use of which we must give a strict account. How we ought to use them he has likewise told us; as to our fortunes in the most express terms, when he commands us to feed the hungry, to clothe the naked, to relieve the prisoner, and to take care of the sick. Those who have not an inheritance that enables them to do this are commanded to labour in order to obtain means to relieve those who are incapable of gaining the necessaries of life. Can we then imagine that every one is not required to assist others to the utmost of his power, since we are commanded even to work for the means of doing so? God's mercy and bounty is universal, it flows unasked and unmerited; we are bid to endeavour to imitate him as far as our nature will enable us to do it. What bounds then ought we to set to our good offices, but the want of power to extend them further? Our faculties and our time should be employed in directing our donations in a manner the most conducive to the benefit of mankind, the most for the encouragement of virtue and the suppression of vice; to assist in this work is the business of speech, of reason and of time. These ought to be employed in seeking out opportunities of doing good and in contriving means for regulating it to the best purpose. Shall I allow much careful thought towards settling the affairs of my household with economy, and be careless how I distribute my benefactions to the poor, to whom I am only a steward, and of whose interests I ought to be as careful as of my own? By giving them my money I may sacrifice my covetousness, but by doing it negligently I indulge my indolence, which I ought to endeavour to conquer as much as every other vice. Each state has its trials; the poverty of the lower rank of people exercises their industry and patience; the riches of the great are trials of their temperance, humility and humanity. Theirs is perhaps the more difficult part, but their present reward is also greater if they acquit themselves well; as for the future, there may probably be no inequality.'

'You observed, sir,' said Miss Trentham 'that we live for others, without any regard to our own pleasure, therefore I imagine you think our way of life inconsistent with it; but give me leave to say you are mistaken. What is there worth enjoying in this world that we do not possess? We have all the conveniences of life, nay, all the luxuries that can be included among them. We might indeed keep a large retinue; but do you think the sight of a number of useless attendants could afford us half the real satisfaction that we feel from seeing the money which must be lavished on them expended in supporting the old and decrepit, or nourishing the helpless infant? We might dress with so much expense that we could scarcely move under the burden of our apparel; but is that more eligible than to see the shivering wretch clad in warm and comfortable attire? Can the greatest luxury of the table afford so true a pleasure as the reflection that instead of its being over-charged with superfluities, the homely board of the cottager is blessed with plenty? We might spend our time in going from place to place, where none wish to see us except they find a deficiency at the card-table, perpetually living among those whose vacant minds are ever seeking after pleasures foreign to their own tastes and pursue joys which vanish as soon as possessed; for these would you have us leave the infinite satisfaction of being beheld with gratitude and love, and the successive enjoyments of rational delights, which here fill up every hour? Should we do wisely in quitting a scene where every object exalts our mind to the great Creator, to mix among all the folly of depraved nature?

'If we take it in a more serious light still, we shall perceive a great difference in the comforts arising from the reflections on a life spent in an endeavour to obey our Maker and to correct our own defects in a constant sense of our offences, and an earnest desire to avoid the commission of them for the future, from a course of hurry and dissipation which will not afford us leisure to recollect our errors, nor attention to attempt amending them.'

'The difference is indeed striking,' said Lamont, 'and there can be no doubt which is most eligible; but are you not too rigid in your censures of dissipation? You seem to be inclined to forbid all innocent pleasures.'

'By no means,' replied Miss Trentham, 'but things are not always innocent because they are trifling. Can any thing be more innocent than picking of straws, or playing at push-pin; but if a man employs himself so continually in either that he neglects to serve a friend or to inspect his affairs, does it not cease to be innocent? Should a schoolboy be found whipping a top during school hours, would his master forbear correction because it is an innocent amusement? And yet thus we plead for things as trifling, tho' they obstruct the exercise of the greatest duties in life. Whatever renders us forgetful of our Creator, and of the purposes for which he called us into being, or leads us to be inattentive to his commands, or neglectful in the performance of them, becomes criminal, however innocent in its own nature. While we pursue these things with a moderation which prevents such effects they are always innocent and often desirable, the excess only is to be avoided.'

'I have nothing left me to say,' answered Lamont, 'than that your doctrine must be true and your lives are happy; but may I without impertinence observe that I should imagine your extensive charities require an immense fortune.'

'Not so much, perhaps,' said Mrs Morgan, 'as you suppose. We keep a very regular account, and at an average, for every year will not be exactly the same, the total stands thus. The girls' school four hundred pounds a year, the boys' a hundred and fifty, apprenticing some and equipping others for service one hundred. The clothing of the girls in the house forty. The almshouses two hundred. The maintenance of the monsters a hundred and twenty. Fortunes and furniture for such young persons as marry in this and the adjoining parishes, two hundred. All this together amounts only to twelve hundred and ten pounds a year, and yet affords all reasonable comforts. The expenses of ourselves and household, in our advantageous situation, come within eight hundred a year. Finding so great a balance in our favour, we agreed to appropriate a thousand a year for the society of gentlewomen with small or no fortunes; but it has turned out in such a manner that they cost us a trifle. We then dedicated that sum to the establishment of a manufacture, but since the fourth year it has much more than paid its expenses, though in many respects we do not act with the economy usual in such cases, but give very high wages, for our design being to serve a multitude of poor destitute of work, we have no nice regard to profit. As we did not mean to drive a trade, we have been at a loss what to do with the profits. We have out of it made a fund for the sick and disabled from which they may receive a comfortable support, and intend to secure it to them to perpetuity in the best manner we can.'

'How few people of fortune are there,' said Lamont, 'who could not afford £1200 a year, with only retrenching superfluous and burdensome expenses? But if they would only imitate you in any one branch, how much greater pleasure would they then receive from their fortunes than they now enjoy?'

While he was engaged in discourse with the ladies, I observed to Mrs Maynard that by the account she had given me of their income, their expenses fell far short of it. She whispered me that their accidental charities were innumerable, all the rest being employed in that way. Their acquaintance know they cannot so much oblige as by giving them an opportunity of relieving distress. They receive continual applications and though they give to none indiscriminately, yet they never refuse any who really want. Their donations sometimes are in great sums, where the case requires such extraordinary assistance. If they hear of any gentleman's family oppressed by too many children, or impoverished by sickness, they contrive to convey an adequate present privately, or will sometimes ask permission to put some of their children into business, or buy them places or commissions.

We acquainted the ladies that we should trouble them no longer than that night, and with regret saw it so soon ended. The next morning, upon going into Lamont's room, I found him reading the New Testament; I could not forbear expressing some pleasure and surprise at seeing him thus uncommonly employed.

He told me he was convinced by the conduct of the ladies of this house that their religion must be the true one. When he had before considered the lives of Christians, their doctrine seemed to have so little influence on their actions that he imagined there was no sufficient effect produced by Christianity to warrant a belief, that it was established by a means so very extraordinary; but he now saw what that religion in reality was, and by the purity of its precepts was convinced its original must be divine. It now appeared evidently to be worthy of its miraculous institution. He was resolved to examine whether the moral evidences concurred with that divine stamp which was so strongly impressed upon it and he had risen at day break to get a Bible out of the parlour that he might study precepts which could thus exalt human nature almost to divine.

It was with great joy I found him so seriously affected; and when we went to breakfast could not forbear communicating my satisfaction to my cousin, who sincerely shared in it. As soon as breakfast was over we took leave of the ladies, though not till they had made us promise a second visit, to which we very gladly agreed, for could we with decency have prolonged this,

I know not when we should have departed.

You, perhaps, wish we had done it sooner and may think I have been too prolix in my account of this society; but the pleasure I find in recollection is such that I could not restrain my pen within moderate bounds. If what I have described may tempt any one to go and do likewise, I shall think myself fortunate in communicating it. For my part, my thoughts are all engaged in a scheme to imitate them on a smaller scale.

I am, Sir.

The first Virago Modern Classic was published in London in 1978, launching a list dedicated to the celebration of women writers and to the rediscovery and reprinting of their works. While the series is called "Modern Classics" it is not true that these works of fiction are universally and equally considered "great," although that is often the case. Published with new critical and biographical introductions, books appear in the series for different reasons: sometimes for their importance in literary history; sometimes because they illuminate particular aspects of women's lives, both personal and public. They may be classics of comedy or storytelling; their interest can be historical, feminist, political, or literary. In any case, in their variety and richness they promise to confuse forever the question of what women's fiction is about, while at the same time affirming a true female tradition in literature.

Initially, the Virago Modern Classics concentrated on English novels and short stories published in the early decades of the century. As the series has grown, it has broadened to include works of fiction from different centuries and from different countries, cultures, and literary traditions; there are books written by black women, by Catholic and Jewish women, by women of almost every English-speaking country, and there are several relevant novels by men.

Nearly 200 Virago Modern Classics will have been published in England by the end of 1985. During that same year, Penguin Books began to publish Virago Modern Classics in the United States, with the expectation of having some 40 titles from the series available by the end of 1986. Some of the earlier books in the series were published in the United States by The Dial Press.